CHASING

DAYLIGHT

by

JEREMY M. WRIGHT

STONE

GATEWAY

PUBLISHING

Copyright © 2020, 2007 by Jeremy M. Wright

Cover design by Lance Buckley

First paperback edition by Stone Gateway Publishing October 2020

ISBN-13: 978-1-7340887-5-5

Printed in the United States of America.

For my wife, Cindy, and my sister, Jennifer.

With love, admiration, and utmost appreciation for your support. Thank you for being an incredible part of my life.

So many evils by Satan's prince will be committed that almost the entire world will find itself undone and desolated.

~ Nostradamus ~

Also by Jeremy M. Wright

Young Adult Fiction

THE GOOD SHIP

CHASING

DAYLIGHT

Prologue

Although he couldn't see her, he could feel the warmth of her sleeping body. He quivered at the thought of how close he was to the seventeen-year-old celebrity. Hannah Jane Hillcrest was within easy reach. Tonight she slept uncomfortably, shifting positions for hours. He wondered if maybe God sent her a premonition warning her of impending tragedy. He thought that would be unfair of God, because like everyone else, God also has to play the game.

Over the last five days, he meticulously mapped a layout of the house and furniture. He could have easily walked room by room blindfolded.

During the past four hours, he played the scenes over in his mind. He was about to begin another game with the FBI.

Even after thousands of years of constructing one detailed plan after another, he still felt a certain degree of uneasiness. The game depended on one domino toppling the next and so on down the curving line. Even after thousands of years, the authorities around the world have never won the game.

He had been waiting since dusk in the darkness of the bedroom. Around eleven o'clock, Hannah Jane and her friend Michael McKay had come home. Michael was a second-rate model, once a poor slum kid with handsome features fortunate enough to bring him some celebrity status and a modest career. The gossip magazines currently battled back and forth over whether Hannah Jane and Michael were romantic.

Both were asleep. It was time to begin the game.

With stealth movements, he slid out from beneath the bed. The menacing shadow rose in the moonlight and gently sat beside Hannah Jane. The bedsprings creaked slightly, which stirred Hannah Jane, and then she settled again.

In the dark, he watched them sleep, their chests rising and falling. He wanted to kill Michael McKay. He wanted to mutilate the arrogant little bastard bad enough that Michael's mother would turn her sight in disgust, but Hannah Jane was the one he wanted.

Ready, get set, go!

He pulled a syringe from his overcoat pocket, removed the plastic cap, and leaned toward Hannah Jane. The needle pierced the crook of her neck. Her eyes suddenly popped open. Her big, beautiful emerald eyes studied the darkness, frantically searched the night, and then found him. A scream nearly tore loose, but he expected it and quickly smashed his gloved hand over her mouth. The fluid was fully injected, quickly racing through her veins, consuming the young woman.

Just before she slipped back to unconsciousness, he leaned in close, his lips a light touch against her ear. In a gentle whisper, he said, "There's no reason to be afraid. There's no need to worry, child. Everything is going to be all right because I've been sent by God."

Michael McKay sat up. "What's wrong, baby?"

A hulking figure stood from the bed. The figure reached for something. In the moonlight, Michael could only watch in complete disbelief, transfixed by what was happening. Something sliced through the air with a hiss, coming at him like a fine-edged sword. Michael felt pure agony as the object struck the bridge of his nose. He let out a howl of pain and threw up his arms to ward off another attack. The effort did little good because he could hear the object coming at him again.

Michael quickly dodged the second blow by rolling off the edge of the bed and collapsing to the floor. He couldn't find focus. His legs wouldn't hold him up. He scampered on his hands and knees, fleeing like a frightened and injured rat toward the bedroom door. The intruder cut off his escape. The assaulting object came swiftly down on him once, twice, and a third time. Michael felt a sickly crunch as his left arm broke. Bones also gave way as his shoulder blades were struck.

When the assault ceased, the intruder knelt beside Michael and leaned in close so that he would hear the words clearly through the pulsing anguish.

"I'm going to let you live, Mr. McKay. You're going to live because you're a person of sadness and distaste, not a true thing of beauty. You're not like Hannah Jane, nor will you ever be. Her misery and torment will give me the strength and motivation to continue doing all the terrible things that I do because I'm the corruptor of humanity. No one seems to understand that because of me, millions have died."

Chapter 1

I'm not going to tell you about the first time I died. I certainly don't feel the need to tell you about the second time I died. Not right now, because I've never really convinced myself that either of those deaths had anything to do with the events leading up to the disappearance of Hannah Jane Hillcrest.

Instead, I'm going to tell you about the third time I died. That was the death that changed everything.

The National Center for Missing and Exploited Children reports that nearly eight-hundred thousand children under the age of eighteen go missing each year. It roughly amounts to two-thousand children vanishing every day. This statistic does not decline each year. Instead, it follows a steady increase.

The majority of those children are runaways and typically return home unharmed within the same day. A percentage of the missing is the result of painful custody issues of divorced parents that usually resolve quickly. Some children are even victims of abandonment. The remaining numbers are victims of non-family abductions. Those figures are compiled into the groups of sexual predators, other sexual exploitations, ransom demands, intentions of mentally adapting the child as their own, and, of course, sinister murders of the young and innocent. The list goes on and on.

To find the total statistics of children retrieved from non-family abductors, someone would need to search many databases proudly announcing successful recovery stories of the missing. Some children, fortunately, return home on their own. Some children are discovered by local police, the FBI, or other devoted child agencies. Other children are rescued by people like myself who specialize in such difficult tasks.

I've researched those databases for those who don't return home. The numbers are staggering. There are thousands every year. When you think about it, a large number of these children will never be seen again. These children are gone but never forgotten by those who still cherish the captured memory of an innocent child now long lost.

Statistics like those make people in my line of work extremely busy. My name is Jack Calloway. I'm a private investigator specializing in finding missing and abducted children. I opened a child recovery agency fourteen years ago. Since then, I've single-handedly brought one hundred and fifty-four children home again. Of that total, nearly seventy-five percent were the victims of a random or pre-meditated kidnapping. The remaining percent were runaways. On occasion, I'm also an outside consultant with the FBI and other child recovery agencies. I've assisted these agencies in hundreds of cases, resulting in the safe retrieval of an additional seventy-seven missing kids.

It's my dedication in life to find these children and bring them home to their loved ones.

For now, I'm home again, where I belong.

It's been ten days since I've seen my wife Caroline and my daughter Reanne. I hate being away for such long stretches. I feel like a traitor of sorts. It's possibly because my work, on occasion, tends to come before my family, which translated to the fact that other families sometimes come before my own. My girls understand the reasons. Children's lives were in danger.

I called Caroline yesterday and told her the good news about a little girl named Melissa Gardner and her safe return.

I had promised my girls that I wouldn't take another case for at least a week, maybe even two. I was going to take a vacation in December. Or so I thought.

I stood at the front door and peered through the oval window. My daughter, Reanne, was busy at the dining room table doing homework. Reanne had just turned eight a month ago. She's growing up so fast. Children always seem to do that even when you don't want them to.

I also saw my wife, Caroline, shuffle back and forth in the kitchen as she occupied herself with preparing a Monday victory supper. Melissa Gardner was home safe and sound, and we celebrate each child's safe return. My girls didn't expect me home so early. I had planned a pleasant little surprise.

I rang the doorbell. Through the oval window in the door, I could see Reanne stand up from the table. Her blond ponytail was swaying back and forth as she came to the door. As she pulled the door open, I greeted her with a genuine smile.

"Hello, young lady," I said. "I'm going door to door, offering hugs and kisses. Can you call your mother over so I can get started?"

She looked at me, irritated. She turned and yelled down the hallway, "Mom! There's a strange man at the door asking for you!" She then giggled and leaped into my arms. I held her tightly. I missed her so much.

"Well, let him in then!" Caroline called back. "I sure do enjoy the company of strange men. Besides, your father won't be home for a few more hours."

"Oh, you must be the comic relief part of the show this evening," I said as I walked in the kitchen and put Reanne and my luggage down. I then gave Caroline a long hug and an even longer kiss.

While we ate a delicious lasagna, I was catching up on lost time. Reanne enthusiastically explained current events circulating the school. Instead of going with the typical Christmas play, the teachers and students unanimously decided to go another route. The top choice was Cinderella, with a Christmas theme twist added in for the season. Reanne had landed the part of one of the mice. The goofy fat one, she told me. I had to smile because I knew it was going to be a terrific show.

"You have to promise me that you won't miss it, Daddy." She gave me a stern look she inherited from her mother.

"Hey, I'm officially on vacation. I promise I won't miss it for anything in the world. Cross my heart," I said and made the motion with my finger.

It was good to be home. Tonight I had a light heart. No burdens of the world could harm my mood.

When I tucked in Reanne, I found my usual place next to her. I retrieved the book from the nightstand I had started to read to her before I left. The book was an old, tattered copy of *Alice's Adventures in Wonderland* that we found at a garage sale. Someone once read this book over and over, maybe to their children. I completely understood why, because it was a remarkable story.

"Daddy, I think you have to start all over again. It's been so long since we started it, I forgot what happened!" she said matter-of-factly.

I knew she hadn't forgotten. She was scorning me a little for leaving on another case. I was more than happy to agree with her request. I smiled and opened to page one.

"As you wish, young lady," I said and began the tale.

When Reanne drifted off in my arms, I closed the book and placed it on the nightstand. I turned out the bedside lamp and eased from the bed. I gently kissed her forehead and told her how much I loved her in a low whisper, and then quietly slipped from the room.

Caroline was waiting up for me. She was curled under the comforter reading a spicy romance novel. "These have been keeping my sexual needs in check while you've been away."

"Do you have any urges you need me to work my magic on now that I'm back?" I asked and rubbed my hands together to warm them.

She pulled back the covers and revealed red lacy lingerie from one of those secret stores. Caroline always had one of the most fantastic bodies I've ever seen. She frequented a fitness center several times a week and a tanning salon a few times a month, which kept her skin a light bronze. She certainly could have modeled lingerie in magazines if she wanted to. Instead, Caroline works as an emergency room nurse. It was the place we met so many years ago when my life had spiraled out of control. Caroline had saved my life in more ways than one.

"I'll let you figure something out," she said.

"You asked for it. Prepare for an invigorating one-hundred and twenty seconds of pure ecstasy," I said as slithered out of my clothes and slid beneath the covers.

My fingers gently caressed her cheek, and I lightly pressed my lips to hers. Our bodies warm against each other. An emotional wave moved through us as desire started to climb. Anticipation climbed higher and, in unison, controlled our every motion.

We've never lost the passion in our relationship. The fire has never roared so greatly.

We spent the night making love, holding each other, talked about family, friends, and Melissa Gardner's safe return home. We finally slipped into the deep realm of sleep a few hours before the sun peeked out over the horizon.

For the briefest of moments, my world made sense again.

Chapter 2

I remember thinking that nothing on earth would destroy my glorious return home. I felt that nothing would take me away from the work-free week I was going to spend with my girls and catch-up on overdue chores. All of that, unfortunately, changed early Tuesday morning.

I wasn't entirely sure if I was awake when I answered the phone. It was shrieking like a vindictive banshee. I snatched it up so that Caroline wouldn't wake.

"Hello?" I whispered.

"Um, Mr. Calloway, I'm so sorry to disturb you at such an early hour." The voice on the other end seemed nervous as words quickly tumbled over each other.

"Then, why did you?"

I was sure the caller was a journalist wanting the first crack at an interview about my recent kidnapping case. I receive a lot of calls like this. Every so often, newspaper rookies called and promised a sensational column about my successful investigations of missing and abducted children. I usually grant interviews with the idea that information raises awareness for everyone in the community.

"It's an urgent matter, sir. One that doesn't have the luxury of time," the caller said with a little more confidence.

My head was swirling. I wasn't entirely sure which way was up or down. I was desperately trying to fight off the fierce grip sleep had on me.

"Who the hell is this?" I asked.

"My name is Nolan Windell. I'm a personal assistant to California Senator John Hillcrest. We left Washington D.C. yesterday morning. I'm calling from his residence in California. I don't want to beat around the bush, so I'll get right to the point. Sunday night, someone kidnapped Hanna Jane Hillcrest from her Los Angeles home. I'm sure you know Senator Hillcrest is her father. Are you aware of who Ms. Hillcrest is?"

I gently slid from the bed, brought the cordless phone with me to the bathroom, turned on the faucet, and splashed frigid water in my face. I hoped it would wake me. This conversation is apparently one I needed to have some focus on.

"Yeah, my daughter is a huge fan of hers."

"At the time of the abduction, she was in the company of a young man named Michael McKay. He's a good friend of Hannah Jane's and was a guest at her home. He sustained a severe attack. Paramedics took him to St. Peter's Hospital. He's in the ICU now, but right now, the doctors won't allow the FBI to interview him."

A U.S. Senator's daughter kidnapped? Does the kidnapper want a ransom? Was there possibly a political agenda?

"You want me to get involved?"

"Yes. Senator Hillcrest personally asked for you. You've come highly recommended by everyone we've spoken with regarding the recovery of abducted children. Of course, Hannah Jane is seventeen now, hardly a child anymore. Senator Hillcrest has already spoken with FBI Director David Gill, who cleared the request for additional assistance. Senator Hillcrest wishes for you to come to Los Angeles ASAP."

I toweled off my face, returned to the bedroom, and sat on the edge of the bed. I couldn't believe this was happening. I closed my eyes and tried to pin down a single thought. I couldn't turn down this case, could I? It's my career, my obsession to find the missing, and safely bring them home. Even though I promised I wouldn't take another case for at least a week, I couldn't ignore any case brought to me.

I turned and looked over my shoulder at Caroline. She was fully awake, propped on her elbows, and watching me like a hawk. She had no doubt overheard the entire conversation and anticipated the direction of my decision.

"Mr. Calloway, are you still there?" Nolan Windell asked.

"Yes, I'm still here."

"I need to know if you'll take the case. Will you come to Los Angeles and help the FBI find Hannah Jane?"

I turned away from Caroline. I couldn't stand looking into her disappointed eyes. For the first time in my life, I would have to break a promise to my girls.

"Yes, Mr. Windell, I'll come to L.A."

Chapter 3

My mind and body were reluctant to leave so quickly after my return home. The good moments in life always seem so short-lived. However, the situation in L.A. won over all of my mental rejections of accepting the case. Hannah Jane Hillcrest is a nationally recognized young woman. Now she has vanished in the middle of the night. Her friend was brutally beaten and left for dead.

Hannah Jane started as a child star. At the tender age of four, her first television break was on a show called *Casey and the Clan*. Hannah Jane had played the know-it-all and always trouble-seeking middle daughter of a single mother. The show only lasted two seasons. At the age of eight, she landed a spot as a lovely co-host on a kid's game show called *Maze Craze*. From that point on, her career flourished. She later went on to several big-screen movies and added modeling and professional singing to her repertoire. Hannah Jane is an inspiration to young women worldwide to seek everything you genuinely want out of life.

Reanne adores Hannah Jane. She even has several movie and concert posters pinned up on her bedroom walls.

Nolan Windell, the man who had rudely awoken the household, arranged a flight on American Airlines bound for Los Angeles under the assumption that I agreed to take this case to find Hannah Jane. My plane departed in just over three hours, which gave me only enough time to shower, pack, and, at the very least, make breakfast for my girls.

Several red flags shot up in my mind when I spoke with Nolan Windell. First, why would Senator Hillcrest request the assistance of a private investigator from Atlanta when there are possibly dozens of others living in Los Angeles? Second, why would the FBI allow the senator to bring a private investigator into this delicate case?

At this point, I didn't know the answer to the first question.

The answer to the second question was possibly simple. The FBI most likely granted Senator Hillcrest's request to bring me in because he's a man with money and connections. I always figured that going against men like that was never a wise choice, no matter who you are.

By allowing me to work closely on the case, Senator Hillcrest wanted to know that things were progressing in a manner that wouldn't jeopardize his daughter's safety. He wanted an inside man. He needed the truth when the case either stalled or pushed forward and was not sugar-coated by the FBI's overwhelming natural ability to conceal facts. I've worked with the FBI many times before, and I understood Senator Hillcrest's method of thinking.

I might get the answers I wanted when I got to L.A.

The flight from Atlanta to Los Angeles was uneventful. I had too much time to think about how much I let down Caroline and Reanne. They put on strong faces of understanding and love, but I knew they were hurt nonetheless. I broke a promise and whisked away on another potentially dangerous case.

No matter how much I tried to sleep during the flight, I couldn't let my mind rest. My thoughts raced at a hundred miles an hour. I've only managed a few hours of sleep in two days.

Nolan Windell met me as I passed a security station and headed for baggage claim. He knew my face because he stepped right up to me and introduced himself. As we shook hands, his jacket sleeve pulled up, and I noticed a small tattoo on the outside of his right wrist. Nolan was in his early thirties, skinny frame, close-cropped brown hair, and intense hazel eyes behind wire-rimmed glasses. He walked with a sense of importance, moving through the crowd of travelers with little regard. When he spoke, he did so with a hint of cockiness, as if Hannah Jane's abduction were simply nothing more than an irritation to his daily routine.

"Senator Hillcrest will be meeting us at Hannah Jane's house. The FBI has already been over the crime scene. I think it will be okay if you want to look inside and understand how the kidnapping took place. Senator Hillcrest spoke with FBI Agent Harper Caster and made it clear that you'll be working with him on the kidnapping. This whole ordeal has just been terrible for everyone. The Senator and his wife are devastated over this."

"I'm sure they are. Unfortunately, parents suffer great emotional pain and a sense of helplessness when their child gets abducted."

As we left LAX, we slid into a sleek white limousine. I've never been in a limo or Los Angeles before. Killing two birds with a single stone, I suppose.

After an hour of battling L.A. traffic, we finally pulled up to Hannah Jane's house. I was surprised to see that the house was modestly simple. It was a two-story with cedar shake siding and a terracotta roof. Although it was large, it certainly wasn't anymore extravagant than the rest of the neighborhood. You'd never know it by looking at the house that a millionaire with credible fame lived here. Hannah Jane felt no need to flaunt her wealth and popularity. It's a simple statement that told me a lot about her character.

I followed Nolan Windell through the house with a different perspective. My investigative wheels were rapidly cranking. I noticed every little thing, and each household item told me a story about Hannah Jane. I filed away all the crime scene's raw material, giving my left-brain something to chew on for a while. Within the next hour, I would know Hannah Jane more intimately than the general public would ever get the chance.

"This is where the attack happened," Nolan said as we walked into the master bedroom.

Five feet from the door were several pools of blood on the beige carpet. I was sure this was the place where Michael McKay lay beaten and helpless. My mind analyzed the before, during, and aftermath of the attack. I wondered why the intruder had left Michael McKay alive. Why risk leaving a witness behind?

"Horrible to see so much blood, isn't it?" Nolan asked.

I forgot Nolan was standing behind me. My mind caught up in the crime scene.

"I don't mean to be rude, but could you leave me alone for a while? I need some time to think things through," I said.

"Of course. The senator is being dropped off out front. I'll wait for him there."

"Thanks."

I felt like a creep as I walked around Hannah Jane's bedroom and searched through her things. I searched the walk-in closet, her dresser drawers, jewelry box, clothes hamper, and beneath the bed. I found nothing incriminating enough to clue me in with who the intruder was or why he took Hannah Jane. I didn't doubt that the FBI had already collected all possible evidence.

I was sitting at the foot of the bed staring at the spray pattern of blood on the walnut headboard and wall when someone walked in the room and startled me.

"It makes me shudder. I'm not entirely sure if all this blood is Michael's or if some of it might be Hannah Jane's blood."

I turned and faced Senator John Hillcrest. Typically, I would have thought of him as an impressive man of power and respect, but today he looked twenty years older. His black suit was unkempt, his shirt untucked, and his tie hung loosely around his neck. His face was pale, his hair messed up, and deep wrinkles gathered under his swollen red eyes. He looked as if he badly needed sleep.

I stood and shook his hand. I said, "I wish our meeting were under different circumstances, Senator. I'm sorry about your daughter. I want you to know that I'll do absolutely everything possible to get her back safely."

"That's kind of you to say. You've come highly recommended. I respect your integrity. You've rescued a lot of families over the years."

"Thank you."

"Kids seem to grow up too damn fast. Hannah Jane wanted to prove her self-reliance at an early age. She was always stubborn about showing how she could make it in life. After maybe a year of nagging, I agreed to let her live here in L.A. Her entire career is here, and it certainly wasn't fair for me to keep her trapped in D.C. I eventually gave in to her requests and allowed her to move out here and live independently. She's only seventeen, still a child in my eyes, but far more responsible than most adults I've known. I have unconditional love and trust in her. I figured that I couldn't keep her tethered to my little finger her entire life. We have to let them go eventually. We have to let them spread their wings and fly."

"Yes, sir, it has to be a difficult thing to do. Can you tell me if anyone has called you with ransom demands yet?"

"The FBI assures me that there wouldn't be a ransom demand. Agent Harper Caster is in charge of this investigation. He told me that this is a highly unusual case. I suppose the agent found something here at the crime scene that told him so. Even though she's my daughter, he still won't tell me what's going on. He's secretive. That's why I want you here. I need someone trustworthy on my side. I need someone I can talk freely with and get straight answers about what's happening. I want you to work closely with this agent and keep me in the loop the entire time. I want, no, I *need* you to uncover the whereabouts of Hannah Jane. I need you to bring my child home alive. Money certainly isn't an issue. I'll pay whatever you want. Can you do that for me? Can you bring Hannah Jane home?"

Chapter 4

"I can read it in your eyes that you're a kind and caring person. I believe you want to find Hannah Jane as much as I do," Senator Hillcrest said.

We headed out the front door. A government vehicle was parked in the driveway as we came down the front cobblestone steps. A man was leaning against the fender.

Feds, I thought.

Senator Hillcrest followed my gaze and said, "That's Special Agent Harper Caster. I met him yesterday. I received a call around nine o'clock yesterday morning from a maid who comes to the house twice a week. She was frantic while she told me about Michael McKay lying bloody on the floor. She thought he was dead. She said she didn't know where Hannah Jane was. I flew across the country in a state of shock to find out that my daughter was missing. I don't know how, but the FBI knew Hannah Jane was missing before I did. That's why I insisted on having someone brought in to work the case with Agent Caster. The FBI knows a great deal about what has happened so far. I know next to nothing. I'm counting on you to change that. Please, don't let the FBI intimidate you or make you feel like you don't belong in this case. You do belong, Mr. Calloway. You're the only link I'll have to any facts."

The kidnapping of a child generally falls under the FBI's jurisdiction, especially the abduction of a senator's daughter. By doing what I do for a living, there are many cases in which I have no choice but to work with the feds. Senator Hillcrest's statement was correct. The FBI are professionals at trying to make me feel inadequate in every joint investigation.

"I'm not too concerned," I said.

"Well, you let me know right away if he's playing unfair and breaking the rules. I'll call Director Gill and settle things immediately."

"I don't think there will be a need for that. We may not like working with each other, but we're out for the same goal. We want to bring Hannah Jane home to you safe and sound."

"Thank you," Senator Hillcrest said with sincerity, shook my hand, and gave me a business card. "I'll leave you two alone. My cell number is on there. Please keep in touch as often as possible."

Senator Hillcrest walked to the limo without speaking with Agent Caster but offered a quick wave. Nolan Windell closed the limo door after the senator slid inside. Nolan moved to the opposite side, gave us what seemed to be a mocking salute, got in, and the limo sped away. There was something strange about the whole departure, but I let it go. I had other important things to wrap my mind around.

I walked down the drive to where the agent leaned against the front fender of a black sedan. My luggage was moved from the limo to the driveway at Agent Caster's feet.

I observed him closely as I approached. His clothing was straightforward and simple, black slacks, a white shirt with a black tie, a black jacket, polished black dress shoes, and finishing out the outfit with black shades. The image was so strange and humorous at the same time that I had to struggle to hold back the laughter. I wondered if he was aware that he mirrored the image that Hollywood movies gave FBI agents. His salt and peppered hair were receding, considerably extending his forehead, and combed back to cover the balding crown. He was too thin for his body structure, with broad shoulders and long arms and legs. I guessed his height around six feet, two inches. I estimated his age around fifty or maybe a little older.

As I approached, he thrust out his hand and said, "I'm Special Agent Harper Caster. It's been a while since I've teamed up with someone, but I welcome you to the hunt, Mr. Calloway."

I shook his hand. He had caught me off guard. I certainly wasn't expecting politeness, probably because the FBI never willingly displayed it before.

"Thanks."

Agent Caster must have read the mistrust on my face. He said, "I suppose you thought I was going to tell you to stay out of my parade?"

"I thought you were going to tell me to go fuck myself," I corrected.

"Not today," he said and laughed.

I thought I had grossly misread Agent Caster. So far, he seemed straightforward. Of course, it could have been a clever ploy to pull me into a false sense of security.

Agent Caster caught me even more off guard when he said, "We've got a lot to discuss. Are you hungry, Mr. Calloway?"

Chapter 5

We were in Agent Caster's government sedan rolling down the San Bernardino Freeway. I kept shifting in the seat, uncomfortably gazing out the window and then to Agent Caster. I hated working in these conditions. However, the investigator in me needed answers.

"What's the current condition of Michael McKay? Has he been able to give any information that would be of help?"

"Michael McKay has had surgeries off and on since being admitted. The assailant brutally beat him with a blunt object, probably a baseball bat or a pipe. Michael suffered broken bones and a major concussion. It's truly is amazing that Mr. McKay is alive. I don't believe he'll be able to speak with us for some time. We probably won't need to interview him anyway. I don't think he has any part in the game. He's probably not the clue we need to follow. Whatever the clue is, we'll have to wait for it. That's why we're getting something to eat while we have the chance."

"I'm not quite getting it. What game?"

"The game of life, death, Heaven, and Hell. Welcome."

"Look, if you're not going to be straight forward with me, then I'll go my own way with this investigation. I'm not going to play mental games with you when there are far more important things to focus on," I said. I was shooting venom now.

"I'm as honest as I can be. I'm not going to hide anything from you about this case. This case is extremely confidential, but we're working together now, and whatever I know, you'll know, I promise, Mr. Calloway."

"If you're serious, then I apologize. Since we'll be working together, you might as well call me Jack."

Agent Caster removed his black shades and looked at me. He had the most intense blue eyes I've ever seen. They were a pale, cool blue that dramatically stood out from the blackness of his clothing.

"My name is Harper."

"Now we're on a first-name basis. It's starting to sound like a partnership," I offered.

"Yeah, I guess it's time to fill you in, partner. He called me early Monday morning after he took Hannah Jane."

"Who called you?"

"The kidnapper."

"The kidnapper called you Monday morning?" I asked, a little stunned.

"Yeah, he always does when he takes a new one."

I shook my head slightly. "He who?"

Harper furrowed his brow. "The kidnapper. Didn't I say that?"

"Let me get this straight. The kidnapper calls you when he takes a new victim?"

"Yeah, he called around four in the morning. I figure it was right after he used Mr. McKay as a baseball and snatched Hannah Jane from her home. He told me he'd taken her, and the chase was on again."

"He's done this before?"

"Yeah, lots of times before."

"Then he's a serial kidnapper?"

"Killer."

"A serial killer?"

"Yeah, kidnapper and killer. He's first and foremost a killer. Hannah Jane is the prize if we can reach the end of the game by the time daylight falls on Sunday. If we don't, he'll kill her and start a new game."

"So you've played this game with this serial kidnapper slash killer several times before?"

"Yeah, going on four years now."

I felt like I was flying through *The Twilight Zone* at insane speeds and only catching snippets of one bizarre frame after another. Nothing was making sense to me. It had to be one of the most surreal conversations I've ever had.

"Four years? In all that time, you still aren't even close to capturing him?"

"Oh, no, we've caught him before."

"You caught him? So then he escaped?"

"No, he died."

"Died?"

"Yeah, pushing up daisies. I know it's all too confusing right now, but don't worry, because as soon as I get some food into me, I'll start making a little more sense. By the way, we're here."

Chapter 6

"I found this place a few years back. The food is excellent, and the atmosphere is comforting, so whenever I'm in these parts, I swing in," Harper said as we slid into a quiet corner booth.

It wasn't a typical restaurant like the ones I frequent with my family. Instead, the lighting was dim, several televisions were propped high in the corners broadcasting various sports stations, and the clientele kept to themselves while nursing drinks. I was surprised that only a moderate crowd filled the bar. The sounds of Billy Joel softly played over the speakers. It was a perfect place to get away and talk.

When the waitress popped over and gave a gentle smile, Harper said, "I'll have a double blackjack, and we'll take two plates of ribs smothered in the finest sauce."

"I'll take a Coke, thanks," I said.

When the waitress went to get the order, Harper turned to me and said, "I would have taken you for at least a light beer kind of guy."

I smiled at him. "You feds sure aren't very good at reading people. Besides, if I still consumed alcohol these days, I certainly wouldn't do it on the job."

I could read Harper's eyes and the dig about his drinking on the job he took to heart.

"After all I've seen over the years, you don't have a right or understanding to label me. I have images and feelings I live with every day that I'd rather see blurred out of existence," he said. His eyes were challenging me.

"I don't want you to think I'm judging you. I'm not. But I do know what you mean."

"How so?" he asked.

I was about to disclose something important to someone I hardly knew. Something like this was highly unusual for me. I have trust issues with everyone I meet. If I'm going to work with Harper, I need to begin a partnership of understanding. I decided that giving him a glimpse into the universal construct of Jack Calloway wasn't necessarily a bad thing.

"A long time ago, I was getting into a steady rhythm with my career. I was at the point of which I convinced myself that I was virtually unstoppable. I was working on a new case in Colorado. A young, precious girl named Connie Christensen vanished one day. My reputation at that point was considerably high. Her parents contacted me and brought me into my new quest to save Connie. This case both destroyed me and eventually saved me."

"Here you are, guys," the waitress said. She placed our drinks down, followed with two plates of ribs that pleased the nose as well as the eyes.

"Thanks," Harper said. He sipped his double blackjack and silently watched me.

"I spent over a week investigating her disappearance. I interviewed neighbors and potential witnesses to the kidnapping. I frantically worked with the police to quickly uncover her whereabouts. Nothing was working. She had completely vanished without a trace. Then, when it seemed like the case would never break, we get a phone call from a man who said he had discovered the body of

Connie Christensen. Connie was eight doors down from her parents' house the entire time. A man they knew and trusted had taken her. I had even spoken with him earlier that week. I never even suspected. If I had been a more thorough investigator, I would have done a background check on all the people in the immediate area where Connie lived. I would have discovered that Lawrence Richardson was a known child sex offender. If I had done my job correctly, the research would have probably led me there, and I might have been able to save one more child. From that point on, everything changed."

"What did he do to her?" Harper asked.

"Unspeakable things that I'd rather not describe. Connie was only fifteen, and he stole her innocence and eventually her life. One day Mr. Richardson's nephew made a surprise visit and found Connie's body in the basement. The night we got that horrible news, I crawled inside a bourbon bottle, and I didn't find my way out for nearly two long years."

"That's just terrible, Jack. I couldn't even imagine the burden of guilt that fell on you. You and I are in that same boat, on the very same ocean. I've suffered along with you. That kind of misery is ours to share. We're losing the battle to a world full of hate and complete disrespect for human life."

I then realized how devoted Harper was to the longevity of the human race. He chose to direct his life, just as I had, to the fight against the many faces of evil. Harper's kindness found the surface at that moment. I now clearly see how he cares about the ultimate goal of saving the missing. The dedication to the job wasn't just a primary career choice, but it was his ultimate struggle to keep hope alive.

After a long pause, I said, "Something good did come out of that entire mess. I began sinking deeper and deeper into depression. I was consuming more alcohol in a day than my body was willing to take in. The last night I had a drink, I'd gone well past my limit, and my body was shutting down. Before I blacked out, I was able to dial 911. It was one last desperate attempt to save my own pathetic life. My heart flatlined during transport. They spent a good five minutes working on me until I arrived DOA at the hospital. The doctors quickly took over. Nothing was working, and they were unable to shock me back to life. I was pronounced dead at 10:32, and at 10:36, my body jolted so violently that I nearly came off the table. The EKG began beeping with a heartbeat. Dr. Phillips later explained that my sudden reanimation shocked one of the nurses so much that she fainted. To make a long story short—"

"Too late," Harper chimed in with a smirk.

"I found my angel. I felt I needed to apologize to the nurse I'd startled so much. She turned out to be the most stunning, the most heartfelt person I've ever met. Nurse Caroline Vaughn. She had the kindest eyes, the sweetest smile, and the cutest tush. Do you know what made me fall in love with her so quickly?"

"The cutest tush?"

"No, that was the second reason. It was Caroline's compassion for human life. It was the same thing I once had and lost somewhere in a bourbon bottle. It wasn't that she was doing her job and taking care of a sick patient, but it was the fact that she didn't know me from any other stranger. She didn't know about the things I had done to save children from the cruelness of the world. As far as she knew, I was some poor street person the medics found and scooped out of the alley. It didn't matter to her because

I was a living, breathing person. She treated me with true compassion. Do you know how rare it is to find someone like that? Sometimes I tell myself that there are higher powers in the universe working in a divine and mysterious way. I sometimes believe that I was supposed to take the Connie Christensen case. As awful as it sounds, maybe Connie was meant to die the way she did. Maybe I was meant to slip into an alcoholic state for two years, which eventually brought me to death for countless minutes, and that I was supposed to be saved by my angel in a white uniform. I would never have pulled through if it weren't for her. I wouldn't have given up the bottle, and I would probably be dead now. My beautiful Caroline saved my life in more ways than one."

Harper gave me a gentle smile. "So, your angel brought you back from the blackness of sorrow to the ambient light of the world."

"That's a weird way to put it, but yeah, I suppose so."

The waitress came by, and we ordered another round of drinks.

Now that my story finished, we dug into the plates of ribs before they got cold. Harper was right. The food was phenomenal and awakened my taste buds as they have never been before. I eagerly tore into the ribs. I paused after each swallow with just enough time to breathe.

"So far in my career, I've brought one-hundred and fifty-four children home safely. Hannah Jane will make lucky number one hundred and fifty-five," I said with confidence.

"I hope you're right, Jack. I really do. No child should have to be a part of something this huge."

Harper's face grew a little sad as he seemed troubled.

"We're here talking a lot about my life and none of yours. You're the one who asked me here for some reason

29

other than food. So, I guess what I'm trying to say is, spill it."

Harper downed half of his double before he spoke again. "Do you believe in God, Jack?"

Chapter 7

I leaned back in the booth. "Man, you're not going to get all Holy Roller on me, are you?"

"Answer the question. It's important, especially to the case."

I wiped sauce from my hands and face. I couldn't have guessed where the question came from or where it might be going, but I played along anyway.

"All right, all right. I suppose you could say that I'm on the fence about a higher power overseeing everything. I see the world for what it is. If there's a God, why is there so much cruelty and hatred around us? Why would God allow a child to get run down in the middle of the road? Why give a child cancer? Or why let a group of terrorists fly airplanes into buildings and killing thousands of people? If it's true that God loves us, why would such things happen?"

"Some of that has a purpose, Jack. *Reasons.* What if I told you that things like murder and war were beyond God's control?"

"I think you've finally flown off the rails. You're implying that God doesn't have control of our existence? That there might even be higher powers?" I wondered where Harper was going with this bizarre line of questions and answers.

"No, I'm not talking about higher powers or even equal powers. I'm talking about influence, a persuasion from those who paid the price for their betrayal. Now they're using this form of punishment to their advantage."

My mind was whirling a bit. I didn't understand a thing Harper was trying to get across to me. "What exactly are you getting at?"

"I'm talking about angels, Jack. Fallen angels. *Killer angels.*" Harper's face was dead serious.

I couldn't believe what I was hearing. *Killer angels?* It was, I guess, practically insane to think. No man who has a strong faith in God would comprehend such a thing. Angels fallen from Heaven are now killing humans? What would possibly push Harper to this method of thinking?

"I think you've been working for the bureau far too many years. I think they've brainwashed you one too many times. Maybe it's time for your annual CAT scan. There could be some irreparable damage if you delay treatment." I watched Harper closely. I was waiting for his exterior to crack and a smile to break out and give me a "just messing with you" kind of look. FBI humor and all, but it didn't come. I don't think I've ever seen a more serious look.

"You're probably not going to believe me when I tell you this, Jack, but we're at war."

"War? Are you saying we're at war with God?"

"No, I'm not saying that at all. We're battling *with* God, not against Him. We're fighting a mistake."

I held up my hands to halt everything. "Okay, let's turn the clock back to the beginning. Let's pretend I don't have a damn clue what the hell you're saying. It shouldn't be too hard, because I truly don't. Talk to me like I'm a three-year-old with ADD."

"All right then. I'll start from the beginning. A three-year-old with ADD. Gotcha." Harper took in a deep breath, trying to focus his thoughts on one specific time in history. "There are some important things that happened throughout history. Biblical stuff that people shouldn't know about."

"You're talking about this mistake?"

"Yes. I'll break it down for you as simple as possible. When God created angels, they were well-loved and honored as a perfect creation. They felt the divine love of their creator every moment of their existence. God's love *is* powerful, Jack. It's a love that's more powerful and fulfilling than anything else in this entire universe. Then came the time when God decided to create the earth and humankind. His glory and love were taken from these beautiful angels and focused on His new creation. He placed humans on the top pedestal of His everlasting glory and loved us above all others. One angel started it all. You know of him just like everyone else. Beelzebub, Lucifer, Satan, or the Devil. He has so many names. He decided to begin a rebellion against God. He built a battalion of followers. Satan challenged the throne, and at the end of the war, he lost everything he hoped to gain. His intentions were simple. He didn't want to be second best. The love he once felt so purely was gone. Satan understood that a creation below all angels now held God's love. As punishment for betrayal, God sent Satan and his followers to Hell, the land of sinners."

"I'm pretty sure that I've heard this all before, Harper. I was once in Sunday School a lifetime ago," I said. I was still a little confused. This subject was certainly far beyond the typical barroom chat.

"Okay, I'm getting there. Just be patient. What you may not know is that time ticked along, and everything seemed fine. Then an overwhelming influence from the evil powers below, Azrael, the Angel of Death, was convinced by Satan to begin another rebellion. Satan told Azrael if he could command a larger army of followers, then victory would be his. The war was long and defiant. In the end, Azrael suffered the same loss as Satan. But this time, as a different form of punishment, each angel who stood against God was sent to Earth, not Hell. Their punishment was more severe than the army who fought before. These angels were forced to live among His proudest creation for all eternity. They are spirits living within humans. They'll never have a body of their own. They take possession of a human body only when a person dies, and the occupying soul moves on. These angels will continue to move from body to body until the end of time. God's goal was to show the angels why He loved this new creation so much. These angels have all the emotional feelings and thoughts that exist within the human form. God meant for them to look upon all of His creation with open and heartfelt eyes. But God's plan, His idea, was a massive failure. Instead of experiencing what He wanted them to, they began a rebellion in a new light. They decided to destroy His creation. It became a front line assault that they brought from Heaven to Earth."

I sunk against the booth. I wasn't entirely sure what I was supposed to be thinking. It was like getting skull thumped with a sledgehammer. I could see it in Harper's face. This conversation was no joke. He firmly believed what he was saying. Harper's convinced that there's no other explanation to the madness in the endless universe.

"So, what you're saying is that we're at war with angels who we can't kill? Spirits occupying a human body, and they continue influencing us in a bad way?"

"Not influencing us, corrupting us. Face-to-face destroying our existence. We were once a creation of absolute perfection, flawless in all aspects, and filled with love and goodwill. We never felt anger, hate, mistrust, and the need to bring violence upon one another. Satan and Azrael and their winged armies showed us how to feel and act out all those emotions. They're destroying a once-perfect creation out of spite."

"So, I'm guessing the archives of top-secret FBI files come spilling out to civilians now? Is this a new method of public relations by getting everything out in the open? Is it a time to air out those dusty confidential file drawers? I think I like that, not having secrets anymore. At least you'll make work much easier for those pesky reporters," I said.

I was irritated by Harper. I felt like he was trying to belittle my intelligence and waste my time. I also felt like he was trying to make a mockery of what we were doing here, our moment of bonding, and the search for Hannah Jane.

"I never said it was going to be easy for you to understand, Jack. I can't blame your denial. I was once in the same shoes you're in now. I didn't believe it either, not at first. It took a lot of time and serious convincing."

I wanted to retreat from this insane conversation of killer angels, human annihilation, and a God with no control over it.

"Just because something sounds extremely far-fetched doesn't make it false. What I've told you is the truth. I've lived and dealt with it for the last four years. The FBI won't allow me to move to any other case, and Azrael won't allow it either. I'm stuck. I've even tried retirement, but Azrael killed my replacement, and he's promised to blink out my wife and daughter's existence if I give up hope, if I give up the chase."

35

Harper slammed his palm down on the table hard enough to rattle the plates and glasses. He looked utterly deflated. He seemed frustrated and sick of this chase.

I raised my hands in surrender. "All right, for the moment, I'll give you the benefit of the doubt until you convince me with proof, ironclad proof. So, where do we go from here?"

Chapter 8

Christine Daniels hadn't experienced such a wonderful day in years. Everything had gone to plan. The marketing pitch to the clothing manufacturer, Tiffany's Style, had gone flawlessly, and the paperwork was signed and sealed by lunchtime.

She smiled to herself as she glanced at the desktop clock. Peter had promised her a victory lunch at Mattela's.

A gentle knock came on her office door. Peter McCabe popped his head inside and said, "Are you ready?"

"Speak of the Devil. I was thinking about you, and some of those thoughts might have even been naughty." Christine said and smiled. She hadn't felt so alive as she did now. Work was perfect, and her romantic relationship was perfect. Life was perfect.

He stepped inside and closed the door. "Would you be interested in telling me exactly what these naughty little thoughts might have been?"

"And ruin my reputation as Queen of Proper Etiquette?"

He approached her, slowly drawing his eyes over her slender body, curves in all the right places. "Because if you tell me, I might do them. Does one of them perhaps involve me locking the door, tearing your clothes off, and making love to you on the desk? If you ask nicely, I could do that for you."

Peter leaned in and kissed her gently on the lips. His hands fell to her waist and then curved around to her butt and firmly squeezed. He felt anticipation rising as the kissing became more profound and more passionate.

Christine pulled away. "My God, are you extremely horny or what?" She laughed as she glanced down to see the bulge in his slacks.

"Don't laugh. You started it. I can't believe how much willpower you have to turn away from temptation like that."

"That's easy," Christine said with a smirk. "I don't have a penis named Kung-Pao, making all of my decisions."

"Hardy-har-har. Does that mean you're ready for lunch instead?"

"Definitely, and maybe tonight, if you're lucky, I'll be in the mood for some spicy Chinese food."

"For sure. You know I'm still whirling from the meeting. We managed to cut right through all the crap, and everyone jumped all over the deal just as we anticipated. I'm proud of you. I couldn't believe how in control you were. Your approach to cover every possible question was phenomenal. You're a hell of a firecracker," Peter said. He gave her a warm smile and a wink.

They reached the elevators. A small lunchtime crowd had gathered. The elevator chimed its arrival, and the group moved in. Christine and Peter managed to squeeze in last.

As the doors began to close, someone down the hall called out, "Hold the elevator, please!"

Peter stuck his arm out and retracted the doors. A young, handsome priest carrying a Bible approached and smiled a note of thanks as he inquisitively studied the elevator and its passengers.

"It seems a little too crowded. Perhaps I'll catch the next one."

"I'm sure we can fit you in," Peter said.

"Quite all right. The next one would be fine." He looked directly at Christine and smiled.

It was something in his smile that sent a shiver up Christine's spine. It wasn't a smile of gratitude or any other type of casual smile. It was a smile that gave her the impression that he knew all of her dirty little secrets. It was as if he read her thoughts and uncovered all the skeletons in the deep shadows of her closet. It was a smile of pure distaste.

"Suit yourself. Have a great day, Father," Peter replied.

As the doors began to close again, the priest mouthed something to Christine. The doors fully closed, and the elevator started its descent.

Christine thought of how odd it was that a priest was on the Bennett Tower's fifty-sixth floor.

What possible mission would have called him here? No one else had even noticed the strangeness of his presence in a business building. Perhaps he's just visiting a friend or a member of the church. Maybe he's visiting someone in need of counseling. But what had he said to me?

The elevator halted, and the doors parted to a small crowd waiting. None were able to fit, and the doors closed again.

A sickening feeling churned in Christine's stomach as she closed her eyes and saw the priest again. He said something to her, only her. She didn't think the other passengers were supposed to see what he mouthed to her. She was now positive about what he had said. But it was something she could have taken in different ways.

39

He had said, "Say your prayers, Christine." But he's a priest. Quit freaking yourself out. He was giving you friendly advice, that's all. But that smile. That God-awful smile told me a different story. The way his eyes looked deeply into me was wrong. He even knows my name!

Christine turned to Peter. Her face had gone pale. He stopped talking when he sensed something was wrong.

"What is it, Christine?" Pete asked.

She leaned in and said, "Did you see the way the priest looked at me? It gave me the creeps, and I feel like something is wrong. I mean, I really think something is wrong."

Suddenly an explosion erupted from above. The elevator car fiercely shook. The ceiling tiles shattered and rained down on the passengers, and then the lights went out and left them in the darkness. Everyone began to scream as the elevator started falling.

The descent was brief, as the emergency brakes activated and halted the deadly plunge.

Christine had a fierce grip on Peter's hand that was nearly hard enough to break bones.

"What the hell was that?" someone asked.

"Did the cable break? We fell a couple of flights. I think the cable might have broken."

Say your prayers, Christine.

Peter was asking if she was all right. He was shaking her, but she couldn't answer because her voice wasn't there. She thought that if only she had stayed in her office with Peter, she could be secretly making love and avoiding this whole awful mess.

Stomach acid crept up her throat. She thought she was going to throw up when she realized that the priest had planned everything. He had brought on this unspeakable madness. That all-knowing smile of his had told her everything. He wasn't giving her advice to say her nightly prayers. He was telling her to prepare for what was about to come.

Four smaller sequential explosions rocked the elevator. The emergency brakes released, and the rapid descent started again.

So did the screams.

Chapter 9

On Wednesday afternoon, Harper and I were hauling ass down the Santa Ana Freeway in post lunchtime traffic trying to get to the Bennett Tower. Getting anywhere fast in L.A. was practically impossible, especially on the freeway.

Twenty-three minutes ago, eleven people fell from the sky. The elevator passengers fell from somewhere near the top floor of the building. It was unclear as of yet, but none presumed to have survived.

Harper and I had been at the library, killing time when Harper's cell disrupted the quiet atmosphere. The caller said three clear words: *Eleven. How beautiful.*

Harper and I had been playing the waiting game since our bar room chat late yesterday evening. Our free time primarily focused on filling my brain with stories of holy wars and angels who had fallen from grace. Being more prepared than not, Harper brought files from previous cases dealing with Azrael and his sadistic games. Harper was using every method possible to give me the ironclad proof I needed.

At first, Harper had spent well over an hour trying to explain to me the ordeal we'd soon be facing. I took it all in for what it was worth. I then asked him for the *Reader's Digest* version to help my mind process everything a little quicker and with a lot more clarity.

The breakdown Harper gave me was simple, just as I asked. The Angel of Death played a cruel and twisted game with the authorities, and the grand prize was Hannah Jane's life. Azrael was going to deliver us a crime scene, and from that, we had to quickly decipher a clue within that would eventually lead us to another crime scene and so on. We had to figure out all the clues left behind to reach Hannah Jane before the deadline. Hannah Jane has until nightfall on Sunday, which is exactly one week from the day he had snatched her. Harper told me that the number of bodies and the clues left behind wasn't always the same. It was one of the many things making the game so challenging. Harper never knew for sure exactly how far ahead or behind he was in the game.

We are now chasing Death, and I'm terrified of the things we'd find in his path.

After Azrael called Harper to announce the number of victims, Harper contacted the local precinct and asked for information on recent tragic events with many estimated casualties. There was an elevator disaster in the downtown area with an unknown number of fatalities.

We arrived on North Hope Street to fire engines, patrol cars, ambulances, and news crews filling the road. Swirling lights were everywhere. The crowd of onlookers crammed in tight along the block. They were restless and far too curious about the tragedy. It all made the scene even edgier.

Harper flashed his badge to a patrol blockade, and they waved us through. We hustled up the flight of stone stairs and inside the Bennett Tower. The scene inside wasn't as frantic. Most of the available FBI agents, patrol units, and building security were scouring the building from lobby to roof, looking for clues left behind.

The L.A. Bomb Squad was also on the scene. They searched for the detonation point to determine if the worst of the attack was behind us or something more severe still ahead. I prayed there wasn't another bomb somewhere.

We walked down the hallway to the elevators. The ground was thick with building debris, and a thicker layer of dust covered everything.

I saw the elevator doors had sustained enough damage that the entire right door had been blown clear from the impact zone and had solidly smashed against the marble tiles of the opposite wall.

As I walked forward, the slender pale arm of a young female reached out. My eyes traveled from her wedding ring to her auburn hair. I couldn't look away, no matter how much I wanted. The woman's beautiful features spattered with blood. My heart suddenly felt a deep ache as I looked into her piercing green eyes, and she lifelessly stared back at me.

The scene was a horrifying nightmare from which I couldn't wake up. I couldn't even blink. There was blood everywhere, with bodies heaped over one another. Azrael told Harper that the victim count was eleven, but it was so hard to tell. It could have been more or less.

The medics and firefighters began to carefully check for survivors as they removed each person from the elevator. The bodies never seemed to stop coming out. They placed them side by side on the marble lobby floor.

Harper and I silently stood next to each other. We were unable to find words for this tense situation.

The medics grievingly shook their heads as they removed the last body. It was a simple confirmation that none of them survived. I wasn't entirely sure of what I was supposed to be feeling. A great sadness, sure, but I couldn't stop thinking of Hannah Jane and the sheer hell she must be enduring. If it's true that Azrael committed this chaos and that the elevator drop was all part of his morbid plan, then there was still a glimmer of hope for Hannah Jane. In a way, these people died for a chance to save her life.

My eyes traveled over the bodies again. These people were bloody soldiers on the front line of a war they didn't even know they were fighting. There *are* eleven victims.

Chapter 10

I turned to Harper. "How do you think this fallen angel of yours knew there were eleven victims in the elevator?"

"I'm not sure. Azrael could have walked by the elevator before the doors closed or stood off in the distance and counted them as they stepped inside. Hell, he could have very well tapped into the security camera going to that elevator. What's most important about this crime scene is that only one of these victims has a trail we're obligated to follow. He killed the other ten simply because they were there."

"This building has six elevators. How would Azrael know which one this special victim would take to the lobby?" I asked.

"Maybe they're all rigged with explosives, but I doubt it. Maybe Azrael even somehow temporarily disabled the other three elevators, but I doubt that as well. He's a creature of precision. He's an expert planner. I figure he watched his target for several days, perhaps longer. Maybe that's what he's been doing the past two days since he took Hannah Jane. The point is that he knew this person would be on that elevator."

A crime scene tech appeared from the stairwell to the right of the elevators and approached us. He handed Harper two clear sealed evidence bags.

"We found these in a utility closest on the fifty-sixth floor. From what we know, the fifty-sixth floor is the last stop to pick up passengers before the explosion."

In the first bag, there was a priest's uniform. In the second bag was a Bible folded open to the cover page. There was a type of poem written on the inside cover of the Bible. It read:

Eleven angels fell from the sky,
It is quite obvious they could not fly.
What a shame it was not me instead,
For those eleven souls would not be dead.
But no matter how innocent they all appeared,
A skeleton in the gloomy closet one of them feared.
She could not run or hide from her past,
For in the tragic end, it caught up with her at last.

Azrael was pinpointing a female individual within the group. The other ten had nothing to do with this unfortunate ending to their lives. They should have been spared from this horrific nightmare.

Although the bodies were removed a short while ago to begin the identification process, I recall seeing six women and five men. Azrael twice mentioned the number eleven in the poem. He knew for certain how many people were in the elevator. Had he written the sadistic poem as those eleven people fell to their deaths?

"I'm going to send several men to retrieve the names and statements of all the employees on the fifty-sixth floor. Someone must have noticed a priest. I'll also have some of my guys review the security footage and see if we can pick out our man coming in or leaving the building. As for us, we need to do a thorough background check on the women in the elevator. We need to kick over every rock. According to Azrael, one of them has something important to tell us," Harper said

Chapter 11

Harper and I were at the L.A. field office. Agents were buzzing around, and the entire floor was like a pissed off hornet's nest. After nearly two hours of Harper, several agents, and myself racking our brains, we had the six women's background information.

I looked over the list. Two women had a police record but only charged with minor offenses.

I saw nothing. None of this information called out to me. Something was missing.

"I give," I finally said to Harper.

"Me, too. This situation isn't usual," Harper said.

"I should hope that eleven people falling to their death isn't usual for you. So, one woman in the elevator has a secret past. From the look of things, I don't see a major offense that would concern us. I certainly don't see anything here I'd consider a skeleton in the closet severe enough for the execution the woman received."

Harper shook his head. He collapsed in one of the chairs, and his body sagged. "I don't either. Of course, whatever this woman did, she didn't get caught, or it would be in her criminal file."

I suddenly had an idea. "If you had a terrible secret, something you couldn't seem to get away from or cope with, how would you deal with it?"

"I suppose there are many ways. Eventually learn to live with it, suicide or changing your identity and running from the law." I saw a light flicker in Harper's eyes.

"Damn, she changed her identity. So whatever name she goes under now is irrelevant. It would be the victim's former name we need to find to dig up the skeleton. We had already checked, and none of the women in the elevator did a legal name change. Our girl went about it another way. She probably paid some big bucks to get a fake birth certificate, Social Security card, and driver ID. Trying to track whoever doctored these documents for her would be next to impossible, but there are other ways."

"Yep." I sat at one of the computers. One of the good things about working with the FBI, I always have unlimited information directly at my fingertips without being denied access to top-secret files and websites.

I accessed several websites at once and crosschecked the social security numbers we had for our six women. I knew of several ways to obtain fake identification. Since I'm constantly bouncing around the country, I always keep my ears open and pick up valuable information from whatever source it might flow.

One of the ways I knew was by assuming the identity of someone who has passed away. If you had a person's social security number, not even the card itself, just the number, you could find a way to get a new identity.

"These days, someone can obtain a social security number over the internet if they know what they're doing." I had quickly found what I wanted.

I printed the pages of the six women.

I scanned the material. "Interesting. According to the social security numbers provided by Hayes Marketing, of the six women, one of them named Christine Daniels died twice. First, I found a death certificate dated 2015, stating she died at thirty-two from leukemia. Today she died again at the age of thirty-seven."

"Died twice. That is interesting. Maybe this girl is related to you?" Harper said and then eyed me.

I turned from the pages and watched Harper closely. Just yesterday, I had told him about the first time I died. I have a strong suspicion he knows about the second death as well. Those FBI guys thought they knew everything.

"I don't recall meeting her at any of the family reunions, so probably not. I think it's highly likely that Christine Daniels is the girl we're supposed to research. We need to find her closest colleagues. Maybe she confided in one of them. Maybe one of them knows about her troubled past. We might get lucky and figure out her former identity. Isn't this the kind of path Azrael wants us to find?"

"That's exactly it. Whoever Christine Daniels used to be, she did something terrible. She then changed her identity to escape it. She altered her life from that point and found a new purpose. Azrael punished her for that. He loves to destroy those who find divine guidance and reinvent themselves from the chaos of their past." Harper took the pages from me and studied them. "This has to be the woman we're supposed to find. All of the other women check out."

It seems like such a crooked road we're heading down. I was slowly learning more about the case of Death.

Truthfully, I still don't believe Harper's theory of killer angels destroying our existence, even though he showed me files from previous cases countering my beliefs. The whole thing sounded extremely left field. For the moment, our unidentified subject was just another ordinary bad guy to me.

Christine Daniels had taken her troubled life and flipped a perfect one hundred and eighty degrees toward a more hopeful future. Christine's rocky past would lead us to someone else, and so on. Eventually, we'd come to the final clue, which would lead us to Hannah Jane's whereabouts. This game is undoubtedly a wicked spider web carefully woven.

Who are you, Christine Daniels?

Chapter 12

Harper and I were driving down Sideways Lane, which hid deep in the outskirts of Los Angeles. The houses were large and widely spaced. It was a neighborhood with a lot of income.

We were on our way to visit with Donna Hayes, the CEO of Hayes Marketing.

Donna Hayes' home was a Spanish style design with a red terracotta roof and a cream stucco siding. Even though it was considered winter, the temperature was sixty-two, and the lawns were lush and green.

As it happened, we hadn't yet tried to seek out Donna Hayes. She found us. I suppose when something as severe as eleven employees suddenly dying in a violent act, the company owner would want to make friends with those leading the investigation.

Donna Hayes was waiting for us and ushered us inside. She was undoubtedly a businesswoman, but today she was dressed down. She was wearing a pair of faded blue jeans with small holes in the knees, a worn gray tee shirt, and her black hair pulled back in a ponytail.

As if she'd been reading my eyes, Donna Hayes said, "I'm sorry for my appearance. I've been taking a much-needed vacation this week, spending most of that time in the greenhouse. I must look like a mess. Can I offer you anything to drink?"

"No, thanks. I'm fine," Harper said.

"I'm good, too," I said.

"Very well. If you could please have a seat in the living room, I'll excuse myself and wash up." She disappeared up the staircase.

I was immediately impressed with the interior décor. Ms. Hayes had undoubtedly taken some of that highly earned income and invested it in her home.

After an extensive view of what the entryway alone had to offer, I turned to Harper and asked, "So, where the hell is the living room?"

"It's got to be here somewhere. Let's wander."

We moved from room to room, studying various artworks that seemed to clutter the walls instead of adding a taste of beauty. There is such a thing as going over the top, and it appeared Donna Hayes had achieved that with flying colors. We finally stumbled into what we figured was the living room. I sat and sank into the sofa. It could have been another work of art as far as I was aware. I felt extremely out of place here.

After nearly twenty minutes passed, Ms. Hayes entered the living room wearing the same thing she had on before. The only thing I saw different was the smudge of dirt that had been on her cheek was now gone. Her eyes were watery and red from crying. I figured she had excused herself and lost her composure in the other room.

"I'm sorry to keep you waiting. You're Agent Harper Caster of the FBI?"

"Right."

"And you are?"

"My name is Jack Calloway. I'm a private investigator."

"The FBI and a private investigator working together on this terrible accident. Interesting, I think." She took a seat in one of the plush armchairs, folded her hands, and crossed her legs.

"I'm sorry to tell you that this certainly wasn't an accident. Someone murdered eleven of your employees today," Harper said.

"So I've heard. It was an explosion of some sort. Someone rigged a bomb on the main cable of the elevator?"

"Yes, and also explosives on the emergency brakes. Once those detonated, the people inside the elevator didn't have a chance. I understand that you were close friends with one of the deceased," Harper said.

For such a stone-cold glare, Donna Hayes' face suddenly softened a little. "Yes. My colleagues have informed me that my friend Christine Daniels was on that elevator. She certainly didn't deserve this."

"I don't suppose any of them did," I offered.

"No, I don't suppose so. I've known Christine for nearly four years. I hired her myself. I met Christine at a local gym I used to frequent. We hit it off pretty well. I think she understood me when no one else did."

"So, you gave her a job because she understood you?" Harper asked.

"No, I gave her a job because she was looking for one. She said that she was in the market for a growing opportunity at a suitable company. I offered her a secretarial position, and it worked out well for quite some time. I was so impressed with her intelligence and creative thinking that I made her my assistant, and later she earned the position as a marketing advisor. She was an all-around dynamite person. She often brought in newer and younger clients who had a lot of money to spend on marketing promotions."

I stood. Being sunk half a foot into the sofa was starting to give me a backache.

"If you want to know the truth of things, I've been divorced for seven years. My husband ran off with a large chunk of my money and the twenty-year-old we hired to clean the house twice a week. I not only hired Christine because she befriended me, but because I was physically attracted to her. I was hoping something else would come out of the friendship."

"Did it?" Harper asked.

She smiled casually. "No. Christine didn't jog down that particular path, if you know what I mean. Our friendship was aces anyway. I think for the last year, or so she's been seeing someone. I don't know who it is for sure, but I think it was someone at the office. It most likely had to be because Christine was a workaholic if ever there was one. There were many days when she was in the office before me and out the door long after everyone else had gone home. I have no doubt she was gunning for the top of the charts and probably would have succeeded if this God awful day never happened."

"Can you think of any reason someone would want to murder Christine? Especially someone angry enough to kill ten other innocent people in the process?" I asked.

"Everyone at work loved Christine. I honestly can't think of a single person on the planet who would do such a malicious act."

"What about someone who wanted to hurt the old Christine, or more specifically, the person she was before she swapped identities with a dead person?" Harper asked in a cut-through-the-bullshit kind of tone.

"Sorry?"

"Christine Daniels wasn't her real name. However, we don't know who she was before, and that's a gem of information we'd like to gather as soon as possible. You're going to help us."

Donna Hayes gave a sly smile. "How original. I know something the FBI doesn't."

Chapter 13

Donna Hayes opened the drawer of the table beside the chair. She retrieved a small silver case, opened it, and pulled out a cigarette. Without asking if it might bother us, she leaned back and lit up.

"Christine was a troubled girl for a long time. She finally stepped over the line that no one should cross. The point of no return, they say. It had taken several years of our friendship to evolve before she would confide in me. The key to earning Christine's trust was not to push too hard. I knew she had something she needed to get off her chest. I could tell when Christine got uncomfortable whenever I asked where she came from and what she had done for a living before we met. She got edgy and avoided the subject by quickly changing it."

I was pacing the room as I listened to Ms. Hayes weave her story of a friendship suddenly bound together and taken apart just as quickly. I felt that she truly missed her friend.

"Was it murder she was running from?" I finally asked.

"If I tell you what I know, will you swear to me that you won't slander her good name? She deserves that at least." She puffed out a cloud of smoke and eyed us carefully.

"Of course, it depends on the severity of the offense, but I can almost guarantee the press won't ever get wind of this. We can't cover up what happened today. The press already knows about the accident, but Christine's past won't see the light of day," Harper said.

"Fair enough," Ms. Hayes said.

I took a seat in one of the adjacent chairs.

"To answer your question, yes, it was murder. Christine's real name was Nancy Stillwell. She came to L.A. from New York City back in 2015. She was formerly in the prostitution trade. She told me that she had many regulars, certain men who gave her frequent business. She had told me about one man in particular. She said that she had grown to trust him as she had never trusted a client before. Christine said that he was a man with great sincerity. She grew more comfortable around him, and every so often, they would go out to get a bite to eat and talk about what they wanted out of life."

"Then everything went wrong?" Harper asked.

"It went wrong in so many ways. Christine's client suggested that they could take a drive somewhere out of the way and secluded one night. As they did their thing, a police car pulls up behind them."

I thought I knew where this story was heading, and I didn't like it one bit. I wondered how Azrael had received all this information. The FBI didn't know who Christine Daniels had previously been until we spoke with someone close to her. How could Azrael have obtained this information?

"I'm sure the cop thought he'd just stumbled upon some young kids making out. But it was worse than that because he was well aware of what her profession was. She said that when the officer had them outside of the vehicle, he searched them, checked their identification, and questioned them. He was leading them to the squad car when the man named Nathan Kline completely freaked out. He jumped the officer, brutally lashing out until the two of them collapsed to the ground in the scuffle. He picked up a rock and struck the officer in the head, just once. Officer Andrew King died almost instantly. The blow nearly caved in half of his skull."

"Holy shit," Harper said disbelievingly.

"I second that," I said. I was quickly writing everything down.

Ms. Hayes stood, went to the small mahogany bar in the corner of the room, and made herself a drink. It was clear that it was hard for her to confess a friend's secret.

"Do you realize that under extreme circumstances, people can do some messed up things? Prison time can scare the hell out of the most sensible people," she said.

"Yeah, I think we understand that. What did the two do next?" Harper asked.

"Christine and Nathan did the only thing that made sense at the time. They dragged the police officer's body into the woods and buried him in a shallow grave. Nathan told Christine that she was just as guilty as he was and that if she told anyone, she'd go down, too. Prison for life. He said he would drive the officer's car and ditch it miles away from the body. Christine departed in her car, and she never saw the man again."

Donna Hayes gave us a moment to take in everything said.

She said, "Of course, the cruiser had a GPS tracking system in it, so the authorities located it right away. However, the body of the officer remained in that shallow grave for almost a week. Two boys playing in Central Park woods found a shoe sticking out of the dirt. I'm sure they were startled as hell when they learned that the shoe wasn't empty.

Christine fled as soon as the news came out about the found body. Maybe she figured she could get lost in another city just as large as New York. The authorities still haven't solved the case."

"Why didn't you ever go to the authorities with this information?" I asked.

"Christine didn't murder that cop. I want to make that very clear to you. Nathan Kline was the one with the rock, and he was the one who ended the officer's life. Christine did help in hiding the body, simply out of fear for her own life. I'm sure almost anyone under the same circumstances would have done the same. The officer was dead. If I spilled what I had learned, it wouldn't have brought him back, and Christine would have gone to prison. She became a better person, and after all that, she deserved a second chance at life."

"You're right. It wouldn't have brought the officer back," I agreed. "But bringing Christine Daniels to the authorities would have announced the killer's name and eventually brought him to justice. It could have given the family of that officer peace knowing that the killer would pay for the crime."

She shrugged defiantly. "So arrest me if you disagree with what I've done. It won't change anything. I've given you Christine's real name. I told you the name of the man who murdered the police officer. I think I've done more good here than bad, don't you?"

I wondered if this woman had always been so cruel, so cold-blooded. If so, I understood why her husband left her for a twenty-year-old maid. He obviously couldn't stand her anymore, and neither could I.

I stood and made my way back through the house and out the front door. I had all the information I needed.

Harper joined me on the front porch a short while later. We silently stood there, watching the final rays of the sun pull away from the California sky. Another day had raced away.

"We're done here, Jack. We now know our next step. We need to find out where Nathan Kline is these days."

"I'm sorry about that. I couldn't stand looking at that woman another second."

Harper said, "I'm not going to have her charged with obstruction. She can live with the death of her friend. Most of all, she can live with herself. I think that seems like punishment enough."

Chapter 14

At ten o'clock on Thursday morning Harper and I arrived at a small L.A. airfield. Fortunately, we weren't flying commercial. It wasn't convenient or productive, and we certainly didn't know what out-of-the-way place we'd need to land. Harper was afforded a private plane and pilot for the duration of the case of Death.

A Galaxy Aerospace C-38A Courier plane waited on the private runway. It was a beautiful piece of machinery, a sleek white mid-sized craft that was certainly accommodating enough for just the two of us. The twin turbofan jets started as the pilot saw our sedan reach the private runway. I thought that these guys were definitely on the ball.

Harper and I had found our clue.

Christine Daniels had taken the task of switching identities the unconventional way, and this had made our job a little tougher to uncover her real name. Nathan Kline took the same approach, killing more time for us to reveal his new name and location. We had finally got in touch this morning with a distant uncle in New York, and he provided the information we desperately wanted.

Nathan Kline now went by the name Richard James.

Richard James had unleashed his wings and took flight from New York to a tiny dot on the map called Treagan, New Mexico.

What was even more astounding about Richard James was that he had joined the priesthood, and less than a year later, he packed up all of his belongings and left New York behind.

"I think I'm still trying to wrap my head around the idea that I'm chasing a fallen angel with a sinister agenda. It seems too complex to take in at once. I've even tried to let your explanation seep in little by little, but that doesn't seem to work very well either," I said as we boarded.

"It's all part of the belief system you've barricaded around yourself since childhood or after a major life event. When you were young, you probably believed in God because your parents took you to church every Sunday, and you sat there for an hour listening to a messenger of God praise the goodness and love He has created for all of us. When you're young, anything seems like a possibility, and we tend to go with the flow. When you grow up, you start changing your perspective of the world and what may lie beyond its borders. You begin seeing things that happen to good people, and you start questioning the logic behind a supreme being that allows disasters to find innocent people. You have devoted yourself to finding missing children only to suffer the loss of your child by the hands of the wicked." Harper glanced at me with a look of pity. It was apparent that he had done some digging into my past and revealed one of the worst things I've ever experienced.

I believed in God as a youth and even up to my early thirties. My faith collapsed when a man named Bill Bakersfield stole my first daughter, Regina, from her bed six years ago and later took her life. That was the moment I knew there couldn't be a God who allowed such cruelty to the truly innocent.

I once failed the most significant case I've ever known. I was unable to save my first daughter from a man strung out on revenge.

Now, at this place and time, I'm given a chance to second-guess the beliefs I've so sternly placed in my heart. I'm facing possible evidence that there is a God. Not only that but a God with little control over the circumstances that ended Regina's life.

"You know you're right, so I won't boost your ego by telling you so. I completely see your point. You're obviously aware of what happened to my daughter Regina, but I don't want to talk about her right now. It would be counter-intuitive to the case to switch my thoughts to Regina when we need to focus on Hannah Jane," I said.

"I'm not trying to tell you what to believe in, Jack. I only want you to keep your eyes open for a greater possibility. Strange things are happening around us every day, and sometimes you need to read between the lines. Most of these things have reasons, but whether they're God's or Azrael's plans, they sometimes have a purpose beyond our understanding. I didn't mean to push about Regina. You can tell me about her later if you're comfortable doing that."

"I understand. Right now, I want to put all of this at the back of my mind. I want to focus on finding Hannah Jane. If that comes through positively, maybe then I'll give God the benefit of the doubt, but not until then."

"That's good, Jack. Focus is what we need to find Hannah Jane within the next four days. You know that we probably won't make it to Treagan on time. I think Father James is going to get his chance to explain his past actions to God personally."

Chapter 15

The Kingdom of Heaven Church in Treagan, New Mexico, was an unusually upscale house of the Lord in this out of the way place. With brilliant white lap siding, gray slate shingles, and a steeple that must have reached five stories high, the church was a monumental work of beauty among the cactuses and tumbleweeds. Above the entrance was a massive stained glass window depicting a portrait of Mother Mary standing with her eyes cast toward the heavens and her hands clasped in prayer.

Azrael was standing before the entrance, staring up at that beautiful colored glass and resisting every urge to seize one of the small landscaping stones, hurl it through the pane and shatter it into a thousand glimmering pieces.

The parking lot was void of vehicles except one, which was a faded blue Ford Mustang that looked as if a scrap yard crusher should have welcomed it decades ago. It was Father Richard James' vehicle, a man with simple needs. He only asked two things from his community: to donate to the church what you can afford and believe in a loving God who believes in you.

Azrael walked up the half dozen steps to the large arched doors and stepped inside. It had been nearly three centuries since the last time he was in the House of the Lord. It felt oddly comfortable. The church was still, and Azrael didn't spot Father James anywhere. He walked down the aisle, passing the vacant pews, lit a candle, and made a brief prayer.

Mend my broken wings, despiteful Father, and the hatred will cease to be.

Azrael stepped to the small confessional, parted the velvet curtain, and stepped inside. A dim red light outside of the booth activated when someone knelt on the padded board, which notified others the confessional is occupied.

Azrael had been kneeling for nearly five minutes before he heard the sound of Father James' shoes clack on the floor, followed by a door closing. Father James sighed as he took his place for confession.

"I apologize, my child. I wasn't aware anyone was here."

"Quite all right, Father. You've only given me time to gather my thoughts and prayers."

"I see," said Father James. "Very well, then. Shall we begin?"

"Of course. Forgive me, Father, for I have sinned. It's been over three-hundred years since my last confession."

Father James must have thought it was a mild joke because he said, "Oh, my. It certainly has been a long time. It's a good thing that my schedule is open for the rest of the afternoon."

"Yes, Father, I have much to confess. However, God already knows all of my sins. He watches me closely, you see. Of all the priests the Catholic Church has to offer, it is your wayward chapel doors that have greeted me. Do you feel pride in my choice?" Azrael's voice wasn't much above a whisper.

"I'm afraid I don't follow. Are you saying that you chose me personally to confess your sins?"

"Confess? No, I believe there are more important matters we must discuss. Although you might find it in your heart to forgive my sins, however, God's heart doesn't match your own."

"I'm sure that whatever sins you've done will be for-
given if you truly repent those mistakes. My heart and
God's heart both beat as one," Father James said.

"Lub-dub, lub-dub, Father. I hear the rickety beat of
those combined hearts now."

Father James did something he has never done before,
something that was forbidden by his own rule. Father
James stood from his seat, exited the confessional, and
pulled aside the curtain to reveal the strangest confessor
he had met in four years of the priesthood.

The booth was empty. The confessor had silently and
quickly gone.

Out of the corner of his eye, something moved.

The man had circled the confessional and came up
from behind. He approached Father James more in a loving way than a threatening one.

"I wish I could say I love you, Father. I wish I could
say that my revenge is finished. I wish I could unfold these
broken wings and take flight back to my beloved home."

"I don't understand. What do you want?" Father James
was a man of God, devoted and also humble to the divine
presence. Although he was these things, he wasn't fully
prepared to meet his creator.

Azrael approached Father James with hands outstretched. He tenderly ran the back of his fingers down the
priest's smooth cheek. It was a touch that chilled Father
James to the core, as if the purest of evil, the first fallen
angel, Satan, had touched him so gingerly, so compassion-
ately.

"No," Father James cried out. He reeled backward,
tripping over his own feet in a mad attempt to flee. He collapsed to the tiles and threw his arms over his face. Prayers
spilled from his lips as the stranger moved closer and
leaned over him.

"I'd give anything to feel even a little bit of the love you feel. It's been so long. I truly do miss it, Father James."

"Please, there's no need to hurt me." Father James began to get back on his feet, but the stranger held out his hand as a gesture to remain where he was.

Azrael removed a scalpel from his coat pocket. The blade gleamed off the sun coming through the stained glass window, shining through the Virgin Mary's heart and soul.

"Redemption has come to terms, my dear Father James. If only your mind had remained twisted and corrupt, we would never have encountered one another. But you've begged for absolution from a higher and divine power. It's these sins of love and good-heartedness that has brought me here. Shh, quiet, Father. There's no need to scream because God is watching you now."

Chapter 16

The scene outside of The Kingdom of Heaven Church was bleak. The police had sectioned off the church grounds, and what lay behind the yellow crime scene tape were lost souls. There was a crowd lined up as far as I could see. I wondered if these were members of the church, members who now mourned the death of a beloved priest.

As I stepped inside the church, I felt a lump catch in my throat. I didn't like the view from the back of the pews, and I was confident that I wasn't going to like it anymore the closer I got.

Harper was ahead of me, walking with a determined pace. I wondered if he felt sadness, too. Maybe he was constantly feeling the entire weight of the world on his shoulders. Perhaps it was the distinct feeling of chasing your tail and never really catching it in your teeth.

Although expected, the sight of the blood smeared across the tiles from the confessional and up the carpeted steps to the altar gave me cold sweats and overwhelming nausea. I remained a pace behind Harper, walking in his footpath, not wanting to risk damaging any crime scene evidence.

Father Richard James was kneeling. His head was bowed before the large crucifix on the far wall. I wasn't sure what I was seeing. Father James didn't appear dead, only in a deep state of prayer. But the blood told an entirely different story.

I circled the body. Father James had a spike driven through each hand and into the altar floor.

Harper and I stood before the kneeling priest. I had to keep averting my eyes from him. The sadness was building in me again. I needed to stay focused on the matter-at-hand and put my emotions off to the side.

Harper had called ahead to have a CSU team collect any possible evidence. It was one of the few rules Azrael would let us bend. With the constant leap-frogging around the country, we didn't have time to get to every crime scene when it was fresh and uncontaminated. Azrael allowed only the collection of any such evidence and processing. However, the techs weren't allowed to move the body until we arrived. Father James was situated in that horrifying position for hours. It seemed like an inhuman thing to do by leaving him there, but it was necessary to save the life of Hannah Jane.

"We followed your instructions, sir. No one shifted the body at all," one of the crime scene techs said.

"Thank you," Harper said.

"I think there's something else you need to see." He walked up the altar and leaned over Father James. "We weren't able to tell for sure what it was without cutting away the fabric, so we left it for you guys to decipher." He pointed to the bare skin at the back of Father James' neck.

I saw a small red line curving out from the collar. It almost looked like a marker, maybe writing on the skin.

"Can you get me scissors, please?" Harper asked.

"Yeah, no problem."

Harper used the scissors to cut the priest's robe down the back carefully. The robe fell away, and what I saw sent a river of chills coursing across my flesh. I stepped back, closed my eyes, and took in a deep breath.

It wasn't a marker. It was blood. Along the entire back-side of Father James were thousands of razor-thin cuts. The cuts weren't deep, only just below the skin layers, enough to draw blood, but not enough for it to flow.

The cuts on Father James' body connected like pencil lines on paper. The cuts were words. The skin of Father James has become a book of blood.

Chapter 17

After I took a few moments to collect myself, I stepped forward and studied the writing. The words carved on Father James were unknown to me. It was some form of language I've never seen before. If I considered what Harper had revealed about fallen angels, it would mean that Azrael has been around since before the dawn of man and cast down from Heaven thousands of years ago. It would also mean that he knew all the tongues of man.

Father James had been threatened, disrobed, written upon with a fine blade, redressed, nailed to the altar, and then murdered in the church he cherished so much. Not even in the most horrific path that my mind could go did I believe that any person, regardless of prior sins, deserved so much torment.

After several minutes, I turned to Harper. "Please, call in the rest of the team. Let's get him undone from this position. We have what evidence we need. There's no reason to leave him here like this any longer."

"I agree, Jack. There's no reason. I think we can just cut the nail heads off and remove him that way."

Ten minutes later, Father James' body was removed and placed on a gurney.

"I've seen this type of horror before. Azrael used this same type of method on a victim in a previous case. But not a priest. Never a priest before."

"Do you remember what he wrote on the other victim? Did it look anything like what's written on Father James?"

"Of course, I remember. No one would ever forget a sight like that. I never thought I would have to see anything like that again. The girl's name was Naomi Lewis. Azrael carved mostly hate words and racial slurs, words I'd be uncomfortable saying. Azrael managed to work in words and numbers inside the message. It took far too long to decipher what he wanted us to learn."

"What were the words and numbers you finally put together?"

"Job 4:20. It says: They are destroyed from morning to evening: they perish forever without any regarding it."

"From the Bible? He gave you a chapter and verse from the Bible scrawled in some poor girl's flesh?

"A mockery if there ever was one. The words of God are the words of blood. Wars have waged over such words. Millions have died in holy wars, fighting for those words they truly believe in."

"I never understood it myself. How could such hate come from people believing in something different? Why can't people believe whatever it is they want to believe? Why slay those who feel otherwise?"

"You already know the answer to that one, Jack. You remember, don't you? From the time we spent in the bar?"

Here came a memory flash. Harper and I had been speaking of the surreal case at our first meeting.

We were once a creation of absolute perfection, flawless in all aspects, and filled with love and goodwill. We never felt anger, hate, mistrust, and the need to bring violence upon one another. Satan and Azrael and their winged armies showed us how to feel and act out all those emotions.

"So in the past, our beliefs, whether the same or different, were of harmony?" I asked.

73

"Right. Azrael and his fallen army brought rage with them. I know you see it, just like I do. Every day the world seems to self-destruct a little more."

I wondered if we found the means to stop Azrael and his battalion, would the violence that controlled most men and women fade away like a virus consumed by the cure.

How can we possibly stop something that can't be killed?

Chapter 18

Sister Hazel Margulies had been called to the crime scene and patiently waited for us just beyond the police barricade. After Harper and I finished our investigation and released the body of Father James to the county coroner's office, we exited the church. We made our way to a group of squad cars where Sister Hazel waited.

She was silently crying and dabbing her eyes with a tissue. I smiled warmly at her and lifted the yellow crime scene tape to allow her to follow us to the front steps of the church and away from the gathering crowd.

"Sister, my name is Jack Calloway, and this is Harper Caster. I want to say that I'm terribly sorry for your loss, and I want to thank you for coming here to speak with us," I said with sincerity.

"I don't understand any of this. Why would someone murder such a beloved priest? What kind of person could do such a thing?" Sister Hazel pleaded for answers.

"That's why we're here, Sister. We want to answer those questions for you. That's why we need your help. I'm about to ask you a series of questions that may not be the type of questions you want to be asked. They're personal questions about Father James' life, both past, and present. Do you think you can handle questions like that?" Harper asked.

Sister Hazel nodded her head solemnly. "Yes, if there's anything I can do to answer your questions, I will."

"Why don't you tell us about Father James' life here in Treagan," Harper said.

Sister Hazel blotted her eyes again and peered up at the church. "Father James was a saint sent by God to provide hope and love to the poor lost souls of this community. Before he came here, crime had been overwhelming. There were burglaries, vandalism, and random acts of violence coming down on the good residents on a constant cycle. Father James came out of nowhere as if he floated down from the heavens. He slowly joined the people of this community and gave them something to believe in other than violence and hatred. At first, each service only held a handful of people. When Father James wasn't at church, he was in town or the surrounding communities and brought faith to those who didn't come to him to find it. He helped people repair their homes, yard work, grocery shopping for the elderly, and many other great things. He never asked them for a thing in return. Eventually, the pews began to fill week after week. I was almost sure that we'd have to expand the church."

I looked at the church with a much different point-of-view. Father James, a man who had once taken a life in New York before his devotion to God, had built this beautiful work of art in the desert. He pulled a community from the edge of damnation and gave them hope for a greater future. He was a pillar that held up those who couldn't stand on their own.

"He sounds like he was a well-respected person," Harper said.

Sister Hazel said, "We will greatly miss him."

"Sister, you knew Father James well, and you worked closely beside him for many years. Is there anything you can tell us about where he came from before he devoted his life to the church? Whatever you tell us, I assure you that we will hold it in the highest of confidence," I said.

Sister Hazel smiled sweetly. "I hope you truly mean that, Mr. Calloway. Father James was a treasured individual, and the people of this community deserve to remember him for who he was when he stepped into our lives, and not for things he may have done in the past."

We shifted away from the front of the church, moving out of earshot from the curious.

"You have our word that none of these people will ever know what you say to us today," Harper said.

"I believe you, Agent Caster." After a moment to collect her thoughts, Sister Hazel said, "Father James grew up in New York. He came from an abusive family. His father was an alcoholic, and his mother was into all sorts of drugs. He once told me that he had been physically abused as a child, beaten by his father's fists, belts, and even burned with cigarettes. He ran away when he was sixteen and has not seen his parents since. He suspected that they were either in prison or dead by now. He said that running away from home was the best and worst thing he could have done at that time. He escaped the abuse from his father, but living on the streets can be unkind to a child who knows nothing of the real world. On his second night in the streets, Father James was beaten and robbed of all his possessions. I suppose living in those kinds of conditions can make one see their surroundings in a different light. To survive the cruel streets, he took to burglary, mugging, and whatever else he could to continue living. It's a primal instinct. We all fight to live at whatever the cost."

"Sister Hazel, I can't explain how or even why we've come to this particular place and time, but I can tell you that the person who murdered Father James did it because your friend had once walked a wicked line. He may have done something that you might consider an influence from Satan. Because Father James did this unspeakable thing, it jarred him so badly that he was able to gather his life back together and became an entirely different person. He became a man of God. He needed to repent for his horrible actions in life. Do you know what I'm talking about?" Harper asked.

Sister Hazel's eyes were tightly pinched shut, but tears still managed to slip through.

"You're asking me about the police officer he murdered, aren't you?"

Chapter 19

There was no degree of shock in the words she spoke. Of course, we already had a brief glimpse of the horror Father James had brought down on a good man, a cop, a husband, and a father. We knew.

"Father James had grown up living the terror no child should, and because of this upbringing, he was more prone to becoming a victim of circumstances. Richard James hadn't been of the priesthood at the time of the encounter with police officer Andrew King. It was many months after that he had decided to devote his life to the church and God. As you said, he wanted to right the wrongs in his life. Not only did Father James bring this community together when it was greatly needed, but he also sent anonymous envelopes of cash to the daughter of that police officer every so often. I figure that he must have sent nearly ten thousand or more over the years. Her name is Jessica, and her mother is Nora. Two poor souls left to pick up the pieces after that terrible crime. Father James told me that he had once sent a letter along with the money."

"Do you know what the letter said?" I asked.

"Only in general. The letter spoke of Father James' horrible actions and that the money sent wasn't so much out of guilt, but of a renewed faith revived within him."

It sounded exactly like guilt to me, but I said nothing.

At that moment, all of us looked up the church's front steps as the gurney carrying Father James sealed in a black plastic bag came out the front doors.

I could hear the gathering crowd beyond the yellow tape groan with sadness. The parishioners had not only known him as a priest but a mentor, savior, and friend.

"Sister Hazel, would you be able to find the current address of officer King's daughter? I'm sure that if Father James sent her money now and then, he would have her address somewhere in his office. If I let you inside, could you find that for me?" Harper asked.

"I'm a little scared to go inside. I want to remember how Father James lived, not how he died."

"I'll bring you in through the back door. You won't have to see the crime scene," Harper offered.

Harper could have made several calls and tracked down the officer's daughter, but time was always a factor. Even seconds seemed to count in this mad game.

We circled the church to the back door and followed Sister Hazel down a short corridor that led to Father James' office. Inside was a neat space Father James had used as a sanctuary. A small walnut desk, several metal file cabinets, built-in bookshelves containing volumes of leather-bound books, and a small table with a lamp set between a couple of chairs was all the moderately large office held.

Sister Hazel moved to the filing cabinet, pulled open a drawer, and searched through the folders.

"Father James was well organized. Ah, here it is," she said.

Harper accepted the file from her and looked over the single sheet of paper within. I was hovering over his shoulder.

The sheet of paper read:

Jessica King
14 Bleecker St. Apt 8
New York, NY 10012

"It's time to head out, Jack." Harper stepped toward
Sister Hazel and gently took her hands. "I can't tell you
how truly sorry I am for your loss. It sounds to me as if
Father James was on the right track for salvation. I'm sure
God has taken all these things into account when He
passes judgment."

Sister Hazel said, "Of course He will. God's judgment
is the foundation to which we all live, whether we believe
or not."

Chapter 20

We were at the McKinley County morgue, which was as drab and depressing as any morgue in America. The atmosphere was grim. The surrounding tile was a gruesome shade of green, and the fluorescence lighting buzzed. Father Richard James had been transported to the morgue and placed on the steel examination table in preparation to release any other hidden secrets Azrael may have left behind.

We were patiently waiting for the county medical examiner. It seems like the people were laid back in this part of the country because there hadn't been a medical examiner on duty. Maybe it's a rare event for a body arriving at this particular morgue. I realize that the county was mostly desert plains spotted with a half dozen small towns, but I still expected professionalism.

"So far as I can see, the daughter is the only lead we have, but I have a hard time believing that Azrael would go after her. Jessica King sounds like she's led a normal life. Azrael hates that, but what he hates more is someone who's on the path of destruction and takes the fork in the road that leads to a much better place. Azrael wants their hatred to keep growing. He thrives on people self-destructing. There has to be something more here," Harper said as he circled the body of Father Richard James. He removed his cell and took a couple of photos of the writing inscribed on the priest.

I was studying the body with a constant wavering eye. I found it hard to look too closely for too long. The method of this murder upset my stomach and my heart. I tried to deal with it the best I could.

"How do you mean?" I asked.

"Okay, Christine Daniels was in the company of our friend here, Father James, during the murder of Officer Andrew King. Now both of them are dead. At this point, I'm not seeing some other connection that leads us to someone else. Azrael has designed this puzzle for us to figure out, but at this moment, I can't begin to comprehend the next step we're supposed to take."

I studied foreign writing carved on the priest's skin. "It has to be something in the writing. Why else would Azrael take the time to do all this? You said before that he had used a similar method to this, that he had concealed the next clue in the writing. I think that's the thing we need to focus on."

"Yeah, I thought that also. I guess I'm just confused about the reason why Azrael used the same murderous fashion as on a previous case."

"Maybe he's running out of ideas, or maybe he wasn't in the mood for originality. You said before that there's always purpose to the things he does. I suspect there's something here, maybe someone's name written within the dialect that covers Father James," I offered.

"No, I don't think he'd be that obvious. Azrael would never outright give us a name. He loves to be mysterious and have the clues drive us mad."

The county medical examiner finally came through the double doors. He was a short man, only topping out around five feet, but what he lacked in his height he made up for in width. He was probably one of the roundest people I've ever seen. His breath was shallow and quick, probably winded from the short walk from the parking lot to the examination room.

"My apologies, gentlemen. We had a death in Midway that I was overseeing. I'm Douglas Wickman." He removed wire-framed glasses from his shirt pocket, put them on, ran his hand over his bald scalp, and shook our hands.

"A death?" Harper inquired.

"Oh, I'm sure it has nothing to do with this case. It was an older woman. I haven't been able to examine her yet thoroughly, but there's no reason to consider it foul play at this time," Dr. Wickman said and then glanced at the steel table. To say his expression was that of shock would be a serious understatement.

"I know it's horrifying," I said as I followed his gaze.

"Dear God. I was only briefed on what to expect when I got back, but I had no idea it would be this severe. I knew Father James well. He was the strongest, kindest person this community had to offer. He shined the light for so many when they saw nothing but darkness. I can't believe someone would do this to such a good man."

I took a shot in the dark. "Have you ever seen writing like this before?"

Dr. Wickman retrieved his white lab coat from a hanger and snapped on a pair of latex gloves. He stepped to the table and hovered over Father James' body.

He said, "Hmm, I would guess it's something like Aramaic. I couldn't say for sure. It's been quite some time since I was in school. I have a computer on my desk if you want to do an internet search. Maybe you'll get lucky."

Harper had left his laptop in the police cruiser that brought us from the crime scene. He wasn't in the mood to retrieve it because he moved to the metal desk in the far corner. He sat on the wooden chair, and his fingers ticked across the keyboard.

While Harper searched for some meaning in the bloody writing, my mind shifted into hyper-drive, and a million and one thoughts rushed me. I knew that I needed to contact Senator Hillcrest soon and inform him that the case was progressing since we spoke last. Of course, I couldn't disclose the insane trail we were following to Hannah Jane's whereabouts, but I needed to let him know that I hadn't forgotten about him.

I also needed to check in with Caroline and Reanne. I wanted to hear their voices and catch up on the time we've been apart. I desperately missed home. I couldn't wait until Hannah Jane was safe and sound. I could then return to my girls and honestly take a well-deserved vacation.

I thought of Azrael and how much I could never understand the overwhelming hatred that grows within his tortured soul. I despised and pitied him.

At the foremost part of my thoughts was Hannah Jane. I was scared for her something fierce. The biggest fear of all was that I wasn't entirely sure if we would make it to her on time. It was a reality I hadn't accepted until now. The fact that Azrael was leaving us stumped by some of his clues ate away at the clock at a rapid pace. We should have deciphered Father James' clue by now and quickly be on our way to whatever destination it was leading us.

The revolving gears of my mind suddenly ceased motion as if someone had thrown a monkey wrench in the works. All my previous thoughts dissipated, and one crucial idea remained.

I enthusiastically looked up at Dr. Wickman and said, "Excuse me, would you mind giving us a moment?"

"I've just begun the examination." After catching the look of seriousness on our faces, he said, "Uh, of course not. I'm going to get a soda. Would five minutes do?"

"Perfect. Thank you," I said. After Dr. Wickman left the room, I turned to Harper and said, "I think this is a diversion. He's purposely trying to get us to waste time."

"You mean to waste time trying to figure out the writing?"

"Yeah, think about it. You said earlier that you were surprised Azrael used the same method on Father James that he'd used in a previous case. You implied that something like that was practically unexpected of him. What I'm trying to say is, what if it isn't what's written on Father James as much as it is the fact that he *is* written on. I think Azrael used this method as the clue, not the words of whatever language that is."

"Shit, you might be right. I was so focused on trying to figure out the words that I may have overlooked the obvious."

We walked over to Father James and exercised our minds in a new light.

"Who was this girl you told me about earlier? The one who ended up like this?"

"Naomi Lewis. She was a schoolteacher. During that particular case, after we found her body carved up like this, we later figured out that she had paid someone to run her husband's car right off the road. The authorities previously considered it an accident before Azrael got to her and revealed the truth. Years after her husband's death, she started feeling bad about what she had done, and she began changing her life for the better. She began devoting a considerable amount of time to soup kitchens and volunteering at a couple of local shelters. Azrael uncovered the truth, and he killed her because the murderous agenda that once overwhelmed her had dissipated."

Our minds were racing into the future as relentlessly as the clock did.

"I believe I know where you're going with this, Jack. You're thinking that he's going after the officer's wife, Nora King, aren't you? Is that what the writing is supposed to be telling us? I found Naomi Lewis carved up like that because I was investigating her husband's death. Azrael directed me on that path to learn the truth. So maybe he's telling us that Nora King played a role in her husband's murder."

I nodded because it was exactly what I was thinking.

"Azrael plainly explained it. Only I looked at it the wrong way. We have to get moving," Harper said.

We left the McKinley County morgue without informing Dr. Wickman. We had another damn plane to catch.

Chapter 21

Harper opened his laptop the second we slid into the police cruiser and began driving back to the airfield. He was sitting in the back seat, and all I could hear were his fingers clicking away at the keys. He would often make a sound as he found the right information or hit a dead end. I couldn't tell for sure. I had no idea what websites he was accessing.

"You're not going to believe this, but I just checked the IRS database, and they haven't received any taxable income from Nora King in the last two years. They can't even provide a current mailing address. It's like she vanished from New York. It's starting to sound a lot like our last two victims." Harper grunted with irritation.

"Okay, so the only thing I guess we can do is head to New York and speak with her daughter. Sister Hazel provided the address for Jessica King. I suppose we'll swing by and ask a few questions," I said.

"I think Azrael knew that we wouldn't find Nora without her daughter's help. Azrael has computer skills like you wouldn't believe, and it probably took some time for him to locate Nora. So he knew for sure that we'd have to track down the daughter first. I'm only guessing. I can't even remotely think straight anymore," Harper said and rubbed his eyes.

We arrived at the airport, boarded, and were quickly on our way to New York.

A big part of me admired Harper. I've only been at this insane game for a few days, and I already feel like I'm going slightly mad. The first case that I failed to bring home a child, and later seeing that sweet young girl's body was enough to push me into a liquor bottle for two long years. Harper had experienced that scene a hundredfold.

I'm a big softy when it comes to my emotions. I'm never embarrassed about this aspect of the ingredients that created me as an individual. I never feel shame about cutting loose tears for the things that truly matter to me. I was experiencing a lot of flashbacks on that long plane ride to New York City. I thought about all the children I've brought home, the ones I wasn't able to, Hannah Jane, and the victims in this crazy game.

Slight turbulence rocked the plane a little, and I felt my fingernails bite into the armrests. Typically, I'm not usually bothered about flying, but the experience I had gone through in the last two days had both set my nerves on edge and left my stomach sour.

I needed to put my mind somewhere else for a while. I needed a diversion during the plane ride. Now I had the time and even felt like opening up a little more.

"I think I'm ready to tell you about Regina now. We have some time, and I want you to understand why I'm so devoted to helping children," I said.

"I only know the basics of the case. I'm sorry for the loss you and Caroline have suffered."

"Thank you. I appreciate that."

"One of your clients kidnapped your daughter, right?"

"Yeah, his name was Bill Bakersfield. Caroline got pregnant soon after we were married. There was no mistake about it. We both wanted children. We had even decided long before the wedding. Regina was such a beautiful baby and full of life. Whenever I didn't have a case,

I'd spend as much time as I could with her. I used to lie on the couch for an afternoon nap with her sleeping peacefully on my chest. I miss those days so much."

I took a drink from a bottle of water and collected myself. What happened to Regina still felt like daggers in my heart. Even after all these years, I felt like I failed the biggest quest of my life.

"Even though the wounds have scarred over, it does help to talk about the past. Talking about it lets us remember the best memories we have," Harper said as he could read the turmoil overcome me.

"I know, and there are a lot of those good memories. I certainly can't agree with the decision Bill Bakersfield made, but a part of me can understand it. His daughter was the third child I failed to save. I took on the case to find Nina. Unfortunately, one of the things I've come to terms with is that no matter how quick and smart I am, I can't save everyone. Some things are simply out of my hands. When we discovered Nina's body, her father mentally lost it. Two weeks after I returned home from the case, he broke into our house in the middle of the night and took Regina from her bed. It was the same method at which he lost Nina. Of course, he wanted revenge for my failure, but I think he also wanted to see if my abilities were great enough to save my daughter. Maybe he wanted to know if I had been at the top of my game when I worked his case and tried to save Nina. By the end of things, I lost Regina just as I lost the fight to find Nina. Regina was only five when she died, but although her life was short, the impact she made in those years was immense. Honestly, if we didn't have Reanne to focus our attention on after Regina's death, things between Caroline and myself would have probably imploded. I probably would have gone crawling back into a bottle. The death of a child is nearly impossible to bounce back from."

"I'd like to see a picture of your family if you have one," Harper said.

I pulled out my cell and selected my favorite snapshot. We were camping at Lake Milliwaka. Caroline was stuffing a large, charred marshmallow into my gaping mouth as she balanced little Reanne on her knee. Regina stood between us, tearing open a chocolate bar preparing for our s'more making party. I handed the phone to Harper.

He smiled broadly and said, "I love pictures like this. It speaks volumes about what kind of person you are when you let your guard down and act naturally. Man, your wife is—"

"Stunning? Hot-to-trot? A ten on the old erection scale?" I tried to finish for him.

"No, I was going to say butt-ugly."

"Thanks. Got a picture of your wife?"

"I'm just messing with you. Caroline is very attractive. You have a nice looking family there, Jack," he said and handed back my phone.

"Okay, so now I'm curious. Tell me about your family if you don't mind."

Harper shrugged. "Not much to tell about recent events. I'm not trying to avoid this conversation or anything, but I think both of us need some much-deserved shuteye. It's only rounding to six o'clock, but I feel like I've only slept five hours in the last month. I hope you don't mind if we pick this up later?"

"I'll agree with that. I'm exhausted, too. Just don't think you're getting off that easy. I want to know a little more about Harper's crazy little world outside of the FBI."

"We'll have more time to discuss the events that are the make-up of my truly complex life." With that final

91

word, Harper slid the window shade down, leaned back, and quickly slipped into a comfortable sleep.

Chapter 22

Unlike Harper, I didn't sleep a wink on that plane ride to New York. My mind was churning so many things at once that not even the dim lighting and the soft, soothing hum of the jet engines could put me down.

After nearly three hours of my thoughts operating at full capacity, I found myself at the beginning again. I hadn't resolved anything during the trip, and I believed that was what Azrael had been expecting. He wanted to leave us utterly dumbfounded until the surprise ending. I momentarily wondered how long it had taken Azrael to work out this truly baffling game and how he had uncovered mysteries that stumped the FBI who had unlimited resources. If Azrael was who he claimed to be, then there was no feasible way we could stop Death, was there?

The jet touched down on a private airfield just outside Manhattan after eleven o'clock on Thursday night. For our time in New York, the FBI field office courteously left us an SUV in the airport parking lot. Harper and I quickly left the airfield, and forty minutes later, we were driving down Bleecker Street. We had found the residence of Jessica King.

The area was upscale, and as I viewed the many brownstone apartment buildings, I guessed that the rent was three times that of my mortgage. It was amazing that people, especially college students, could afford such housing.

We slid from the vehicle, went up the steps of Jessica's building, and found her apartment on the third floor.

"Cross your fingers that she's home, Jack."

I did. After almost five minutes of knocking and response of silence, I said, "Maybe Jessica is attending a late yoga class. Isn't that what people in New York do?"

"Unfortunately, we're going to have to wait this out until she comes home," Harper said.

I followed him back down the stairs to the vehicle. We sat in the darkness for a long while.

"I hope she gets home sometime soon. Her mother's life depends on it," I said and glanced at my watch. It was a little after midnight. I wondered where she could have been this late on a school night.

A long half-hour passed when we spotted a young woman coming down the sidewalk. She was attractive, with baby face features and an overwhelming innocence. As she turned to head up the apartment building steps, I rolled down the window and said, "Excuse me, is your name Jessica King?"

The young woman appeared college student age and slightly tipsy as she stopped and walked back down the stairs toward us. She may have been a little drunk, but instincts were still firing as she remained a safe distance from our vehicle.

"Jessica?"

"Yeah, is that you?" Harper asked.

"No, I'm Bianca. Jessica is a friend. She lives across the hall. Why?"

Harper showed his badge. "We need to speak to her is all. Do you happen to know where we could find her?"

"FBI? Is she in some sort of trouble?"

"No, no trouble. We only need to ask Jessica a few questions."

"Um, she was just with me a little bit ago at Jinx's Club. It's a place about six blocks down that way," she said and pointed.

"Thanks," Harper said, cranked the engine and shifted into gear.

"Wait, hold on a minute, she's not there anymore. She met some cute guy and hooked up. They left before I did. I couldn't say for sure if she'll even be back tonight. You'd probably have better luck catching her in the morning. She'll have to come home and shower and change before class."

"You don't know where this guy might live, do you?"

"Nope. Never seen him before. Sorry."

"Does Jessica have a cell phone?"

"Nope. She's an old-style girl. She doesn't even have a computer. Can you believe that? She does all of her assignments in longhand. Like I said, better luck in the morning," she said and waved. Using the handrail for support, she staggered up the steps and disappeared inside.

"That's just great," Harper hissed and turned off the engine.

"A thought just popped in my head. I hope it isn't Azrael she met. If that's the case, then I don't think she'll even see morning," I said.

"Let's hope that isn't the case. I think it's Jessica's mother that Azrael wants. We'll wait until morning and hopefully get our answer."

It was an unbelievably long night as I felt myself continually nodding off. The little amount of sleep I got was plagued with horrifying imagines of eleven bloodied elevator victims and a priest who had some insane story written upon his flesh.

Harper poked me in the ribs. I jolted upright and looked at him with sleep-dazed eyes. He pointed down the street, and I saw a young girl walking in our direction. She looked as if she had a long exciting night. Her blouse buttoned incorrectly, and her blonde hair was frazzled. She strolled toward us as if she hadn't gotten any sleep either.

I opened the car door and said, "Is your name Jessica King?"

She suddenly stopped and eyed us suspiciously. "Yeah, why?"

Harper showed his badge. "I'm Special Agent Harper Caster, and this is Jack Calloway. We need a few minutes of your time. Do you mind if we talk inside?"

"I think I'd feel uncomfortable letting you inside. What's this all about? I've got to get ready for class."

"Can you tell us where we might be able to locate your mother?" Harper asked.

"My mother? What has she done?"

"Nothing at all. We need to get in touch with her this morning. Do you have an address?"

"My mother's a free bird. She moves around a lot. I don't speak with her very often because she's lost her mind a bit since my dad died."

"Lost her mind? How do you mean?" I asked.

"My dad was a police officer here in New York. He was murdered one night on the job. My mom was fine for a long while, and then she started to get a little crazy. She gave me over one hundred thousand dollars from the life insurance money, and she told me to pick a good college. She's moved around New England over the years and gave away the remainder of that money to perfect strangers. Don't get me wrong, it's nice that she's trying to help out the less fortunate, but she's put herself into a life of poverty. She's broke these days."

"Why do you think she did that?" Harper asked.

"Who knows? Maybe she feels guilty about receiving a lot of money for my dad's death. Maybe having that money reminds her of him. I'm not sure. She never explained it to me. I've got to change before class." She turned and started up the stairs.

"Jessica, we think your mother might be in danger. We think someone bad might be after her. Do you know where she's living now?" I said.

"No, but she called a little over a week ago. She told me that she had given away the last handful of cash from the insurance policy. She said now that it was all done, she could start her life all over again. I don't have an address, but she told me that she now has a new job. She's working as a waitress at the Diamond Dust Casino in Atlantic City."

"That's great, Jessica. Thank you very much," Harper said and moved for the car.

She stepped to the window as I slid in.

"My mother and I aren't on the best of terms these days, but if she's in danger, I hope you can help her out. She's tried hard to help many people and give them a fresh start with some extra money. She's a good person at heart. Please help her if you can."

Chapter 23

Azrael was moving fast this time. The game was rapidly escalating. By Friday morning, he had already reached his next target of destruction. Atlantic City was a place full of lights and mischievous wonder.

He was at a blackjack table at the Diamond Dust Hotel and Casino playing an uninteresting game with a short, plump, redheaded female dealer who never quit goddamn smiling. He spent the majority of his time watching the witless tourists shoving money into the slot machines and getting little or nothing in return.

His mind played games of madness as he waited for the right moment. In his mind, he watched an explosion flash across the casino. He heard the eruption, felt the concussion, and smelled the delightful stench of people on fire. Casino chips and money took flight on the wings of mischief. He humorously saw himself still sitting at the table as body parts blew by him. What an extraordinary vision he has. A picture-perfect snapshot of mayhem.

Of course, this time, Azrael had no such spectacular display in mind. This time it was going to be sweet and simple with a single murder.

"Would you like a hit, sir?" the dealer asked.

He was holding eighteen, and the dealer was showing a queen. He was feeling a little brazen.

"Yes," he said.

She flipped out another card. Three of hearts. 21. The dealer had twenty. It was a sign.

Just then, his next target came into view, a waitress named Nora King. He consulted his watch and saw that it was after eight o'clock in the morning. She had just ended her shift, and now she was heading home.

He gathered his winnings and left the table without offering the plump dealer a tip. He casually followed the forty-year-old. Her sandy blond hair bounced as she strolled through the casino to the parking garage.

Azrael rotated his gaze to another man who had also stood from one of the blackjack tables. The man crossed the casino floor. He stopped beneath one of the bubble cameras, looked up, and gave the watching eyes the finger. Very interesting.

The parking structure was poorly lit and offered him the perfect opportunity to make his move. He planned everything so well. He knew where all the cameras were in the garage. He knew how to mingle among the crowd of gamblers and make himself invisible in the casino. Azrael knew that the FBI would later view the video capturing Nora King leaving the casino and another who had followed her.

You shouldn't always believe what you see, boys. Things are never what they appear.

For this particular act of violence, he was going to have to get right on top of her. Face to face. Personal contact, just like it had been with Father James. The closeness always gave him an essential thrill. He was going to hold her face in his hand as he watched the life slip from her eyes.

Her shoes clicked as she walked to her ancient green wreck of a vehicle. There were no other people in the immediate area as he quickly came up behind her. She may have heard him or sensed that something terrible was about to happen because she abruptly turned around. She was holding a small canister of pepper spray retrieved from her purse. She was fast and prepared.

Azrael instantaneously stepped to the left to avoid a direct blast. He seized her arm, rotated it painfully behind her back, and used his body to pin her against her car. She struggled but couldn't match his strength.

"I'm impressed with your speed. You almost made it. I'm pleased to make your acquaintance. Although I hate to be the bearer of bad news, I'm the Angel of Death, and your time is up." Azrael plunged the ice pick deep. It pierced her skin and flesh just below the sternum.

Nora's eyes went wide, and she drew in a violent gasp. She tried to scream, but he smashed his mouth over hers, a passionate kiss as if they were intimate lovers. She fought harder, trying to use the pepper spray, trying to break free.

He pulled the ice pick free and stabbed her again. This time the sharp instrument penetrated deep in her heart. Nora offered a slight tremble, and her body went slack. Death was almost immediate.

He slid the lifeless body to the garage floor and leaned her against the car. He quickly stood and took a long look at the layout of the structure. He could hear voices, but they were far off, probably on another level. He doubted he'd be interrupted.

Azrael pulled open her white blouse, revealing her average-sized breasts. With a folding knife, he cut away her bra and inspected the small deadly wounds. He was feeling incredibly powerful!

How mad am I? Well, let me show you! I want Harper and Jack to be sick to their stomachs as they observe your remains. I need the image to plague their dreams until the end of time. Jack the Ripper was an English gentleman compared to what I'm going to do to you! How beautiful this will be.

Chapter 24

Harper told me that he has never yet saved one of the selected victims or the primary girl the game revolved around. As it turned out, the statistics remained the same because we were too late to save Nora King.

Someone discovered Nora's body before we arrived. The entire area was already brimming with crime scene units and officers barricading the area while struggling to control the crowd.

Harper didn't have a problem with me lagging back. I waited outside the parking structure for Harper to take in the sight of how bad Azrael had punished Nora King. I couldn't convince myself to view the massacred remains of another human.

The crowd surrounding me was unsettled. The people wanted to know more about what had gone down earlier this morning. I think most of the people only wanted permission to get their cars and get the hell out of here.

After a half-hour dragged by, Harper forced his way through the crowd to where I was leaning against the concrete parking structure. His look was grim and pale as if he'd just eaten something that wasn't sitting well.

"Good thing for you that you had an intuition to stay behind. It was truly horrible, Jack. He practically dissected her right there on the parking garage floor. I've seen a lot of bad things that he's done, but this one has certainly placed in the top five."

"Why do you think he did that? Do you think Nora King being torn apart like that is a clue?"

"It's hard to tell with him. It could very well be a clue, or maybe he did it for the fun of it."

A few minutes later, Harper and I followed the casino Chief Director Kevin Wilcox from the parking structure. We went through the casino and wound our way through drab-colored corridors to the main security room.

"I've only spoken with Nora King once, back when she started a little over a week ago. She certainly came across as a decent person. I can't imagine why someone would do something so brutal. It wasn't even a mugging because I saw her purse lying beside her when I was alerted to what had happened," Kevin Wilcox informed us.

We knew Azrael was in the casino tonight. We guessed that he must have followed Ms. King through the casino to her car. We intended to capture his movements and possibly ID him using the security cameras positioned throughout the entire casino gaming floor.

Fifteen-inch computer screens lined an entire wall of the room. Men and women watched the monitors, changed points of view, and searched for those types of gamblers who didn't want to play by the rules. The watchers were the best at what they did. They knew every trick in the book, even some that weren't in there.

We approached a young Asian man with wire-rimmed glasses, black Dockers, and a white shirt with the sleeves rolled up. He was working feverously at one of the computers.

Mr. Wilcox said, "Agent Caster and Mr. Calloway, I'd like you to meet Thomas Wu. He's my right-hand man. If something is there, he's the one to ask."

"Yep, I'm the super geek of superfly geeks. I even have a diploma that says that very thing. Does this mean that I'm working for the feds, too?" he asked.

"Let's just say that I'll make it more than worth your while if you give me what I need," Harper said.

"All right, a date with Jessica Alba it is then," Thomas Wu said with a smirk. "I've already loaded up what you gentlemen may be wanting. I figured that you guys would probably be wanting the footage of her work shift on the floor."

"I like a man who's on the ball," I said.

Thomas handed me a flash drive. "I've even taken the liberty of making a copy for you. Naturally, I can't get everything during her shift. We're said to have cameras everywhere, but that doesn't necessarily make it true. I copied for you the last three to four hours. I figured they would be the most important. While you guys were over at the parking garage, I've been analyzing the footage. Being an FBI agent and all, I felt that it was my duty," Thomas said.

I liked Thomas Wu. He had a young, cocky attitude but countered it with high intelligence and impressive talent.

"Did you happen to find anything interesting enough that you might want to clue in the rest of us?" Despite the situation and the long day, Harper was in a relatively good mood. It suited him, though I'd never tell him that.

"I'm glad you asked. I sure did," Thomas said. He tapped a few keys and opened a file. "Now, from what I can see, Nora had a usual workday. No one harassed her or tried to play grab-ass or anything like that. She did well on tips for the night, chit-chatted with some of the regulars here and there. Nothing unusual stood out until she was finishing her shift. I then came across this."

The footage showed Nora entering the casino floor from one of the back rooms. She wore a black leather coat and carried her purse. It was apparent that her shift was over, and it was time to go home and unwind.

Thomas paused the footage as Nora was beneath one of the cameras. "Right there." He pointed to a man at one of the blackjack tables. "He watches her from the moment she enters the floor until she gets to this point, and then he gets up and follows."

Thomas continued the footage. We carefully watched the man. It wasn't outright obvious, but the man was wearing a type of disguise. He had a thick brown beard with streaks of white, a Red Sox baseball cap, a tan windbreaker, and blue jeans. I was trying to focus on his face most of all. I was trying to see what was in his eyes, trying to see his face without all that hair. I was looking through his disguise and seeing the killer within.

He then did a peculiar thing. The man following Nora looked up at the camera, gave a sly smile, and then gave us the finger. He exited the casino and disappeared from the camera view.

I asked Thomas to rewind the video to the point in which Nora comes out from the backroom and grabs our suspect's attention. I had Thomas slow down the playback until it was like watching a projector running with just enough juice to crank the reels slowly.

When the suspect was beneath the bubble camera, looks up, smiles, and gives us the finger, I said, "Pause it there."

The picture was frozen in a mocking gesture, giving us a long view of the bird.

Harper said, "I see it, too, Jack."

"What do you see?" Thomas asked excitedly. He was only a temporary FBI rookie, so we cut him a little slack.

"Look closer. More importantly, look at the back of the man's wrist," I told Thomas.

"It's a tattoo. Isn't it?" Thomas asked.

"I believe so. Can you zoom in and clear up the picture a bit, Thomas?" Mr. Wilcox asked. He was as eager as the rest of us to catch a killer.

"Just try to stop me," Thomas said. Within a minute, the video zoomed on the tattoo and began cycling the image through several program filters to clear the resolution.

What we saw was obvious enough. The tattoo was a horrific image of Death. I guessed that it was about three inches in length. We saw a figure cloaked in deep violet, a sickle in a bony hand, and the partial skull visible beneath a hood. The picture of Death had a morbid grin.

"Nice work, Thomas. You, too, Jack," Harper said. "We have a lead to follow. I can have this image run through the database and find out what tattoo parlors do this work. I'm sure it's probably popular, but maybe there's a chance we can track this one down."

I was shaking my head. "To track down a tattoo like this would take forever. The good news is that there isn't a need for a search. I've seen this tattoo before, this *exact* tattoo, and I know the person who has it. This footage is the clue, Harper. He flipped us off so that we could catch a glimpse of the tattoo."

Mr. Wilcox and Thomas looked at each other confused, and then at us.

I needed to continue the secrecy from the public ears, so I leaned in close to Harper and whispered a name.

Harper looked at me with mild surprise. "You're sure it's him?"

"I'm sure of the tattoo. I've certainly seen it before. As for the person, he fits the same physical form as the man on the video and even the same colored eyes. It has to be what we're supposed to figure out. The tattoo leads us to our guy, I think. "

Mr. Wilcox cleared his throat and said, "If you know who this is, you need to tell me so we can get an APB on him before he slides right out of town, and we lose our chance."

"I assure you, Mr. Wilcox, he's already long gone from here," Harper said.

"I've seen a lot of cruel things happen in this town, Agent Caster, but never anything of this magnitude. The world is taking a roller coaster ride straight to hell," Wilcox said.

I thought that maybe Mr. Wilcox was right. This ride made me nauseous, and I wasn't sure if I could tolerate the experience anymore, but I didn't see an emergency stop button anywhere.

I thought of Nora King's daughter back in New York. When we left her earlier this morning, her mother was alive. Right now, Jessica King probably thought the world wasn't such a despicable place, after all. The bombshell would most likely be delivered sometime later by local law enforcement. Her father long ago murdered and left in a shallow grave. Now her mother also horrifically stripped away from the land of the living. Both her parents senselessly murdered, leaving her pieces of a fractured life.

"Thank you, Mr. Wilcox and Mr. Wu. You've helped us more than you'll ever know," I told them.

As we left the casino, Harper immediately called the pilot and told him to prepare the jet for takeoff. I was sure that our man was running back to Los Angeles and we were coming for him.

Chapter 25

There are moments in life when you think you're rolling along smoothly, and then someone slaps the ball from your hands, and suddenly everyone is diving for the fumble.

Harper answered the call as we entered the plane. I could tell from the tone of his voice that there was immediate respect toward the person on the other end. I briefly wondered if it was Senator Hillcrest. Then again, I wouldn't think that the senator would call Harper because he was one of the guys keeping too many secrets.

"I know it is, sir. Yeah, we're in Atlantic City getting ready to depart for L.A. I can understand that, but we're moving fast on this one, and we don't have time to—"

The voice cut off Harper.

"Yeah, I suppose if you're not giving me a choice, we'll be there in a couple of hours. Okay." Harper ended the call and slumped in the seat.

"So, what's the deal now?"

Harper yelled to the pilot. "Hey, Allen, we have a change of plans. We've got to stop in D.C. first."

Allen glanced over his shoulder and said, "Whatever. You point, I fly."

"D.C.? Are you kidding me?" I asked as I tried to comprehend the sudden course change.

"Nope. The strong winds just got pulled from our sails. Director Gill wants us at headquarters. A barrel of shit hit the fan, and he wants a face-to-face conversation."

"Great. I've always wanted to meet the director," I said with little enthusiasm.

I was thankful that the trip to D.C. was just under an hour. Time wasn't our friend, and the less time spent delaying our progress gave Hannah Jane better odds. Washington D.C. streets were heavy with traffic, and the time wasted getting from the airport to the FBI headquarters made me grind my teeth in frustration.

The J. Edgar Hoover Building was a monstrous fortress on Pennsylvania Avenue. The place has an odd architectural design that looked as if giant concrete blocks had been stacked on each other to construct the highly regarded federal building. Honestly, I thought it was one of the ugliest buildings I've ever seen.

Harper and I stepped inside and moved through security relatively quickly. In the elevator, I found myself getting a little edgy in anticipation of the storm that was going to come down on us.

Sensing my discomfort, Harper said, "Relax, Jack. You look as if your underwear is creeping somewhere unpleasant, and you're trying to work it out without using your hands."

"I'm not wearing underwear. I was a child of the seventies, and we spent most of that time running around in the nude and picking flowers. I can't do that anymore. The government made laws that ruined all the fun."

A middle-aged woman in a bright-colored blouse was chatting away on the phone about a cooking recipe in the outer office. She glanced up at Harper, gave a brief smile, and motioned for us to proceed into Director Gill's office. It was apparent she knows Harper and that the director was expecting us.

When I typically think of someone with great power, I always picture him or her as a larger than life person who makes you quiver at the thought of upsetting them. Director David Gill certainly wasn't a man of physical intimidation if you happened to have a bad run-in with him.

Director Gill is a good thirty pounds lighter and four inches shorter than I am. He wore a navy colored suit that fit him loosely as if he hadn't fully grown into it yet. He was bald on top and wire-rimmed glasses perched on his long, humped nose. His face was sallow and seemed drained of life. I couldn't imagine the time someone like him dedicated to the office each week. I would think that a career like that didn't give someone much of a chance for home life.

"You made pretty good time getting here, Harper. I'm sorry to delay your trip to L.A. I want you to know that this decision wasn't mine to make. It came directly from the President," Director Gill said and took a seat behind the massive walnut desk.

"What decision would that be?"

"The President and his advisors have been overseeing certain aspects of this case. Hannah Jane Hillcrest's kidnapping is a cluster of a headache for all of us. Understandably, Senator Hillcrest is furious because he wants immediate results. Let me inform you that Senator Hillcrest is rattling a lot of cages to get those results. The President isn't at all impressed with your previous work file. He said that in the last four years, your track record is an embarrassment. Those are his words, not mine. He doesn't want to see Hannah Jane end up like all of the other girls you've tried to save. The President strongly recommends that we replace you immediately."

I stood there, feeling completely confused.

"Jack and I are kicking ass on this one. I honestly don't believe I'll fail this time. We'd be on our way to Los Angeles if you didn't make me come here and waste time."

Harper's voice was rising as the irritation of being replaced must be grinding on him.

"The long and short of it is that I don't have a say in the matter. Whatever the President commands, I have to follow those orders or start putting in applications elsewhere."

"David, we've known each other for a long time. You know as well as I do that replacing me will only eat away the clock faster. If that's the case, then you might as well call Senator Hillcrest now and tell him to prepare funeral arrangements. I wouldn't even know how to bring other agents up to speed on everything that has gone down so far. It's too complex to spit out in such a short amount of time."

"Sir, I agree with Harper. If other agents take over, I guarantee that Hannah Jane won't survive," I said as I stepped to the desk.

Director Gill eyed me suspiciously. "Do you even know what it is you're chasing down, Mr. Calloway?"

"Yes, sir. I can't say that I'm completely convinced, but I'm getting there."

Director Gill leaned back in his chair and rubbed his eyes.

"There's something else you need to know. Nolan Windell has something to do with Hannah Jane's kidnapping. We don't know for sure if he's Azrael, but we're certain that he plays a part in all this," Harper said.

"The senator's assistant?"

"Yeah. We believe Nolan is on a surveillance video at The Diamond Dust Casino. I even found his name on the United Airlines passenger manifest departing from Atlantic City to LAX. We're ninety-nine percent sure he's involved."

"The senator is going to have a fit when he finds out. Look me in the eyes and give me a sincere answer to my question. Do you believe you can save Hannah Jane Hillcrest?"

Harper's sight didn't waver. His confidence was genuine. "I truly do."

Releasing a deep sigh of indecision, Director Gill said, "All right, here's the current plan. It's too late in the evening to fly across the country to Los Angeles, so I want both of you to find a hotel, take a shower and get some sleep because you both look like shit. I'm going to get the President on the phone and work my ass off trying to convince him not to pull you from the case because time is a huge factor. I'll call you early tomorrow morning and let you know what his final verdict is. Does that sound fair?"

"That's all I can ask of you, sir," Harper agreed.

Chapter 26

"Hello?"

It was all Hannah Jane Hillcrest could think to say. She thought, *Hello? How about letting me the hell out of here!* Despite everything that has happened up to this point, Hannah Jane remained relatively calm. She spent her time pacing the small room, back and forth, and time so well spent it would have made a snail curl up and die of boredom.

The room was a strangely comfortable space with soft colors on the walls, modern style furniture, and thick carpet. Hannah Jane might have even decorated a bedroom in her house this way.

She thought of how nice it was of her kidnapper to leave a bucket for use as a toilet, a case of water bottles, and a cardboard box full of sugar-filled snacks. She figured that at the very least, she'd nominate him for a humanitarian award when the authorities eventually caught up with him and threw his ass in jail.

There were no windows, but there was a wooden ladder at the far end of the room running to a ceiling hatch door.

She needed a weapon she could use against her captor. The only thing she found in the room was a heavy lamp on the nightstand. It would do the trick if she could see the precise time to strike. She thought that maybe she could surprise him whenever he finally made his introduction. Perhaps when he came down the ladder, she would smash the lamp across his back or head. She could then flee through the open hatch to a nearby neighbor or flag down a passing car. It was a complicated idea she'd have to spend some time thoroughly examining. If any part of the plan failed, she knew she would die.

During her time of pacing and considering all current options, Hannah Jane began to hear things. A shuffle here, a scuttle there. The floorboards above her were creaking again. Something was shifting across the floor above. Something was pacing also. She thought that he was here in the house. Was he waiting for her to have a mental breakdown? Was he waiting for her to start screaming, crying, and senseless pleading for her own life? Was this part of his mental competitiveness to see who can outwit who when the game of life and death escalated?

She walked to the ladder. It was something she had been standoffish about since her arrival. She always worried that the wooden hatch would unexpectedly flip open, the madman standing there, gun in hand, and he would put a large caliber bullet through her upturned face.

The creaking of the ceiling came again. Someone was certainly in the house. Her kidnapper was walking back and forth. Was he anxious or worried? She sensed definite tension in the pacing above. Were the authorities onto him, closing in fast, and he was beginning to feel the pressure of capture? She didn't want to mistake those rambling pace-creak-pace-creak noises for a sense of hope. Not yet, anyway.

Hannah Jane took a deep breath and stepped beside the ladder. Her fingers curled around one of the newly constructed rungs. Every nerve in her body told her to climb and see what was what. Hannah Jane didn't know if the hatch door was even locked but suspected it had to be. There was actually little doubt about it. But what if?

The courage was suddenly and gracefully rippling through her bones and muscles. The worst that could happen was a locked hatch. She had to take it upon herself to find out. She moved foot after foot and hand over hand until her head gently knocked against the planks of the thick wooden hatch. Hannah Jane was where she feared most. The doorway of the unknown. Hannah Jane reached up and gently pushed the heavy door and received no positive results. She shoved even harder and found no give.

She stepped down a rung, ready to give up any chance of escape. Looking up, she felt anger, and she was livid about her quick retreat and her less than glorified ability to fight for her freedom.

Hannah Jane charged up with the force only a raging bull could create. She slammed her shoulder into the hatch and felt the wood give a bit under the brute force. She was ecstatic now. The door had moved. Her freedom was now attainable with a lot of willpower. With a shout of anger and biting through the pain, she rammed the door again. It shot upward but didn't fully open.

As Hannah Jane prepared another assault, she heard the floorboards creak beside the hatch. Someone was standing there. Someone was watching her momentous effort of trial and error.

Hannah Jane held back another upward strike and listened carefully. There was no movement, no sound, and certainly no sudden death for her.

"Please," she said. Her voice was trembling. Her body rattled from both fear and the cold of her confining room. "Please let me out of here. I want to go home. I want to see my family. Whatever it is you want, whatever your demands, my family will give them to you. My father is a powerful man. Whatever you need him to do, he can help you as long as you let me go home safe."

There was no reply. The bastard was taunting her with silence.

Hannah Jane did something she didn't think herself capable of doing. She continued her escape attempt, even with the lunatic standing right there.

Hannah Jane placed the palms of her hands against the hatch and used her legs like springs and began nudging the thick door. Inch by inch, the door moved upward. The determination was there. The cry for freedom was there, too. She was damned if she'd let some pathetic twerp keep her from going home.

With all her might, Hannah Jane thrust up. The hatch door came to a dead stop as the sound of metal rattled.

The goddamn hatch door is chained shut!

She cried out in frustration. The man had beaten her. The energy that coursed through her moments ago was now drained. She released her hold of the heavy wooden hatch.

Thick, relentless tears spilled down her cheeks. She was exhausted, and her body was barely able to cling to the ladder anymore.

"Please! Please let me out of here. I'm a good-hearted person. I'll help you any way I can. What is it you want?"

Silence. He was mocking her, tormenting her by being so calm of the situation.

Hannah Jane pushed up on the hatch again, gently this time. She reached through the gap and felt the metal chains with her fingertips. There was a lock, too. She searched the darkness, probing for the signs of someone there.

She felt something like a coarse fiber. Her fingers came across something wet and quickly retreated from exploration. She wiped her hand on her sweater. Whatever it was, it was repulsive to have the liquid touch her bare skin.

"Answer me!" she screamed.

A thundering bark of a large dog came down at her. It startled her enough to lose her hold on the ladder, and she plummeted down the ten feet. The thickly padded floor helped break her fall, and the only thing wounded was her pride.

Lying on the floor, shivering from the cold and uninjured in body but not spirit, Hannah Jane curled into a fetal position, cupped her head in her hands, and wept.

Chapter 27

The trembling had finally stopped, the tears, too. Now, something just as primal began building inside Hannah Jane. She was royally pissed off now as fear gave way to anger.

With anger boiling over, she pushed herself off the floor, embarrassed that she crumpled so quickly because of the stupid dog upstairs. Hannah Jane started pacing the confined area. Her fists balled up, nails biting into her fleshy palms. Her teeth clenched, grinding together to help relieve the built-up tension.

Hannah Jane was about to unleash a blood-curdling scream when a loud noise echoed upstairs. Someone was home.

She ran to the bed, leaned hard against the headboard, pulled her knees to her chest, and wrapped her arms around her legs. She was watching the hatch, waiting for it to flip open, dreading the psycho would come down here and do unspeakable things to her.

She could hear shoes clacking on the floorboards, and the person rummaging through things. She heard mumbling as discarded items clunked to the floor. Are there two people here? She then realized that there was only one angry voice. The person was talking to himself or herself. Someone was in a highly ticked off mood.

Hannah Jane followed the creaking, clacking of the footsteps with her eyes. The pacing was a little frantic, a little nutzo. Whoever it was, she hoped they'd forget that she was even down here.

Suddenly, something possibly made of glass crashed to the floor with a concussion. A scream followed the tantrum. It wasn't a scream of pain, but one caused by frustration or even hostility.

She couldn't be entirely sure that it was the same person who had taken her. Was someone else in the house? Was this a team kidnapping?

The mystery person upstairs stomped across the floor, and then the sound of a slamming door.

Hannah Jane stood from the bed. She closed her eyes so that her hearing would be more acute.

She could hear the crunching of footsteps on the gravel. A car door opened and then closed. An engine rumbled to life, and then the sound of the car rolling down the driveway. With her eyes still closed, Hannah Jane walked the length of the bedroom wall, following the sound until it was gone. She'd heard something else, or rather, something different about the pitch of the car engine. There was a spot at the wall where the car engine wasn't as muffled by the cinderblock foundation's thickness. She thought there might be a hollow point somewhere behind the drywall and framing.

For the next half hour, Hannah Jane stood beside the wall with her ear pressed against it and gently tapped the drywall with her knuckles. The spacing sounded hollow, but one spot, high toward the ceiling, seemed hollower than the rest. She heard something else in this spot. She could hear the outdoors. She was sure there was a window behind the wall.

She went to the dresser, removed a pair of sneakers she found earlier in one of the drawers and pulled them on.

Hannah Jane no longer wanted to wait around. She no longer wanted to be held captive by a lunatic. She quickly walked to the bed and retrieved the lamp from the nightstand. She marked a spot with her eyes and reared her arm back with all intentions of smashing the lamp's base through the wall.

Hannah Jane was going to make a prison break.

Chapter 28

In less than ten minutes, Hannah Jane had destroyed an entire wall. Bits and pieces of drywall littered the carpet, and a thin film of white dust covered everything.

For the first time in countless days, she had a new-found hope. There *was* a window behind the wall. It was several feet wide and maybe a foot in height, more than enough room for her to squeeze through. Hannah Jane wondered if the man claiming to be sent by God knew about the window or if it was a gross oversight on his part. She had considered the fact that this may not even be his place, maybe a friend's house, or even someone he had murdered and claimed ownership of the residence.

After peeling away as much drywall as she could, Hannah Jane saw only one tiny glitch in her whole plan of action—the window was caulked shut. It didn't matter much. She had a heavy ass lamp, and she wasn't afraid to use it.

Standing on the nightstand, she prepared herself for the next move. She gripped one of the bare studs for support with her left hand, and with her right hand, she thrust the base of the lamp into the window. The shattering glass was nearly as jarring as the incident that had earlier taken place upstairs by the unknown lunatic.

Fragments of glass shot into the hedge just outside the window. Hannah Jane caught her breath, listened, and waited. She was straining to hear any signs that someone was inside the house, suddenly alarmed and running for the hatch door. She even expected the dog upstairs to release a thundering bark in surprise. But it was quiet, dead quiet.

No one here but the scared shitless, she thought.

A freezing wind blew in through the shattered window. A snowstorm gripped the world outside of the house where he held her.

Carefully, she used the lamp to break away the remaining fragments of glass. Next, she popped up on her toes and pushed herself through the window. Hannah Jane's freedom cost her nothing more than a few minor cuts on the palms of her hands.

I'm free! Sweet Jesus and all that's good in the world, I'm free at last, she thought.

Her celebration of freedom was stolen just then as headlights pierced the black woods surrounding the house. The single pair of headlights then became two.

She wanted to leap from the shrubs and sprint toward the approaching vehicles, frantically waving arms, screaming for help, but common sense told her to wait. Gut instincts warned her that something wasn't right, and she could very well run toward the people she was desperately trying to escape.

Hannah Jane crouched in the cold shrubs as the vehicles came up the driveway and parked in front of the garage. The drivers got out and walked up to each other. She couldn't see very well in the gloom of the night, but one of the voices she knew well enough. It was a voice she'd be happy as hell never to hear again. It was the man who came to her house, claimed God had sent him, and then he pierced her neck with a needle.

He's come home, and he wants to see his pride and joy, sweet Hannah Jane. Poor defenseless and helpless Hannah Jane.

Surprise! Hannah Jane doesn't live here anymore, she thought.

The fear of getting caught was overpowering. What Hannah Jane feared most was how nutzo the man would get once he found out that she had escaped. He'd come looking for her. If he found her traveling blindly through the woods, things would get really scary.

Hannah Jane couldn't understand what the two were saying. There was a definite tension between them.

Calmly and patiently, Hannah Jane waited for the right time to make a mad dash for the woods. The two figures were walking up the driveway and discussed God knows what when one of them suddenly stopped. He was looking in her direction. He was staring as if he could see her crouching low in the shrubs, but it wasn't her that he was studying. She realized her error too late.

"What the hell is that?" he asked the other in alarm.

"What's what?" the other said.

Death began walking toward her.

What Hannah Jane hadn't realized upon her cunning prison escape was that the bedroom light was still on. Light blazed through the battered drywall, broken window, and the shrubs like a lighthouse beacon on the ocean's dark shores. The glow was a signal flare to all those near.

Unknown Lunatic Number One and Two were coming for her.

Hannah Jane did the next brilliant thing that came to her mind. She suddenly got jackrabbit in her blood and ran like hell.

Chapter 29

Hannah Jane was running like the fires of hell were licking at her heels. As she quickly made a considerable distance from the house, the light died away and left her in utter blackness. Despite the visual impairment, she found her way relatively easy by searching the midnight forest using her outstretched hands to feel the trees and low hanging branches. Her feet were quick but also steady. She couldn't afford a fall or even a stumble. Death would be all over her, and the game would be over.

There was no doubt that her steady but noisy escape was giving off her location. She figured that she had a decent head start, and if the adrenaline kept surging, she'd find herself with a gracious and hopefully mind-blowing gap between her captors.

Some of the thin branches relentlessly slapped at her hands and face as she barreled through the trees, and combined with the bitter cold of winter, it had hurt like hell.

As she ran, she also listened. She didn't want to take the chance to turn and look to see where Death was. In the unfamiliar grounds, she'd crash and burn for sure. So she relied on the telltale signs of his stumbling and uncoordinated effort to retrieve her. She *could* hear him. He was somewhere in the darkness behind her. He was pursuing, and by the sound of it, he was closing in on her.

I can't. I won't. I refuse to let this psycho catch me and take me back to that place, Hannah Jane thought, and then pushed herself even more.

She was breathing harder now, feeling the energy squeeze out of her with each long stride she took. The frozen air stung her lungs, and her legs burned with exhaustion. Her momentum was failing.

A second later, Hannah Jane's left foot rammed between the ground and a fallen log. Her balance went entirely out of whack, and she pitched forward with a bone-cracking velocity as she crashed headfirst into the dormant bushes.

Quickly, Hannah Jane was back up on her feet, but the second she put pressure on her left foot, the nerves in her entire leg screamed out. She muttered a soft cry of pain but didn't concern herself whether her ankle was broken. She needed to get away from this place.

Something tore through the trees behind her. She dared a glance back and saw a hulking shadow closing in on her. One of the men was coming up fast.

Hannah Jane threw herself forward with a hop-slide-hop-slide.

"I see you, my love. I'm coming to get you now. I'm so angry! You're going to pay dearly for what you've done!" he screamed at her.

A dreaded thought raced through her mind as she hobbled through the winter forest. *There's no way I can outrun him now.*

A lightning-fast thought came to her a second later. If she wounded the man, it might give her enough time to make a clean getaway.

She collapsed to her knees and searched the snowy, leaf-covered forest floor. She needed a weapon.

The pursuing shadow of Death broke through the trees. He was right in front of her now, and he wasn't slowing down. He was going to ram into her and crush every bone in her body.

Suddenly, Hannah Jane's numb fingers came across something buried in the dead leaves. She ripped the thick branch from the ground and swung it with the little energy she had left. The branch cut through the air and connected perfectly on the side of his head. He was hurt, and he was going down!

Hannah Jane began screaming in both pain and delight as she back peddled as fast as she could without making her ankle cry out any more than necessary.

Something moved behind her, and a second before she could turn around to see what it was, she felt something hard crack on the back of her skull. Her body immediately gave out. Whatever the object had been, it had drained all the fight from her. She fell onto her back, and with blurred vision, she stared up at the other assailant.

Unknown Lunatic Number Two had circled through the trees and snuck right up behind me. They were hunting me like a couple of damn wolves, she thought.

Death was standing over her now. He was breathing hard. She thought she saw a red fire burning in his eyes.

"I wish you wouldn't have done that. You broke the rules, and you'll need to be punished for it. I'm afraid, my love, this is the end of the road for you."

In the dim moonlight, she saw him pull something from his waistband. He pointed it at her.

He said, "Kiss, kiss, bang, bang. God's will be done."

The object flashed a brilliant blue, and Hannah Jane Hillcrest knew no more.

Chapter 30

After leaving the Hoover building, Harper and I checked in a hotel. I immediately headed for the bathroom and stood beneath the scorching showerhead for nearly half an hour. My body was tired and sore, and I thought that maybe I could wash away some of the evil I had come in contact with this week.

After refreshing myself, I left the bathroom to find Harper collapsed on one of the queen beds. His hands were covering his face, and his fingertips massaged his eyelids.

"I feel twenty whole minutes younger. You should shower and feel like I do," I said as I pulled on a pair of socks.

Harper got up from the bed, unzipped his small suitcase that contained only the bare essentials, and retrieved a bottle of extra-strength aspirin. He moved to the minibar and snared a tiny bottle of Jack Daniels, which would probably sticker shock any average income person, cracked it open, and washed down the pills.

I ignored the fact that Harper was trying to kill essential brain cells that needed to stay active for the time being.

I stood in front of the mirror and combed my hair. I eyed Harper in the reflection and said, "I have to say that the time we've spent together has been quite the bummer lately. Honestly, the grim look on your face is depressing the hell out of me."

Harper glanced over his shoulder and smiled at me, which kind of spooked me a little because a smile like that could be taken in several different ways.

"You're right, Jack. Perhaps it's time to take a breather. I've got an idea. Get your shoes on."

At first, I wasn't impressed with the destination Harper had in mind. Of course, on occasion, even I'm sometimes deceived.

Harper had brought me to a place called Xavier's Bar and Grill. It seemed like a decent place to grab some food, not to mention that the aroma seeping out the front door tantalized my senses, and I was hungry as hell anyway.

The place was larger inside than it appeared. There was a game room to the right of the entrance, and a group circled the billiard tables laughing and having a good time. The bar and dining area were busy with people enjoying a good meal, a few drinks, and unwinding after a long work week. There was even a small stage where three men played a mellow rhythm and blues song. I thought this was exactly the place we needed.

The hostess sat us in a booth along the far wall. A cute waitress with an energetic attitude quickly stopped by and took our drink and food order. To my surprise, Harper ordered an iced tea and gave up the heavy drinking for the night.

What happened next in that cozy, out of the way bar caught me more off guard than anything else that happened today.

A young, handsome black man dressed in black slacks and a silk cream shirt cruised over to our table. I caught a glimpse of him from my peripheral vision as he approached. He strode right for us as if he knew who we were.

He stepped to the table, a broad smile covering his face. He then reached out and shook Harper's hand.

"Hot damn, it's good to see you, Harper. I thought you'd be breaking your word to me again," the man said with a tone of playfulness.

I breathed a huge sigh of relief. Everything was cool as a cucumber again. There would be no more unexpected action for the night. Or so I thought.

"It's not my doing. I wasn't sure if I was going to be here tonight. I got wrapped up in a case. Fortunately, the evil ways of the world just so happened to bring me to this place and time."

I had no idea what was going on. I wasn't sure how these two knew each other and what "word" Harper had made to the man.

Possibly sensing my confusion, Harper turned to me and said, "Reggie, I'd like you to meet Jack Calloway."

I shook his hand. "Nice to meet you."

"Likewise, my man. Tell me, did this old stiff tell you why he dragged you into this joint tonight?" Reggie asked.

I had thought so. I figured we were taking a quick break from an active case of a high profile kidnapping and an ongoing Heavenly war. I thought we would talk more about fallen angels with darkened hearts. I also hoped Harper would air out some more dusty confidential FBI files. I wasn't entirely sure of Harper's intentions tonight. I guess drinks and a good meal was just a ruse to bring me here for something bigger.

"No, he didn't," I finally said.

"Well, well, well, it looks like the surprise is on our friend Jack." Reggie turned to Harper. "We're ready when you are, my man."

"I'm ready," Harper said.

"All right," Reggie said.

"Just sit tight a few minutes. My food will probably be cold by the time I get back. If your plate doesn't fill you, be my guest and dig into mine," Harper said to me and stood.

"Where the hell are you going?" I asked with more curiosity than worry.

"The man is ready to create some magic," Reggie told me.

I watched as Harper and Reggie left me behind. I couldn't believe what I was seeing. Harper stepped up on stage, removed a guitar from its stand, and took a seat on one of the stools with the rest of the band.

I watched with an unwavering gaze as the band began a song that all members, including Harper, knew from memory. The music was light and full of heart. Reggie's voice carried throughout the room and seized everyone's attention. My sight had been so focused on the stage that I hadn't even noticed that our waitress dropped off our plates and drinks.

Sometimes, just when you think you have people figured out, something comes along and knocks you back a few steps. Harper's fingers smoothly moved across the guitar strings and released sweet sounds that significantly increased the melody with the rest of the band.

Harper *was* human, after all.

I leaned back in the booth. The food looked and smelled terrific. I eagerly dug into the chicken parmesan and enjoyed the atmosphere.

Today seemed to be winding down to a degree of normalcy.

Chapter 31

A few hours later, I left Xavier's Bar to head back to my hotel room and get some needed shuteye. Harper had stayed behind to play some more and catch up on lost time with old friends. It made me smile to see the unexpected lighter side of Harper. It made him seem more human in some strange way. Until tonight, I believed he was an android secretly built by the government and capable of working twenty-four-hour shifts. But he was just a human. Possibly.

Winter has so far been kind to our nation's capital. Maybe the whole global warming has something to do with it. Whatever the case may be, it made for a pleasant walk back to the hotel.

Even though it was just after eleven at night, the streets were buzzing with people. I watched a couple holding hands, chatting away about whatever interested them, and enjoying the night just like me. I also spotted a man in greasy clothes leaning against a building, a bottle of whiskey between his feet. He was begging for handouts to all who dare to pass him. There were a couple of kids, long bleached hair hanging in their eyes as they did tricks with their skateboards.

As I approached the entrance of the Marriott Hotel, I heard someone walk up behind me.

"Excuse me, but aren't you that good looking gentleman I've seen before on television?"

What now? I thought. I wasn't prepared for what came next.

When I turned around, I saw one of the most beautiful things ever molded into existence. It was my incredible wife.

She stepped up to me, smiling broadly and obviously proud of her sneak attack. She could be sly when the desire came along. Before I could even open my mouth to throw out a baffling question, she wrapped her arms around me and planted her lips on mine. Confused but going with the flow, I hugged and kissed her in return. It felt so good to see my lovely wife and hold her tight. It was something I desperately needed right now.

"How?" I finally managed to get out as we parted.

"Oh, didn't I ever tell you I have FBI connections? Sorry to say that I'm a girl of many secrets."

"Did that crafty partner of mine call you here? He did, didn't he?"

"Guilty. Agent Caster had a stakeout on you. A cute, lonely, and desperate woman has been watching this hotel for nearly an hour for you to show up, and now the chill has finally got to me. Let's go inside."

"A warm-up session, you mean?" I teased.

"Whatever you want to call it. If it involves heat, I'm up for it." Caroline wrapped herself around my arm, and we walked inside.

In the room, I removed my coat, tossed it on the bed, and then kicked off my shoes. I asked, "Where's Reanne?"

"She's staying at some cute boy's house while I'm with you. She said they'd just play games and hang out. I told her that I recommend spin the bottle and anything goes in the mystery closet."

"Funny lady," I said. She was playing on my fear of my little girl growing up too fast. Sometimes I was over-protective of Reanne. It seems that if you took a long blink, they were hitting high school and then college. The next thing you know, they're getting married and having children of their own. It's was one of the only downfalls to my career choice. I couldn't be there every day for Reanne.

"She's with my parents, of course."

"I miss her bunches."

"She misses you, too. But don't worry, she'll be standing there with open arms when this foolish case is over, and you come home."

I held my tongue. It wasn't a foolish case, and Caroline knew that. I think she was still a little angry about my broken promise and jetting off across the country.

I remember thinking earlier about how much I wanted to go back to my room and slip into a comfortable sleep. Now my mind was thinking of something entirely different. I pulled Caroline to me. I gently stroked her cheek and lightly kissed her face all over.

"My heart is dancing tonight. You have no idea," I said.

"Mmm, I hope it's the Tango. I simply love the Tango. It's so romantic."

I remember a line Al Pacino said in *Scent of a Woman*: "If you get tangled up, just Tango on."

So I did. I did the Tango in mind and spirit. The way I saw it, it *was* romantic. I began to peel off Caroline's clothes slowly. She peeled off mine, too. A few minutes later, we had a heap pooled around our ankles.

I pulled her even closer to me if that were possible. I gently kissed her bare shoulder. My tongue traced up the delicate curve of her neck, and I kissed and teased her ear.

Her fingernails began to dig into my back in a good way. She was enjoying this. So was I.

We collapsed on the bed. We didn't need words anymore because our bodies said everything. Rhythmic motions and soft touches were all we had now. In Caroline's special way, she pressed gently on my shoulder, which told me to slow down a little bit. I was anxious, but I didn't want this fantastic moment to be over too soon. I slowed down just as she wanted. I don't know how much time had passed, but it seemed like a lifetime. When my arms finally gave out, and the last bit of my energy had wilted away, I rolled over to the empty spot on the bed.

Caroline placed her head in the crook of my arm and ran her hand up my chest. "That was wonderful, Jack. I think it was just what I needed."

"Me, too," I agreed, out of breath. "I'm especially pumped that I got my first booty call ever," I teased.

She lightly slapped my forehead. "That isn't what it was. I just wanted to see you."

"Are you telling me that you flew all this way and in no way whatsoever had naughty sex scenes in mind?"

She groaned. "You're impossible sometimes."

I told her about the evening I had spent with Harper. I explained how much he had thrown me a curveball and had shown me the brighter side of his personality. Caroline didn't know much about the man, only what she learned from our brief phone conversations, but she was glad to hear that the feds weren't so inhuman after all.

"When Harper called me at home earlier this evening, I was shocked as hell. I was so scared that he was going to tell me that something bad happened to you. Maybe that you weren't coming home ever again," Caroline said.

"Nothing is going to happen to me. This case will end, and I'll come home as I always do. I promise. I'm not going to break this promise either."

"Although I was happy and excited when he said that there was an airline ticket waiting for me. He said you guys had a layover in D.C., and if I hurried, I could see you for a while. I'm glad I could be part of an FBI undercover operation."

"Literally undercover and naked," I commented.

After a while, we made love again. It was probably only a few hours before sunrise when we finally drifted off in each other's arms.

Sometime later, my cell rang. I glanced at the other queen bed. It had been unoccupied last night. I guess Harper must have crashed elsewhere to give us some private time.

I figured it was Harper as I reached for the phone. The fun was over. It was time to get back to the grind.

Harper said, "Time to get dressed and kiss the wife goodbye, Jack. We've got ourselves a bad guy to catch."

Chapter 32

We were back in Los Angeles by Saturday afternoon. We parked down the block from Nolan Windell's modest townhouse.

I turned to Harper and said, "Thank you for last night."

He chuckled and said, "Don't thank me. Thank your wife."

"I did. Twice," I bragged.

"It was a silly little thought that popped into my mind when Director Gill ordered us to stay put until morning. I stayed away last night because I figured the two of you would be eager to oil up and wrestle. Even though my apartment is on the other side of D.C., I drove down there for the night. I figured you deserved at least that much for all the crap I've put you through."

Several things bothered me. Who is Nolan Windell? Why did he push so much for Senator Hillcrest to bring me into this case? Is Nolan really the Angel of Death this time around? Or is he only taking orders and ushering this case the way Azrael wants it to go? Or are we following a hunch leading to nowhere? I know for a fact that the tattoo seen in the surveillance footage is identical to the one I spotted on Nolan's right wrist during our first introduction at the airport. Of course, I wasn't sure of anything right now, but I'm going to ask Nolan personally in a short while.

We'd been staking out Nolan's home for nearly six hours. He finally came home late in the evening. He parked the Mercedes in the garage, and with only the occasional shadow passing by the windows, we didn't see much else going on. I don't know what we were expecting to happen. I didn't think anything dramatic would take place tonight.

"So, tell me about the nickname," Harper said while eyeing me from the passenger seat.

I knew what he was talking about, but I played the game of stupidity for the hell of it. I had nothing else to do.

"Whose nickname?"

"You know what I'm asking, Jack," Harper said with a little irritation.

"I can't believe she told you that."

With a furrowed brow, Harper said, "Who?"

"Caroline. Did she tell you my nickname when you called her and brought her to D.C. for my surprise visit? I can't believe she told you that. She only calls me that in bed, you know."

Harper gave another confused look.

"You know when we're romantic, Caroline calls me *The Hurricane*," I said with a little pride.

Harper snorted in disbelief. "Yeah, exciting at first and always ends in disaster."

I lost my composure, and so did Harper. We broke out in laughter like a couple of long-time friends. It was good to laugh, to cut loose a little. The past five days have been hellish beyond belief. It was an excellent way to let it slide away for the briefest of moments.

"No, P.I. Jack-ass. I'm talking about the nickname the press labeled you all those years ago. It certainly isn't something you've forgotten, have you?"

Harper watched me closely. He was digging a little bit more. He wanted to know more about me. I thought that was all right. I think Harper is starting to let loose and put a little faith in a new partner.

I grinned. "You already know the answer to that. I'm sure you've done some digging into my past before I was allowed to join the chase."

"Of course, I did. But I want to hear it from you. The difference between what you read in a newspaper and what you hear from the first-hand experience is a line as wide as the Amazon River."

Harper didn't speak again but waited and listened. He was real good at that.

What the hell. We definitely have time to kill.

"Ah, you must mean the other nickname. My friends at the Atlanta Press thought it up after I had several bad life experiences. They put a label on me after my second death. They started calling me Jack Everlasting, never aging, never dying, and granted eternal life. Except I never drank from a special spring as did the family in the novel *Tuck Everlasting*. The press ran several articles about my experiences with death and how I found my way back from the reaches of the unknown. After the articles saw the light of day, hundreds of reporters, faith believers, and the outright curious came to our house. They even called at all hours of the day and night, begging for an interview. I declined every time."

"Jack Everlasting. It has an intriguing ring to it, I think," Harper said as he stroked his chin.

"It's true that I've twice returned from death, but I do age just like everyone else. My hair has started to thin in places, not to forget that some of it turned gray. The wrinkles on my face seem a little more defined these days. Every time I look in the mirror, I see a tired man staring back at me. I'm getting older, and despite the name they labeled me, I've never had any delusions of immortality.

I've survived two deaths, but I'm certain the third one won't let go."

"Yeah, I wasn't going to say anything, but you do kind of look like shit. I bet you could use a vacation."

"Thanks. Your comment is well noted. If you want to take the gloves off, I've got a few digs about you that I could get off my chest. So that you know, I was starting a vacation just before Nolan called me and brought me into this insane case."

"Not that I had anything to do with it, but I'm sorry your plans were ruined. I know you must need a vacation as much as I do. Spending time with family is the most important thing you should do. Unfortunately, I figured that out far too late."

"It's never too late to get it all back, Harper."

"Yeah, I know you're right, but Azrael doesn't let me breathe long enough to correct those errors in my life. Maybe someday things will turn around." After an awkward moment of silence, Harper said, "Let's not switch off the subject. You've already explained to me about the first death. If you don't mind, I'd love for you to tell me all about the second time you died."

Chapter 33

I looked into the distance. The blackness of the neighborhood surrounded the sedan. It seemed like the two of us were alone in the world.

I finally said, "Ah, the second time. Unlike the first one, I remember this one well. Sometimes the details still play in my head like an old film reel."

Harper was watching me closely.

"Caroline and I had spent the week in Corpus Christi. On our late-night drive back home, a semi-truck following the downgrade curve as we approached the same curve in the opposite direction, except the semi-truck was wide on the turn. The front left fender of our vehicle exploded as the semi slid into our lane. We were rammed hard to the right as the semi continued downhill. Caroline was able to roll free from the vehicle just before the car went down a steep embankment. My door was badly damaged, and I wasn't fortunate enough to get out in time. I had a momentary blackout. I wasn't sure what had happened, but the next thing I saw was the headlights bobbing up and down the surface of the Mississippi River like a horrifying amusement park log ride. Freezing water was rushing in through the shattered windows. I was momentarily hung up as I tried to get free. I lost my breath, and the river came in."

"How long were you gone?" he asked.

"No one can say for sure. From the time the water filled my lungs to the point of revival was a large gap. Caroline later told me that the truck driver we collided with was uninjured, and he quickly called for help. A rescue team and helicopter were probably on the way before my lifeless body drifted from the car. Caroline said the air search team found my body hung up on a thicket of branches along the shore. I was hauled to the helicopter and airlifted to the hospital in Baton Rouge, about fifteen miles from the crash site. I didn't recover until I was at the hospital. A ballpark guess would probably be somewhere around eighty minutes or more. The doctors said that if it hadn't been for the near-freezing temperature of the water, resuscitation would have been impossible."

Harper didn't say anything. He simply gave a satisfying *"hmm"* sound as if everything made perfect sense to him. Alive, dead, and then alive again.

"The doctors were baffled. I never received a good enough answer that I could chew on and swallow."

"You don't recall anything while you were dead?"

"No," I said plainly. "No heavenly lights or angels with harps. Nothing. I don't remember a thing. Almost as if I completely ceased to be anything."

"What the hell?" Harper said.

I followed his eyes to Nolan's house. The garage door was opening, and the cobalt blue Mercedes came to life. The car backed out of the driveway and onto the street.

"Where the hell is he off to at this hour?" Harper asked.

Although it was just after nine on a Saturday night, I wondered the same thing. It seemed strange that Nolan had first appeared done for the evening, but he had someplace to go whatever purpose. Many questions are rolling around in my head, and I hoped soon they would be answered.

Is Nolan the Angel of Death, after all? Where the hell is he going? Are we going to follow Death on a late-night rampage?

I'm not convinced that Nolan is Azrael. It's more likely that Nolan knows whose identity Azrael has taken. Maybe Nolan would lead us right to Azrael tonight, and we could finish this thing once and for all.

I waited until the taillights disappeared around the corner until I kicked over the engine and started to follow. I'll be the first to admit that I'm not the best at tailing someone. I was confident I'd do something incredibly stupid and blow our cover well before we found out where Nolan was heading. I should have let Harper drive, but it was too late. We were already in motion.

I wasn't sure if Nolan had spotted us from one of the house windows. Maybe he decided to play some sort of game with us, or perhaps he really did have a purpose this late on a Saturday night. In either case, I was willing to go all the way to find out for sure.

I did pretty well for a while. I allowed a considerable distance between the two vehicles, but not enough to lose Nolan if traffic flow suddenly picked up. He was heading for the on-ramp leading east on the 210 Freeway. As I turned onto the ramp twenty seconds later, I realized we could be doing this tailing thing for a while. There were so many places he could go from this point. The good news was that I was thrilled with the late-night chase. The bad news was that we only have half of a tank of gas. Motivated, I was; prepared, I wasn't. Damn, I could have already blown this thing from the beginning.

Traffic was moderate, and it was easy to follow Nolan in the stream of cars.

Fifteen minutes later, Nolan eased the Mercedes to the far right lane and banked down exit 35A. Good, we weren't going to run a long stretch of the road tonight. I was happy that I hadn't fouled things up after all.

Nolan's Mercedes turned right on South Mountain Avenue and quickly took another right into the parking lot of a club called DeeDee Digg's. I drove past the busy bar. I didn't want Nolan spotting us pulling in the packed parking lot. Cars were also lining the adjoining street. The club was a happening place tonight.

I went down the street and turned into the parking lot of a closed gas station. From this position, we could see the bar perfectly.

Nolan weaved his way through the parked cars. He suddenly looked too young to me. He no longer looked like a thirty-something man with a reputable career, but more like a kid fresh out of college and looking for a little excitement. I only wonder what kind of excitement he has in mind.

Without glancing our way, he reached the front door and disappeared inside.

Chapter 34

"So, what are you thinking?" Harper asked impassively.

"Part of me thinks Nolan is here meeting Azrael. Another part of me thinks he could be our guy, and he's come to scope out his next victim. We know for a fact he was in Atlantic City, so that also means that he's either a small or large part of Hannah Jane's kidnapping."

"Yeah, I kind of thought those things, too. If Nolan is the clue we were supposed to figure out in Atlantic City, I can't understand in what way he had anything to do with the murdered police officer," Harper said.

I had thought that exact thing. Where's the connection?

I looked at Harper. I could tell how wiped out he was. He appeared tired of chasing shadows all these years. He has followed this maniac's trail of blood and mayhem for four incredibly long years. Harper once told me that Azrael seemed to spend ninety percent of his time playing his games in the states. I wondered why that was.

"If anyone spots us with these steamed up windows, they're going to think something naughty is going on," Harper said after a long pause.

He was hinting that we were wasting time, and not a thing was being accomplished.

"Well, I'll draw little hearts on the fogged up windows to set the mood while you work up the courage to make a move and grab my ass," I countered, and we both chuckled.

"All right then, rock, paper, scissors?" he asked.

"No need. I'll go," I said. "Besides, have you looked in the mirror lately? You look like shit barely warmed over. I'm the only spring chicken in this car, so that means I'll go."

"Piss off, Jack. You're only three years younger than me!"

I stared at him in mock surprise. "Man, I thought you started in the bureau while J. Edgar Hoover was in office. You could *really* use a vacation, you know?" I found myself laughing inside.

"Thanks, smartass. I'll pencil that on my calendar. Now get out of my car."

I opened the car door and stepped outside. The wind bit at me a little. The night had considerably cooled off. It was definitely winter, even in California.

"By the way, the gas pumps are still on, and they'll work with a credit card. Why don't you fill up just in case Nolan is planning another drive somewhere," I said.

"Yeah, I'll do that. Just remember to keep your excitement down in there, cowboy. Keep your head low. Remember that Nolan knows what you look like."

I walked the short distance to the club. There were several people outside smoking, drinking, and chatting away. They didn't pay any attention to me as I opened the front door and went inside.

I quickly scanned the bar for Nolan. I was trying to stay covered in the crowd of people. I didn't want to bump into him accidentally. There wasn't any possible way he would believe our meeting was purely coincidental. I stepped to the bar, casually keeping my head low, but not enough to draw attention. Between the amount of alcohol being served and the constant shuffling of people, I didn't think even Bruce Willis would get a second glance in this place.

The bartender approached me. "What'll it be?"

"Make it a Jack Daniels on the rocks," I said. I had no intention of taking a single sip. The two Jacks parted ways many years ago. We weren't even on speaking terms and could even be considered mortal enemies. The alcohol was only for blending in.

As I waited for my drink, I finally spotted Nolan. He was at the other end of the bar, partially turned away from me. Unbelievable, he's talking to a cute brunette girl in a yellow sweater and a matching yellow scrunchie in her ponytail. Was his only goal tonight trying to get his rocks off with some barhopping girl?

The bartender brought the drink. "Thanks," I said as I dropped a ten on the bar and walked out.

Chapter 35

Harper had moved the car to the gas pumps and just finishing topping off the tank as I crossed the street.

"You're not going to believe this," I said as we both slipped back in the sedan. "Nolan's sitting at the bar trying to get some play."

"Female, I hope."

"Yeah, cute brunette. Nice scrunchie."

"Do you think it could be Azrael?"

"No chance. Body language suggests they feel a little awkward around each other. They're into each other in a possible sexual way. It's kind of comical watching them flirt back and forth. It just seems like he's out to unwind and trying to have a night of stress relief sex."

"Shit," Harper said with irritation. "I was hoping we'd get somewhere tonight, some kind of lead anyway. Instead, we're trotting in circles while the clock keeps running forward. The signs are pointing right at this guy, but now I'm not so sure about anything."

I was annoyed, too. I wanted a giant leap forward in the case tonight. I needed to end Azrael's terror this time around, find Hannah Jane, and go home to my girls. It didn't seem like that would happen anytime soon.

Harper turned to me. "Let's call it a night, Jack. We're both tired as hell, and this isn't getting us anywhere. We'll get a hotel, catch a few hours of some well-deserved shut-eye, and get a fresh start early in the morning. We'll let

Nolan enjoy his night of fun, and then we're going to corner him in the morning and make him talk. Nolan knows who Azrael is, and I'll use any means necessary to get the information from him. We have to figure this out as quickly as possible because tomorrow night, Hannah Jane is going to die if we don't."

I was about to agree until I noticed Nolan step out the front door of DeeDee Digg's, and the brunette bar bunny was with him. Nolan had his arm around her waist. They were nuzzling close in the bite of the wind. They certainly had grown real close fast.

"Holy crap," Harper muttered. "I need to take some pointers from this guy. He's only been in there twenty minutes, and he's already caught a beauty."

They slid in Nolan's car and drove out of the parking lot right by us. He was heading in the opposite direction of his house.

"Where the hell is he going?" Harper asked.

"I don't know. But I'm guessing our much-needed shuteye just got thrown on the back burner."

I shifted into gear and followed as carefully as I had before. After a while, the houses grew farther apart. We were trickling out of the city limits and into the beautiful California mountain countryside. I assumed it was beautiful anyway. It was dark as hell outside, and I couldn't see anything except the distant red glow of the taillights.

The road was starting to wind through the hills. The trees were growing dense, and it was hard to keep up without giving ourselves away.

"Damn. Can you see him?" I asked.

"No. But he's got to be up ahead. I haven't seen any splitting roads. Just keep driving."

A moment later, the curse of Harper's words found us. The road forked. We had lost him.

I cursed under my breath. I had let Nolan get away from us. Being cautious had cost us considerable time and effort.

"Look," Harper suddenly said.

I followed his finger to the road cutting off to our left where distant taillights flashed through the trees. I hit the gas, steering down the left side of the fork. I safely followed until we approached a gravel road. It was a long driveway leading to a large log house tucked securely in the woods.

I quickly killed the lights. I didn't want to alarm Nolan, informing him that he has company in this secluded emptiness.

"This can't be the girl's place," Harper said. "It's got to run quite a few million dollars. It can't be Nolan's either."

"It belongs to Hannah Jane," I said confidently. "Senator Hillcrest mentioned this log house during our long conversation at Hannah Jane's house in the city. He said she has a place in the hills that she uses to escape from work and the press from time to time. I guess Nolan decided he needed to get away, too. A retreat to a missing girl's private home."

"It makes me wonder. If Nolan is Azrael, he could be keeping her prisoner in her own home this whole time. But I have a hard time believing Hannah Jane is in there. I think Azrael knew we'd figure out that the tattoo belonged to Nolan, and we'd follow him tonight. Azrael has planned this game so well that it's scaring the hell out of me," Harper said.

"Hey, at least the evening has gotten a little more interesting."

I let the sedan crawl on its momentum. I didn't want them to hear the engine or a squeal of brakes.

I found a split in the trees, and I carefully angled the vehicle into a cozy hiding spot. It was a prime viewing position, for what, I had no idea.

I killed the engine but left the radio playing at a low volume. I scanned the stations. Not many channels would come in without severe static. We were now out in no-man's-land. I found a station that came in clear enough. A soft, soothing Barry White song played to us.

Harper smiled. "Thanks for setting the mood, Jack."

Lights began flicking on one window at a time. Nolan must be showing her around the impressive residence.

I was trying not to get too comfortable. I wanted to be alert with no slacking on the job tonight, but the music made me feel too relaxed. The fact that I've hardly slept in the last week was taking a significant toll on my mind and body. What did I need to prepare myself for tonight? Nolan wasn't going anywhere for a long while. So, I let myself ease up, muscles beginning to loosen from the tension.

"It's difficult to tell on this one. Azrael has so many personalities that you never can tell who's who. I just can't place my bets on this one yet. Honestly, I think things have been too easy," Harper said

"Too easy? Shit, then I guess I wouldn't want to be involved in one of those cases that were too hard. I couldn't imagine what the hell that must be like."

"I know Azrael, and he hasn't yet been satisfied with enough killings for this particular game. Nolan can't be him because we still have nearly a day until the finale. It's always a showdown to the wire, a showdown he always wins, by the way," Harper said.

I could sense the anguish coming from Harper. So many years and so many graphically slain bodies have depleted the man he once was.

"You're probably right. Nolan might just be the next clue and nothing more, but we can't move on it until we know for sure," I admitted.

Is Nolan the Angel of Death, or is this a ruse by the puppet master tugging on the strings?

Chapter 36

Twenty minutes later, I got an answer. Only it wasn't an answer I necessarily wanted.

Someone started screaming inside the house. The sudden and frantic scream tore through the peaceful countryside and made both of us jump.

"Christ," Harper said as he shoved the door open, yanked his Glock free, and ran for the house.

I was only a few steps behind and preparing for whatever sadistic thing waited for me.

As we charged the house like a couple of runaway trains, I thought, *what had he done to make the girl scream like that?*

As we ran up the front porch and paused at the front door, the screaming abruptly stopped. I feared the worst. I could only imagine a dead girl inside and an angry, bloody Nolan Windell standing over the body.

I turned the doorknob, and we maneuvered inside. The foyer was empty. Harper was directly behind me, our guns searching the area. Cautiously, we crept through the house room by room, clearing each area. We reached the kitchen and saw dishware, pots, and a rack of steak knives on the floor.

Where the hell are they?

I listened. I could just make out the tiniest whimper coming from one of the back rooms. We quietly went through the kitchen. We had no choice but to surprise Nolan. We couldn't take the chance that he might panic and take the girl as a hostage if things were already that bad. The truth is, I didn't know what the hell was going on or how bad the situation was.

We paused at the doorway to the bedroom, and I could hear the brunette softly crying. I also heard Nolan breathing heavily.

I swiveled around the threshold, my gun in front of me. I wondered if I'd see the face of Death staring back at me with an insane smile and all.

The girl, who I judged to be in her late thirties, was lying on the floor. Nolan was sitting on her stomach and leaning close to her face. His eyes were wide and insane. He had a large kitchen knife pressed to her throat.

"Freeze, Nolan," I said as calmly as I could.

He quickly turned in our direction with a surprised look. Despite my earlier thoughts, he hadn't heard us come inside or suspected we followed him to this secluded retreat.

"What the fuck are you guys doing here?" he spat at us. The instant of fear quickly transformed into a thundering rage. He was furious that we had disrupted his twisted and morbid sacrifice.

"Drop the knife and get face down on the ground," Harper said.

The girl's eyes rapidly switched back and forth from the two of us and then to her suddenly demented host. Tears spilled down her face into her hair. Other than a shattered sense of trust, the girl appeared unharmed.

"Don't do this," I said. "Whatever the deal is here, it can be worked out. No one has to die."

His rage suddenly swapped placed with insanity. Nolan began to laugh as if I'd just told a joke. The laugh worried me. He didn't seem like the guy I met at the airport and rode with over to Hannah Jane's house. He seems to have a separate identity altogether. Does this man have multiple personality disorder? Does he have a legion of identities rolling around in his head? Or is this, in fact, Death, and we've pounded our way to him well before Hannah Jane's deadline?

"I didn't see this coming. But it's a cool change, I suppose. I guess I can say goodbye to my career. I have no doubt John will request my resignation tomorrow morning. As for putting the knife down, I don't think that's going to happen anytime soon. Honestly, I'm going to leave with the girl, and you're going to let me."

"I don't know how you reached that conclusion. You aren't going anywhere, especially with the girl. She stays here," Harper countered.

Nolan slowly stood and pulled the girl up with him. The knife never left her throat. I didn't like how this was going, and I was terrified of how it might end.

"You can shoot me, but I'll still drag this blade across her neck before I go down, and you'll be responsible for that. You'll have to live with her death if you do something stupid."

"We're not going to do anything stupid, Nolan. But I don't understand any of this," I said. "What possessed you to do something like this? Why would you jeopardize everything you've accomplished in your life to throw it all away now?"

Harper took a step inside the room. I cringed, expecting the blade to start slicing, but Nolan showed no fear of Harper's advancement.

"I've accomplished nothing! My life has been completely pointless until now. It's the defining moment I've been waiting for the last thirty-three years. I was just another pathetic, walking through life asleep drone of a human being. I followed my daily routine and never feeling alive, but instead feeling half dead. Azrael is showing me the way to overwhelming power."

I shuddered at the name. Nolan does know Azrael. These days, Azrael has become a mentor by teaching human destruction and chaos to all those eager to learn.

"Everything Azrael told you, everything he has done is for his glory, not yours. He's using you like he uses everyone. When he's used you up, he'll kill you. You may believe in him, but that's because he's brainwashed you so he can control you better. He wants to corrupt the man you are," I said in desperate pleading. I didn't want this day to end in bloodshed.

"He told me that I would understand him, that I would feel the power that he feels if I sliced away her soul from her body. I desperately want to feel what he feels."

"Hate and greed are the only things he feels. You don't need that. You're better than that, and you know you are. Just let the girl go, and we'll talk this thing out," Harper said.

Nolan began backing up. He was against the sliding glass door. Without warning, he shoved the uninjured girl at us. I reached out and caught her in my arms. When I looked up, the glass door was wide open, and Nolan was gone.

Chapter 37

I found myself racing out the open door in fierce pursuit of Nolan. I badly wanted him. He would have taken the life of an innocent girl tonight if Harper and I hadn't intervened.

My legs scissor beneath me. I couldn't let Nolan get away from us. He knows Azrael, and either he has met him in person or is in contact with the killer angel. Either way didn't matter to me. He has information I desperately wanted, information that would unmask our nemesis and lead us to Hannah Jane's whereabouts. Nolan was going down at any cost.

Nolan rounded the house and was now out of sight. He was going for the Mercedes, trying for a fast getaway.

As I began to round the same corner, my foot slipped on the wet grass, and I went down hard. My right side screamed out in pain as I did a body slide down a slope in the yard. I pushed myself up in frustration and began to hammer my way to the front of the house again.

I heard the Mercedes roar to life, followed by the bite of tires on gravel as he tore away from the house and down the driveway.

Harper came out of the front door. We were both now running back to the sedan tucked away in the trees nearly a hundred yards away. Nolan had a substantial lead on us, but I was one hell of a madman behind the wheel when the adrenaline was pumping.

We quickly reached the sedan, and I reversed out of the nest of trees and onto the main road. I slammed into gear and shot down the gravel road in pursuit.

The Mercedes had one hell of a highly tuned engine. I knew that the basic sedan we had was no match for German engineering. The only way I could catch up was by cunning maneuvers, cutting sharp corners, and with a little luck tossed into the pot.

Nolan already had a significant lead on us, but he was driving too erratic. He was all over the road. With every curve he took, the rear end badly fishtailed on the gravel. Tires skidded to the edge of the road and nearly dragging the entire car down the steep embankment into the thick trees below.

"He's going to lose it on one of these turns, Jack," Harper said.

"I'm trying not to lose it myself," I shot back.

"I think we're going to get him. He doesn't know how to handle that car well enough. He's panicking. He's risking death to get away."

"Nolan isn't worried about death. He's already met Death, remember? I think he's trying to get away because he doesn't want us to beat the truth out of him. He doesn't want to ruin the ending for us."

"Look! He's losing it!" Harper yelled.

The Mercedes was out of control. The rear end spun wildly on the road, pitching a hard left, then right and left again. The brake lights flashed, and I knew it had been a deadly mistake.

The Mercedes slid on the gravel toward the edge of the road. The right front tire dug deeply in the soft ground of the shoulder. With such velocity, the car turned in the air like a tightly spun football. It came down just beyond the tree line with a deafening crunch as it rolled.

I skidded to a stop fifty yards from the wreckage. Harper and I got out, and we did a painful slide down the embankment.

Nolan's Mercedes would never again be mistaken for a well-crafted piece of machinery. The car was now a twisted mess of steel. It was upside down and, although I saw no fire, the vehicle billowed a cloud of smoke.

I knelt beside the shattered driver window. Nolan was still inside. He hadn't been wearing his seatbelt, and the mangled metal punished him for it. His face was a bloody mess. His nose was cocked sickly to one side, and deep lacerations covered his bare skin. His right arm was rotated at an odd angle. He looked as if he'd gone too many rounds with a heavyweight contender.

"Harper, help me get him out."

Harper raced over and reached inside.

"Okay. You got him, Jack?"

"Yeah, let's do it."

I knew that moving him too much could cause even more bodily damage, but I was afraid that the car might suddenly catch fire or explode if we didn't get clear.

We dragged Nolan away from the vehicle. He was still conscious, which amazed me. We collapsed in the tangle of weeds in pure exhaustion. Nolan's breathing was raspy and labored. I knew he must have sustained severe internal injuries from being tossed about in the car. Harper was on his cell, calling for immediate assistance. I didn't think they'd make it on time.

Although I knew it had to hurt like hell, Nolan Windell, assistant to Senator John Hillcrest, began to laugh. It was a deep, know-it-all kind of laugh. Even in his condition, he was mocking us. He had secrets, and he wasn't in the sharing mood.

"Where is she? Where's Hannah Jane? Are you Azrael? Are you Death?" I asked.

"You'll never figure out the ending. It'll shock the shit out of you." Nolan coughed fiercely and spat blood into his hand.

"Redeem yourself, Nolan. One last chance to go to Heaven," Harper said.

Nolan wouldn't say anything, not anymore. His blank eyes stared up at the clear night sky.

Chapter 38

Los Angeles *Times* crime reporter Rita Sowell was standing at the back of the open ambulance doors. She watched the circus scene with the eyes of a reporter. Instead of digging deep to find her daily story, she became a major part of it. Her mind had already been churning the words together that would make a sensational front-page story. She couldn't wait to get to her laptop, office computer, or even a pencil and paper. She had nearly died by the hands of a maniac an hour ago. She was vibrating from the adrenaline surge. She has never been this thankful to be alive.

It was a shock to the system when Nolan Windell had called earlier in the evening and disclosed the abduction of Hannah Jane Hillcrest. She agreed to meet at the bar and discuss the bombshell topic. Now Nolan tossed her another humongous story at the moment of his death. These were her big headlines. These would be her breaking stories she has patiently been waiting for, and it all fell right into her lap. So far, she only knew small facts of tonight's entire mess. Of course, the relentless investigator in her knew that in only a short while, she'd have all the necessary dirt on Nolan's mental instability.

The local police were here, but they knew little more than she did. The real information would have to come from the two FBI agents who had stopped Nolan from cutting her throat.

The thing intriguing her most was that these guys had followed her and Nolan to this out-of-the-way retreat. It was evident that Nolan had done something big enough to warrant the FBI's attention and pick-up a secret tail following them out here.

What struck her odd about Nolan was that it seemed as if he had some level of multiple personality disorder. At the bar, he was charismatic and full of humor. On the drive from the bar to the secluded house, he was calm and level headed. However, in only a matter of minutes from when they stepped in the front door, his personality switched into something she never expected. Insanity like that was something she only saw in the movies or wrote about in her daily column. She never suspected she'd become a central character in one of her crime stories.

These FBI guys probably had the dirt on the self-proclaimed Angel of Death whom Nolan referenced in their conversations. One way or another, Rita was going to drive the information out of these guys.

A few people were busy tending to Nolan's body. Another crew worked on right siding his vehicle to tow it from the ditch. An even larger force was back at the house of horrors, searching for whatever incriminating things they could find on Nolan. Rita knew they wouldn't uncover anything. Nolan had told her on the car ride that the country house belonged to Hannah Jane. Nolan said he'd give her a chance to peek inside Hannah Jane's private life for added authenticity when she wrote the headline exclusive.

Rita moved to the driver's door of the ambulance and peered in the mirror. She thought that she looked like hell, but under the circumstances, no one would blame her. Rita worked her fingers into the frizz of her hair and attempted to pull it seemingly straight. She used her thumb to wipe away the smear of mascara. After a few minutes, Rita figured it was the best she would look for the remainder of the night. Sure, it was still a scary picture by her standards, but she wanted this story. The FBI guys would just have to accommodate the sight of horror that was Rita Sowell.

Rita slowly walked toward the FBI agents as they observed the clean-up of the crash scene. They were talking, and Rita was able to grab pieces of what they were saying. She honestly didn't consider what she was doing an act of spying. It's regarded as public information when people are out where everyone could overhear them.

With her ears finely tuned and her brain recording with precision, Rita thought, *Come on, baby, give me the story of the century.*

Chapter 39

"Excuse me, gentlemen. I wonder if one of you might be able to tell me exactly what the hell this whole whacked out evening was about?" Rita said as she approached Harper and Jack.

"Ms. Sowell, I'm sorry we haven't been able to speak with you yet, but we've been managing over this crash site and trying to piece everything together," Harper said.

"Have you managed some sort of conclusion from this mess? If so, I'd love to know why I was involved and why that man tried to kill me tonight."

"I apologize, but we're not at liberty to discuss an ongoing case with civilians."

"Okay, how about a reporter? Have you ever heard of the right to free press?" Rita said.

"You're a reporter?" I asked and glanced at Harper.

"That's right. I'm a crime reporter for the Los Angeles *Times*. This kind of thing just happens to be my area of expertise. I'd love to sit down with both of you back at the house of horrors, have a cup of coffee, and chat."

"Ms. Sowell, I'm sorry for what you experienced tonight. I'm happy that we came at the right time and stopped the situation before it got worse. However, you're well aware that we're unable to disclose anything at this time. We'll have an officer take you to the station. They'll have to get your statement, and then you'll be able to go home," Harper said.

Surprisingly, I recognized sincerity in Harper's voice.

"Fine. I'll answer your questions, but then I have questions of my own. I hope we can reach some sort of compromise?"

I ignored her question and said, "Why were you with Mr. Windell tonight?"

"Hmm, can't a gal like a guy and hope for some romance?"

"I bet this wasn't the type of romance you were looking to find," I said.

"Oh, we talked a lot about our favorite things like food, vacation spots, and things like that. Oh, yeah, we were also discussing exactly how we were going to release the information of Hannah Jane Hillcrest's kidnapping."

I staggered back a little. *Shit, shit, shit!* I figured Harper thought the same thing.

Rita's brown eyes watched us closely, searching for a telling confirmation to the inside story.

I couldn't believe Nolan released the information of the kidnapping to a reporter. What was behind his entire plan? Why contact a reporter, spill everything to her, and then attempt to end her life? Was it a power trip for him? What kind of connection did Nolan have with Azrael? What was Azrael's purpose for becoming partners with Nolan? It couldn't have just been the simple reason of influencing Senator Hillcrest to bring me into the case, could it? There has to be so much more behind this mystery.

"Hannah Jane Hillcrest?" Harper said, offering a look of confusion that fooled even me. "I wasn't aware that she *was* kidnapped. Who told you that? Did Nolan Windell say that?"

"Don't play stupid with me. I know a lot more than you think," Rita shot back with a degree of resilience.

Harper offered a genuine laugh. "Are you telling me that the man who aimed to sever your head from your shoulders an hour ago told you that Hannah Jane Hillcrest was kidnapped, and you believed him? Did you happen to take into account that he might have delivered you a sensational make-believe story like that so he could get you out here alone? He probably brought you to this secluded area to dismember you and then bury your remains somewhere in the woods, and never to be heard from again. I don't know what you're thinking, but that sounded like his plan to me. I don't typically trust people who hold a large blade to my throat. You should check all your facts before driving out into the middle of nowhere with a stranger. I don't think we'll be able to be there for you next time. If this happens again, that is."

"You guys were watching Nolan Windell. Why is that? Maybe because you suspect him in the connection of Hannah Jane's disappearance?" Rita asked.

"I honestly haven't heard anything about Hannah Jane Hillcrest. It isn't my department if she is missing. Maybe you should call FBI Director Gill and ask for the department that handles high profile kidnappings. I'm sure they can hook you up. We've been investigating Nolan Windell for some time. I won't go into detail about the case, but let's just say the word embezzlement is on my mind. He suddenly has a lot of money on hand, and we want to know where it's coming from."

"Embezzlement? Are you saying he's stealing from the government or the American people?"

"No, Ms. Sowell, I'm not saying."

Chapter 40

Sleep was pulling at Rita. She wasn't necessarily tired, but her body was kicking in a defense mechanism against the shock of the evening. Her body told her that sleep was the best method to calm her nerves and lower the anxiety levels. The soft motion of the police cruiser also assisted in the attempt to draw her into unconsciousness.

The FBI agents gave her little to go on. If anything, they confused the matter even more. Now she wasn't so sure if Hannah Jane was even missing at all. Even if Hannah Jane wasn't missing, Rita certainly had one hell of a story to begin writing as soon as she got home. The feds won't be able to stop her from writing about the insane night she experienced.

The most significant case she reported on so far in her bleak career was back in her early years in New York. A police officer had gone missing and eventually turned up in a shallow grave in the woods. It was one of the only cases she had covered receiving nationwide attention. Rita always felt there was a lot more beneath the surface of that particular case. Every lead she received ran into a dreadful dead-end. She wrote several columns about possible theories that she believed to be the truth. The editor even allowed the stories to run. The paper fired her when the police department threatened with lawsuits for slander and false accusations. She had many suspicions, but nothing ever panned out for her or the police. The case remains active to this day.

"I guess you had one interesting evening," police officer Howard Nivens said and glanced at her in the gloom of the cruiser.

"Not really. I do this kind of thing every weekend," Rita said as she tried to resist the pull of sleep.

She sat up and gazed out the windows at the darkness that gave her a certain discomfort. The winding road she'd taken earlier was in front of them, and the glowing edge of the city lay a dozen miles beyond that.

"You must be one of those wild girls who need an adrenaline rush every so often," he said and laughed at his joke.

"I guess. Sometimes you have to inject your life with a thrill so that you know you're still alive."

The officer was saying something else, but Rita's mind had tuned him out. She suddenly started thinking about the man Nolan referred to as Death. Not Death, as explained in the Bible, but another quack believing he was something more than just human. Azrael, the Angel of Death.

Death has Hannah Jane Hillcrest. That's what Nolan had told her.

Did Nolan conjure this elaborate hoax of a story to get me somewhere secluded and murder me? Why would someone do that? Nolan, or any madman for that matter, could kill someone at any time if he knew the daily habits of that person. Maybe the FBI agents were right. Maybe Nolan wanted quiet and seclusion as he dismembered me. I guess nothing would spoil a hacking party more than a close neighbor who rings your doorbell and tells you to keep the slaughtering noises down, she thought.

"Does that sound okay to you?" the officer asked.

"I'm sorry, what did you say?"

The officer's face glowed in the dash lights as he watched Rita. "I asked if it was all right with you if we get you to the station and take a little time to get your statement while it's fresh in your mind, and then I'll run you home. It's what the feds want. I can ignore the order if you'd rather go home to clean yourself up and get some sleep. I understand what kind of hell you've been through, so I could always take your statement later."

"That's nice of you, but I'd rather give the statement now. I'm not sure if my sleep will be very relaxed anyhow. I'm going to have a busy day at work."

"Huh, I'd have to take some leave if I had been in your situation. What is it you do for a living?"

Rita wasn't able to answer because intense bright lights suddenly fired to life at the edge of the forest ahead and to their left. Rita threw up her hand and shielded her eyes from the blinding intrusion that broke the night. She caught a glimpse of the lights drawing closer and heard the roar of another vehicle on this lonely stretch of road. There were no other cruisers or rescue vehicles following them from the house. They were alone, and Rita felt fear leap into her throat and catch her breath.

"What the hell is this joker doing?" the officer asked.

When the vehicle hit the incline connecting the tree line to the road, the front bumper skimmed the shoulder's gravel and sent small rocks airborne. The vehicle was now on the road and charging right for them.

Officer Nivens switched on the siren and flashers.

The large truck hit the police cruiser's left fender with such a jarring force that Rita was violently thrown hard to her left and recoiling equally hard to the right. With such velocity, her head snapped against the passenger window and shattered the tempered glass.

The impact crushed the cruiser's entire left side and practically shoved the engine into the passenger compartment. The windshield spider-webbed but held in place.

The cruiser shoved down the road into a small ditch beside an empty field.

Rita's head was ringing from the impact. She held onto consciousness by sheer willpower. She thought that if she blacked out, she'd never wake again. Aside from a fierce full-body ache, she felt that she was all right. She would pull herself from the wreckage with nothing more than minor cuts, bruises, and a throbbing goose egg on the right side of her head.

She turned to Officer Nivens and was about to ask if he was all right, but it was apparent that he had endured more of the impact than she had. He was unconscious or dead. Rita couldn't immediately tell for sure. Blood was seeping from a long laceration in his forehead. The blood ran down his face, giving him a horrific mask of red. With a trembling hand, Rita reached for him and gently shook his shoulder. He didn't respond. As she watched him with eyes of shock, she could see his chest slowly drawing in a breath.

"Thank God," she said.

Rita's eyes searched the interior of the cruiser. The CB radio had become dislodged from its mounting bracket and was lying on the floorboard. The light still glowed on the unit's face, which told her that it was still operational. She seized the mike and brought it to her mouth as she was about to begin a frantic cry for help to anyone or everyone, something passed by the single working headlight.

She heard footsteps crunching through the twigs and fallen leaves. A figure suddenly appeared from the night to the broken passenger window.

"I don't think I'd make that call if I were you, Rita. I don't believe you want to be responsible for the death of any more officers tonight," a man said.

"He's—he's—he's not dead," she stammered and glanced at the officer again to confirm the statement more to herself than to the stranger.

"No? Huh, good for him, I guess. I suppose he's going to have one bastard of a headache when he wakes up. I hope you don't have any broken bones or internal injuries, do you, Rita?"

"I'm not sure. I don't think so. Why did you do that? Why would you crash into us like that? You had the whole road to pass, and you just hit us. How—how do you know my name?"

"Not very bright for a reporter, are you? I think you know the answers to those questions. I crashed into you on purpose. It's an all-new part of the plan. I'm improvising because I wasn't expecting you to survive tonight. I apologize, I haven't introduced myself. My name is Azrael, and I'm the Angel of Death. I suppose we should be going before more company comes along."

With that said, the man called Death brutally struck the side of Rita's already injured skull, and the blackness of the night quickly surrounded her.

Chapter 41

Harper and I had left the crash site soon after Nolan's car was pulled back onto the road. We drove back to L.A. and found a cheap hotel so that we could shower and take a breather before our next move. The trouble is, we weren't entirely sure what that was.

Time was running away from us, so we slept very little.

Just after three o'clock on Sunday morning, Harper and I went to Nolan's house. We intended to turn his place upside down to find anything that would link Nolan to Azrael or Hannah Jane's current position.

There was no need for a search warrant because we had probable cause. Besides, I didn't think the owner would object.

I held my tongue as Harper delivered one swift kick just below the door handle, and the front door of Nolan's house splintered open. I cringed from the echoing sound and glanced around the dark neighborhood. I didn't see any lights suddenly flick on. I wondered if the police would soon show up and halt our search with drawn guns.

We walked into Nolan's house and flipped on the lights.

What was so odd about Nolan's home was that it was outright ordinary. The entertainment center, lamps, couch, and throw rugs all had a basic design and could probably be purchased at any local retailers.

"Sure doesn't seem like I walked through the front door of a house whose owner was over-eager to kill last night. It's like cramming a square peg in a round hole. It just doesn't seem to fit, no matter what," I said as I browsed the living room and opened cabinet doors.

"Be patient, Jack. We haven't found a box of horrors yet, but it doesn't mean there isn't one. Besides, remember that Nolan was an average guy with a prominent career, all before a sense of evil got its grip on him. That evil controlled him, twisted his mind, and made him believe in things that weren't necessarily true. I would find it strange if his home were different from this. Nolan still controlled many aspects of his life. He went to work each day and probably did everything exceptionally well. What Azrael controlled was the part of his brain that wasn't set by routine. I bet Nolan going to that bar last night was highly unusual for him. He probably went there only to meet with Ms. Sowell because it was part of Azrael's well-constructed plan. Nolan's rage to inflict pain, terror, and death on a completely innocent person last night was all implanted by Azrael. He's done it for thousands of years. Corrupting humans is his unfortunate God-given ability."

"There's so much stuff I just can't wrap my head around," I said.

"Join the club."

We went upstairs and poked through Nolan's closets, cabinets, and any other place we could find in hopes of uncovering something. Being in someone's bedroom reminded me of the first day of this case. I had been digging through Hannah Jane's bedroom, searching for some sort of clue that would get my wheels spinning. It was the day I had left my girls, flown across the country, and met Senator Hillcrest and Harper. It was also the day I catapulted into something that was way over my head.

As I pulled open the bureau drawers in Nolan's bedroom, Harper's cell rang. I closely watched him. The call quickly jumped to an intense one-on-one. His face morphed from surprise to fear and then to rage as the conversation continued.

"Yeah, do what you can and let me know the moment there's any new development. Thanks," Harper said and ended the call.

I said, "What's the deal now?"

He sighed with exhaustion and said, "Our efforts last night were all for nothing, Jack. Rita Sowell is now missing. She was being taken to the police station after we left, and the police cruiser she was riding in had some sort of collision. The officer is in pretty bad shape, but he's still alive. I think Azrael got to her after all."

"Why would he do that? I don't understand his method of thinking. First, he wants Nolan to kill Rita, and when that doesn't pan out, he takes matters into his own hands to kidnap her?"

Nothing Azrael does shock me anymore. I expected the worst with each passing hour, and it's what I usually get.

"I couldn't hazard a guess right now. A group of officers has been searching the area since they discovered the wreckage. They'll let me know the second they come up with anything. We need to let them do their job so that we can concentrate on ours."

"I can't imagine what Senator Hillcrest is going to say when I break the news to him about Nolan. He's going to go nuclear, that's for sure," I said.

"Yeah, I guess anyone would. I think finding out that a man he greatly trusted was part of this chaos from the beginning will definitely set him off."

Harper suddenly halted beside the nightstand. He stood there like a statue for a full minute and then leaned toward one of the framed pictures. In a voice that was barely an octave above a whisper, he said, "Jesus Christ."

I stepped up behind him. Over his shoulder, I saw the photo grabbing his attention. The picture was of a slightly younger Nolan and an attractive blonde female I didn't recognize. They wore colorful swimsuits, standing knee-deep in the breaking surf and smiling for the camera. Imprinted on the frame below the photo read:

Siblings Until the End of Time.

"Doesn't look like Jesus Christ to me," I said.
"No, not Jesus. Better."
"Better than Jesus Christ?" I didn't get the punch line.
"Not just better. *Way* better."

Chapter 42

Unfortunately, Harper and I were shooting across the country bound for D.C. again.

When Harper caught a glimpse of the photo in Nolan's house, the clue immediately became known, well at least known to Harper anyway. Harper knew the blonde in the bikini. Things were connecting so well now that it was insane to understand how Azrael had pieced every single detail of the game together with patience and precision.

As we jet streamed to D.C., Harper laid it all out for me.

"I was partners with Hunter Jacobs four years ago when we first learned about killer angels. We were partners for three years before that. Hunter is one of the few who knows about this fallen army. Soon after we killed Azrael for the first time and learned the truth of everything, Hunter cracked up when the relentless game began again. He said he couldn't take it. He didn't want to be a part of fieldwork anymore, especially cases involving a heavenly war. He mostly stayed in the office and did a lot of research for other field agents. I haven't had a partner since, and I rarely speak to Hunter because I'm always on assignment. Hunter turned in his badge and resigned from the FBI last week."

"Damn, another good person destroyed by Death."

"What everything boils down to is that Hunter's wife is Virginia, and Nolan is apparently her brother. She's the one in the photo. I'm at the point in my mind where I don't have enough information to tell me if Virginia or Hunter might be the next clue or if one of them might be Azrael. That's why we have to go back to D.C."

"Yeah, I understand all that. We need to follow the clue, and I think you're right. One of the two has to be the clue."

"Not only that, I feel that I have to be the one to tell Virginia about her brother's death. Of course, I'll have to leave out all the details of the attempted murder of Rita Sowell. Honestly, I had no idea that Virginia and Nolan were siblings. I think Hunter had once told me her maiden name. It didn't click in my head until I saw the picture of her and Nolan. I knew her, but not well enough that we discussed things like family. I only saw her on occasion when Hunter wanted to get together with my family and go out for dinner. Of course, that was before my wife and daughter left."

After another long plane ride over the states, Harper and I finally reached the house of Virginia and Hunter Jacobs. It was a modest home in the outskirts of D.C. At the corner of the house, the gutter was pulling loose, the blue paint of the siding was blistering and peeling in several areas, and the front screen door had a long tear in it and needed replacing. The household chores had gone neglected for some time. It reminded me of my own home. I spent too much time away, and it was starting to build regrets in my mind.

We went up the front porch and rang the bell. Virginia Jacobs answered the door. She was in her late thirties, pretty, shoulder-length blonde hair, and dressed in a tan jogging suit. Her face and hair were damp with sweat. She looked like she'd spent the last hour running a marathon.

Despite the weariness on her face, she offered us a warm, sincere smile.

"Hey, Virginia," Harper said, leaning in for a hug.

"Hey, you." She affectionately hugged him back.

"This is Jack Calloway. He's my flunky," Harper said.

"Actually, he's *my* flunky," I countered. I gently shook her hand.

"It's nice to meet you, Jack. Would you like to come in for some coffee? I'd like some company, good or bad. Just get your tails in here."

Virginia seemed overwhelmingly earnest, a true to heart kind of person. She struck me as a woman with a lot of affection and love to give, but the recent worry lines on her face told me another story.

The entryway and living room were pleasantly decorated with modern as well as antique paintings and tabletop sculptures. Seeing the artwork, the furniture, and throw rugs told me the family had extra money to kick around. They had accessorized with a taste of bringing delight to the home without going to extreme overkill.

We settled on the couch as Virginia disappeared to the kitchen and returned moments later with a tray of coffee and a plate of sugar cookies.

"It's good to see you. I hope things are well," Harper said.

She forced a smile. "I apologize for how I look. You guys caught me right in the middle of a workout. It helps to take my mind off of things. I've also been keeping myself overburdened at work. I can't seem to give myself two seconds to breathe. You know how it is these days, crazy, crazy, crazy."

"Crazy is an understatement. We were hoping Hunter would be home. I was just wondering how he's doing."

"I've kind of wondered that myself, Harper. I haven't seen Hunter in over a week. When I called his cell last Tuesday, he only offered ten seconds of his time to tell me

177

to piss off. I haven't heard from him since." A couple of tears slipped from her eyes, and she swiped them away.

"I don't understand," Harper said with obvious concern.

"Hunter is a different person these days. He's a man on a mission."

"What kind of mission?" Harper asked.

"Saving the world, I guess. I don't know. Hunter has changed so much since the accident. He never clarified what he was talking about before he left. He rambled on a lot, gibberish that didn't make much sense to me. He packed up some of his belongings, and just before he left, he said, 'I'm going to save us all.'"

Chapter 43

Harper furrowed his brow as he looked from Virginia to me and back to her again. "I didn't hear anything about it. What accident?"

"You never heard about the accident? I figured he would have called you." Virginia said.

"No, I've been away on assignment. I spoke with Hunter on the phone a little over two weeks ago for a few minutes. He sounded fine."

"He's okay now. He was in a car accident nearly a month ago. Another driver crossed into his lane on the highway. It was practically a head-on collision. The other driver died, and so did Hunter. Someone passing by stopped and pulled Hunter from the wreckage. They performed CPR until he revived."

Simultaneously, Harper and I looked at each other to confirm the thought that had just leaped into our tired minds.

Hunter had momentarily died. His brief death would have given Azrael a chance to slip into Hunter's body. Hunter is Azrael, after all. It has to be the clue we needed.

"Hunter said he was going to save us all? Who do you think he meant?" I asked. I thought I already knew the answer.

She gave me an exhausted glance. "As I said, I'm not sure. Humanity, I guess. Hunter didn't make any sense ever since coming home from the hospital. His personality changed after the crash. When I went to see him in the hospital, he didn't seem to care that I was there for him or that I love him so much. He kept talking about preparing a plan. I told him that he needed to rest and build his strength. He told me that he would punish everyone. I figured he meant all the people who did bad things."

"Do you still think that now?" Harper asked.

"Now?" She gave a nervous laugh. "Now I'm not so sure. It's just that he seemed so angry. I've never seen him like that before, with so much hate and mistrust. When he came home from the hospital, his rage only seemed to grow. Against the doctor's recommendations, Hunter didn't take it easy or give himself time to recuperate. Instead, he traveled a lot. He didn't tell me where he was going. I assumed he just went back to work."

"Virginia, Hunter quit the FBI."

"I don't understand. Hunter didn't leave the FBI. He's been traveling and working on cases. I'm sure he has." Virginia shifted her sight from Harper to me as if we were trying to pull a fast one.

"It's true. Hunter resigned."

"I knew something was wrong, but I didn't realize it was this severe. I know one of the places Hunter went to was Los Angeles. I caught a glimpse of an airline ticket before he left. Oh, and he went to see his mother, too. The poor woman, such a terrible thing that happened to her."

"What happened to Hunter's mother?" Harper asked.

"She passed away during his last visit. She suffered a massive heart attack right in front of Hunter. He hired a private jet to have her body flown to St. Paul, where she grew up. His father is also buried there. Do you know what hurts the most out of all this? Do you know how he inflicted the most emotional pain for me?"

"How?" Harper asked.

"Hunter wouldn't even allow me to go to St. Paul for her funeral yesterday. He told me that I was no longer part of the family. I loved that woman like she was my own mother. She was the sweetest person you'd ever want to know. He wouldn't even let me say goodbye to her. I hate him for that. Whatever his reasons were, it doesn't matter. It still hurts all the same."

Harper and I glanced at each other again. Things were adding up a little faster. Hunter had experienced a brief death and sudden behavioral changes. His odd disconnection, ranting like a maniac to his wife, and speaking about a hidden agenda also helped draw our conclusions. It started to appear that we were on the right path to our killer angel.

Virginia retrieved a pack of cigarettes from the coffee table, shook one loose, and lit it.

"So, do you want to cut through the crap and tell me the truth, Harper?" Her state of anguish seemed to melt away and quickly replaced with suspicion.

"We need to speak to him. We believe he has some information concerning the current case we're working on. I thought he could help out."

It was simply amazing how a seemingly frail and heartbroken woman could suddenly turn so defensive and gritty within seconds. Her guard sprang into action, and she was ready to fight for the man she still obviously loved.

"Horseshit. I want you to be honest with me, Harper. You owe me that much."

"You're right, I do. But the fact is, you know I can't do that. The FBI won't allow me to disclose any information on an active case. However, I will tell you that we believe Hunter may have done some bad things. That's why we need to speak to him. We need to clear him of all suspicion. You know how it works. If you know where he is or where he might be heading, you need to tell me now."

"If I did know, Harper, I'd tell you. I want you to find him. All I want is for him to come home. Why can't you find him and bring him home?" she pleaded. Tears were running down her cheeks again as the emotional pressure became too great for her to carry.

Harper went to her. He wrapped his arms around her with the comfort I'd never have thought him capable of doing.

"You don't have any idea where he might have gone?"

"I honestly don't know. As I said, the last time we spoke, Hunter told me he has some things that needed a final touch. He then said for me to get on with my life while I still have one. That's all he told me, and then he hung up. I haven't heard from him since. I swear to God."

Harper held her tightly, trying to soothe her. He then delivered the unfortunate news about her brother, Nolan, and his untimely death.

Chapter 44

We had about four and a half hours to kill as the jet headed for Ironside, Oregon. We were on our way to discover what madness would unfold in the wake of Death.

I honestly didn't mind these slingshot trips across the country anymore. The time of jumping from one clue to the next gave me time to think, to work out unsettling and confusing steps we've taken. It also gave me time to think about my girls, and the next time I'd see them. I had made a promise to the most beautiful girls in the world. Even if Hell froze over, I wouldn't miss Reanne's play on Monday evening. Breaking another promise in a lifetime just wasn't going to happen for me.

Harper decided that I wouldn't let him off the hook, so he began telling me more about his wife and daughter and the on and off-again relationship. He told me that the job had already firmly wedged itself between him and his wife long before the Angel of Death brought Harper into this twisted and illogical game.

"She always knew I was doing good things, that I was improving our country one case at a time. But it was certain cases that consumed my time and energy. I became obsessed with these cases, and I couldn't ease up until they were solved. Those were the weeks and months that began to crack the pillars. Azrael and his winged army of destroyers not only corrupted my marriage and being a decent father, but shook my entire life down to the foundation."

"Tell me more about the first time you dealt with Azrael," I said.

"As I told you earlier, Hunter was also involved with the investigation. The entire thing began with a kidnapped young girl. We followed evidence leading to another crime scene, and so on. Just like we're doing now. All the clues brought us to a desolate spot in the mountains of Idaho. We were completely unaware that we were playing a horrific game with a killer angel. Unfortunately, we arrived too late to save Christie Anderson, and we took Azrael down for the first time in our strange career. At that time, being naïve and certainly not expecting to become part of a heavenly war, we thought the chaos of the case was over when Azrael fell to the forest floor after half a dozen slugs tore through him."

"But it wasn't over, was it?"

"The case in Idaho was just the beginning. Three months later, a similar case showed up on our radar, and a new chase began. Everything about it screamed copycat, but Azrael had called me, taunted me, and explained that the body we had put down in those Idaho woods was nothing but a shell to him. Suddenly, Hunter and I begin to think that it was some sort of cult that picked up the game after the passing of one of their members. The idea was short-lived. By the director's orders, the secret files the FBI has on killer angels suddenly opened wide for me. From that point on, I became the primary agent dealing with Azrael and his maniacal plans for human destruction. These cases have been my life since then, insanity at its finest."

"Hannah Jane is going to live, Harper. I made a promise to Reanne, and I'm going to see that promise fulfilled."

"I've never won the game before, Jack. It would be best if you don't get your hopes up only to have them come crashing down. We have until sunset today, and I couldn't even guess at how close we are to the end."

"You haven't worked with me before. I can be completely relentless when I want something so bad. It's been that way ever since I lost my daughter, Regina, to the murderous hands of a madman. Hannah Jane is going to live."

Chapter 45

Beverly Jacobs' home was nestled in a cove of maples. The beautiful property spread out over acres of lush woods with an incredible view of the mountains to the east. The snow-covered landscape made the scenery even more pleasing.

Dr. William Jenkins, who had been a long-standing physician and friend of the family, accompanied us from town to the residence. He was a large man, with thin gray hair brushed back on his scalp and wire-rimmed glasses perched on his stumpy nose. He was polite and accommodating and showed no resistance to allowing us inside to have a look around.

Inside the home, something struck me right away. Death has been here. There was no mistaking it. Wherever he went, he seemed to leave a mark lingering in the air. The essence gave me the shivers.

Dr. Jenkins said, "Bev was one of a kind. She'd go out of her way to do anything for someone. Well, up until her arthritis got so bad. She always had a wonderful sense of humor. I don't think anyone will miss that old firecracker more than me."

"You said that her son didn't visit very often?" I asked.

Looking somber, Dr. Jenkins slowly shook his head. "Naw, he was too busy working with the FBI. He never seemed to find the time to come up. I understand, though, because it's an important job for him. I even remember him wanting to be an FBI agent or a detective since he was knee-high. It's a shame Hunter wasn't able to visit more often. He was all the family Bev had left, real family, I mean. Heck, Bev was a mother to everyone in town. God bless her sweet soul."

"Did you have the coroner perform an autopsy?" Harper asked.

With a look of shock, Dr. Jenkins said, "Autopsy? Why in heavens would I do that? Bev was seventy-seven years old. She had a history of heart problems, and there wasn't any funny business that had gone on to warrant an autopsy. You can take my word on it, Bev died of heart disease. I'm not going to allow that poor old gal to be hacked up just to confirm what I already knew."

"If you knew what I know, an autopsy would have been first on your agenda," Harper said.

"And what is that? What's here that has captured the interest of the FBI? What are you hoping to find?"

I said, "Dr. Jenkins, do you mind if my partner and I have a look around the house alone? I just don't want you getting upset that we're searching through Mrs. Jacobs' things."

"No, I suppose that would be all right. I'll be waiting outside. Just let me know when you're finished." Dr. Jenkins left through the front door, obviously agitated.

I turned to Harper, who was busy searching through the bureau drawers. "You sure do tend to make friends wherever you go."

"You're the only friend I need, Jack," Harper said without even glancing up from his frantic search for *something*.

His tone was sarcastic and rolled out in a careless way that almost placed him back in the co-worker category.

Sometimes it was hard to tell whether or not he even considered me a friend or if I was simply an aid to his greater goal.

"You can be such a prick sometimes," I said. "In the course of your busy days, do you even take into account the feelings of anyone else? Or are you so focused on what Harper is doing that the rest of the world is a blur?"

He closed the bureau drawer and eyed me. "That's where you're wrong. The fact is, I've considered everyone else's feelings in the entire world first before I even thought of myself. Why do you think my wife left me and took our daughter with her? I'll tell you why, because I always put everyone else's fucking problems before my own. It's one of my greatest downfalls. My wife realized that I was obsessed with strangers' problems and not caring enough about my loved ones. I single-handedly ruined the only thing I cared for in my life. I never blamed them for leaving."

It was easy to see the heartache in his features. I began to understand the torment Harper has been through the last four years. In the course of only six days, I had run myself to the brink of exhaustion and fried my mind trying to put the pieces of a complicated puzzle together. I've even managed to go two full days without speaking to Reanne. It's the longest stretch I've ever gone without talking to my sweet little girl and telling her that I loved her. I understood Harper now.

I shook my head. "I'm sorry. I shouldn't have said that."

"Don't worry about it. In the quest of this thing, I've made a lot of enemies along the path."

"You know, it's never too late. If you find the time, you can get your family back."

"Clara will never come back. Besides, with them staying away from me might be the only thing that's keeping them safe from Azrael. Let's not focus on my problems right now. The clock is ticking, and we still have a lot to figure out. Hannah Jane is the one who needs us right now."

The main floor of the house revealed nothing vital that we could use to lead us to Azrael. The only thing of interest we discovered was old photo albums in which we saw Hunter's pictures as a child and through his high school days. He'd been an outgoing, well-liked person. Many photos were showing us that Hunter was highly active in school functions. Hunter's soul is no longer here on Earth, but hopefully somewhere much better. A killer angel occupies his body now.

The basement floor and walls were concrete and stark white. A set of fluorescent lights flickered overhead. Except for a large workbench cluttered with an assortment of odds and ends, a steel sink against the wall, and a stack of cardboard boxes in the far corner, the room was completely bare.

As I walked over and inspected the contents of the boxes, Harper said, "What's this?"

I stepped beside him and looked. It appeared as if someone recently replaced half a dozen of the foundation cinderblocks. Unlike the rest of the wall, these were unpainted.

"Someone's been up to no good, I think," Harper said.

Chapter 46

It wasn't until Harper slammed the head of the sledge-hammer through the unpainted cinder blocks that I realized how far over the edge he has gone. He was more than a man on a mission. Harper needed a complete understanding of the reasons behind Azrael's madness. As he beat away the house's foundation, I suddenly felt extremely sorry for the wreck of a man he has become over the years.

I was shielding my eyes from the flying debris. I was also holding back the protests. Provoking a man dancing on the last thread of sanity and swinging a ten-pound sledgehammer was never a good idea.

The cinder block foundation crumbled under the massive blows. Within a minute, Harper reduced the newly replaced blocks to a jagged pile of rubble, and a thin gray cloud filled the room.

"Jesus, I think that might have been a little excessive, don't you? There could have just been a plumbing problem behind that wall. Maybe that's why the bricks are new," I offered.

Harper was on his hands and knees, now digging at the rubble, shoveling it between his legs. He looked like a dog searching for a lost bone. I would have laughed at the sight if I hadn't been so afraid.

Harper was throwing dirt all over me. I could hear him breathing with exhaustion. I moved to the right of the hole and knelt beside him.

"That's enough, Harper. Please stop this. We'll find our next clue, but we'll do it with a certain level of sanity." I softly spoke as if I were trying to talk a child out of a tantrum.

Harper suddenly stopped.

I heard the clacking of footsteps on the basement stairs.

"What on earth are you boys up to down here? I heard a fierce commotion outside." Dr. Jenkins reached the bottom step and said, "Sweet Jesus. I said you could look around. I didn't say it was all right to tear the house down around our ears!"

"We need to go, Harper."

"Jack."

I held up my hand. "We've done enough here. We have to go."

"But Jack—"

"Harper, the clue isn't buried behind the goddamn foundation. We need to go!" I was watching him closely, expecting him to lose it on me.

"Dammit, Jack, just turn your head and look!"

I did. What I saw wasn't more dirt. What I saw was a sheet of plastic, and behind that clear plastic were bulging eyes and a face I didn't recognize. The sight frightened me so much that I rolled right off my heels and fell backward.

Dr. Jenkins recognized the face. "Good Lord. It can't be. It simply can't be. How is that possible? That's Beverly. But Hunter flew her body to Minnesota to be buried in the cemetery right next to her husband. I simply can't believe this."

After a minute of mentally collecting myself, I said, "Azrael switched the bodies. Somehow, he must have put Hannah Jane in the coffin, sedated maybe, and flew her to St. Paul. That's why he rented a private plane to take the body to St. Paul. Airlines have regulations with transporting caskets. Hunter might have figured they would check the casket contents, and they would find Hannah Jane alive inside. He left that part of the foundation unpainted so we would get curious. It has to be the meaning behind it."

The clue before us was such a vile act of cruelty. Beverly's son, now plagued by the spirit of Death, had murdered this poor woman and left her in one of the most morbid graves I've ever seen.

"I think you're right, Jack. I think Azrael buried Hannah Jane in a grave that doesn't bear her name. We have to get to the airport now."

Chapter 47

"Call the authorities in St. Paul, Harper. They need to get to that grave right away and get Hannah Jane out of there," I said.

"No, Jack."

"What? You can't possibly think about leaving her in there."

"We're going to get her out, but we can't let the local police do it. You and I have to do it. We have to play the game by Azrael's rules, whether we like it or not. There will be severe consequences if we cross any lines."

The private plane lifted off the runway with a fierce momentum and a sudden eagerness to land in St. Paul. A young life hangs in the balance.

"Forget the rules, Harper. What if she's almost out of air? What if the coffin is buckling under the pressure, and she's getting crushed to death? If we get the locals there right now, dig up the grave and get her out of there, she'd be protected, and there's nothing he can do about it."

Harper consulted his watch, and then he was on his laptop and punching away at the keys. "It says here that sunset is at 5:22 p.m. in St. Paul. Because we're now on Pacific Time, it's 1:33 p.m. in St. Paul right now. That gives us nearly four hours until the deadline. This plane should get us to St. Paul in under three hours. With the car ride to the cemetery and the time it takes us to dig, we'll make it there on time, I promise. I don't want this entire week of running down the clues to blow up in our faces.

There could be many deaths as a penalty for ignoring his rule book."

"You said that breaking the rules in the past has cost extra lives. I won't let that happen if I can help it. I'm sorry, you know this maniac better than I do. I won't question your motives or decisions again," I said.

"There won't be a need to question again. I'm fairly sure Hanna Jane is in that casket, and this will be the end of the game for you. Hopefully, anyway."

I watched him closely. I could see immense sadness in his eyes. The large gap that had formed between himself and his wife and daughter had weighed heavily on him. Harper has no one at home. No children would come running to him and shower him with hugs and kisses the second he got home. His wife and daughter had moved away and moved on.

The worst part of all was that Harper knows a new game would begin in a matter of weeks or a month. There was nowhere he could run from it. Azrael would deal another hand, and Harper had no choice but to pick up his cards and see what kind of hand he'd be dealt. I felt a great pity for him. He certainly didn't deserve any of this.

Finally, I said, "Despite the first impression you gave me, you've kind of grown on me. Hell, I might even be brave enough to call you a friend."

"You'd be the only one I have. Everyone else just calls me an asshole, but friend sounds much better," he said with a hint of playfulness.

I said, "Let's not get too far ahead of ourselves. Let's get Hannah Jane home safe and sound first."

Harper opened his cell and made a call to Director Gill. He explained the current situation and asked for arrangements to be set up and ready on our arrival in St. Paul. It was going to be close, but I thought Harper was right. I thought we'd just make it on time.

Chapter 48

It was snowing in St. Paul when the jet kissed the lightly salted runway. A private car and a four-car police escort were waiting for the only two men who could go near the grave of Beverly Jacobs. We wasted no time with pleasantries as we exited the jet, passed the waiting patrolmen, and slipped inside the black sedan. We had a life to save, and time is critical. Only twenty-two minutes of Azrael's deadline remained. The flight had taken a little longer than Harper anticipated. We were cutting it close, but I was sure we'd make it.

The local authorities had located the grave at Rolling Green Cemetery. The place would be lit up like a Monday night football game.

Paramedics were standing by. I was sure that even the press had caught wind of the incredible events of the evening. They would be armed to the max with cameras to capture the miraculous rescue of the beloved celebrity. I was sure the tabloids would have record sellouts.

We didn't bother introducing ourselves to the driver. He was only there to get us to the cemetery as quickly as possible. Harper was in the front seat, and I took the back. The sedan was off and running.

It was the second to last weekend before Christmas, and traffic was heavy. Police cruisers shot ahead of us and blocked off cross traffic. They were trying to get us to the cemetery with little delay.

The driver turned to Harper and said, "I got a call just before you landed, sir. Senator Hillcrest and his wife are on their way here. We've got everything ready for you."

I wondered who the hell had called the senator. Had Director Gill informed him? Or had Azrael called the senator to disclose Hannah Jane's whereabouts, only for Senator Hillcrest to arrive in time to witness our failure? I thought that he had because it sounded just like Azrael.

There were lights everywhere. It was a strange thing to see from nearly two blocks away. It was a peaceful stretch of land usually cloaked under cover of darkness, but the roaming souls across the land would find no rest tonight.

The last rays of the sun had given way to the relentless night. I glanced at my watch before I slid out of the car. Zero hour had come and gone. We were too goddamn late. Because of the street conditions, the ride to the cemetery had taken longer than expected. However, I wasn't giving up until I knew for sure what's buried out here.

The cemetery was filled with more people alive than dead. Police, firefighters, paramedics, civilians, and even those pesky reporters I had worried about were standing at the police barricades. Somehow, our race to save Hannah Jane had leaked out.

The snow was coming down in a wind-battering torrent. I hadn't adequately dressed for a night of grave robbing, so I was shivering from the cold and my unsettled nerves.

The authorities surrounded a particular gravesite.

Harper and I snatched up the shovels and began to work frantically. I remembered how insane Harper had looked only hours ago as he hammered away the brick wall and clawed away the dirt to discover the real resting place of Beverly Jacobs. I saw that same look now. He was a man in motion, and nothing would slow him down until he found the very end of this thing.

The top layer of the earth was frozen, which made our task all the more difficult. With each jab of the shovel, I heaved out only a little dirt.

The deeper we dug, the softer the ground became. We found ourselves quickly sinking in the ground foot after foot. I couldn't imagine what we'd find beneath our feet. Both terror and delight filled my thoughts that this game was at the end. I was praying a little, to whom I wasn't sure, but if someone wanted to listen, they were more than welcome.

What happened next caused both Harper and me to stop digging and glance at each other. We struck something hard. We quickly used our shovels to clear away the remaining clumps of dirt. I went down on my knees and swiped away the loose soil from the lid. It was a casket.

Harper used his shovel to pry at the gap separating the upper and lower lid as I worked my fingers along the edge and pulled.

Light from above brightly shined down on us. When the wood finally splintered apart and released the lid catches, there was no hiding what we saw inside.

We were face to face with Hannah Jane Hillcrest. She was buried beneath blankets where only her head was visible. Silver oxygen tanks were on each side of her. Tubes ran from those tanks to the mask covering her mouth and nose. She was sickly pale, her eyes were closed, and she wasn't moving at all.

I suddenly got the feeling that we were duped as I moved in closer. Reaching out and touching Hannah Jane's cheek, I realized it wasn't a trick at all. Her skin was still warm. I moved my fingers to her throat and found no pulse.

"Harper, help me get her out of here. Hurry!"

We pulled Hannah Jane from the coffin. We hoisted her up to the emergency techs at the edge of the grave. I stuck my foot in Harper's cupped hands, and he lifted me out of the grave. I reached down, seized his outstretched hands, and yanked him to the surface.

Harper and I quickly shoved the EMT's aside. If anyone were going to save Hannah Jane's life after this long, crazy ride, it would be us.

I knelt over her lifeless body. With my left hand over my right, I thrust sharply down on Hannah Jane's breastbone, trying to jolt the still heart back to life.

"1...2...3...4...5..." I said with each compression.

Harper pressed his lips to hers and blew warm breath deeply into her. Hannah Jane's chest rose and then fell as the air seeped out.

We continued the process for what seemed like a lifetime.

Hope was dying in me. I didn't know how long she'd been gone. With each passing second, the chances of recovery were more unlikely.

I've experienced the kind of grip death has, but I also believed that if someone's will to live is great enough, no grip within Heaven or Hell can hold them.

I held her hand as Harper delivered three more sharp breaths. My eyes were closed, and I found myself silently praying again. Was there something in me, maybe something in my mind, heart, or soul that wanted to believe that something powerful could hear those prayers?

Harper sat on his heels, closed his eyes, and somberly shook his head.

Hannah Jane was gone. Our efforts to bring her back to the beautiful life she had once led had failed. *We* failed.

If someone with such a pure soul deserves to live, it's Hannah Jane. My heart twisted in agony. With so much beauty and kindness she brought to the world, she deserves life.

Chapter 49

Dreaming, of course, you're dreaming, silly. You're always dreaming these days, except when you're working, and you seem to work too much. It's okay because I love the work, and it's fun, an all-natural blast of a good time, except now. Something changed because someone bad had changed it. Someone real bad.

Hannah Jane saw her brother, Thomas, playing in the sand. The tide came in and washed over his toes, and he screeched with surprise and delight. He danced in the water until it rolled away again, and then he continued digging at his hole that was refilled by the rush of water and sand.

Hannah Jane's mom was smiling so brightly on this lovely day. Her face turned up to the sky, observing the spotted white clouds that drifted lazily across the brilliant blue. She giggled to herself as she saw Thomas dancing in the water as if he were in a low budget Broadway show.

Her father came strolling down the beach to them. He was wearing orange flip-flops, faded green swim trunks, and a dorky Hawaiian shirt unbuttoned and showing off his muscles. His hands were full of sodas and hot dogs from the local vendor.

"Hot dogs! Hot dogs! Hot dogs!" Thomas chanted as he ran up the beach, leaving his hole to be filled in once again.

Hannah Jane giggled as her father began to run in circles with Thomas chasing. She loved to see her father so happy. He was like a big child most days.

In her heart, she wanted it to be real, but it wasn't. It was a dream or maybe a memory that had been buried deep in her mind. She thought that just perhaps this day had taken place so long ago, but she couldn't be for sure. Everything seemed so fuzzy now. She wasn't entirely sure what was happening to her.

She stood up from her sandcastle and stepped into the ocean. The cool water rushed forward, curling around her ankles, and then pulled back. It didn't feel like what water usually feels like. It was *different*.

She turned and watched her family farther up the beach, eating, drinking, and laughing. It didn't even appear as if they saw her.

Hannah Jane averted her eyes from those she cherished most. She walked a little way down the shore, her feet splashing in the water that didn't feel quite real. She wondered what this place was and why she was here. She vaguely remembered terrible things that happened moments before she found herself kneeling before a sandcastle.

She remembered the man who called himself Death. She escaped from his house of torment. The man called Death had caught her again, and he had punished her. He had shot her with a Taser gun and then used his fists to punctuate his rage. Had he taken her to this place? Is this where people go when Death comes for you? But there were no other people, no other families. They were alone.

That's when Hannah Jane glanced up and saw the man down the beach. She thought it was odd that he was wearing winter clothing on such a warm day. He was looking right at her. She didn't recognize him, and for some reason, she didn't fear him. He was maybe in his early forties, handsome features with short brown hair. She couldn't tell for sure because of how far away he was, but she thought he was saying something to her.

Hannah Jane started walking toward the man. She found that the more she went to him, the more he seemed to drift away as if he were on a cloud.

"What did you say?" Hannah Jane called out as she ran faster, trying to catch up to him.

His voice, or a voice, came to her from all around as if it were from a loudspeaker.

"You need to come back to us, Hannah Jane. Come back."

"Come back to where?"

"To those you love," came the answer.

She stopped running, looked over her shoulder, and found that her parents and Thomas were no longer there. They weren't eating hot dogs and laughing. There was nothing behind her. There wasn't anything here for her anymore.

She wanted to go back to the place she had been before she came to the beach. She remembered that it had been a good place. Only recently it hadn't seemed so wonderful. That's okay because the bad things that usually happen never really seem to stay for long. She loved the place she came from, and yes, she wanted to go back.

It was so beautiful here, but it wasn't home.

Suddenly Hannah Jane felt as if she were spinning. Her eyes couldn't focus on anything because there wasn't anything to focus on here. The beach, crashing waves, and the brilliant sky above blurred together as if a tornado had captured the scenery and mixed everything up, making a surreal painting bound by no rules.

Chapter 50

Hannah Jane suddenly drew in a stuttering, violent breath. All those surrounding the girl pulled backward in complete surprise. Hannah Jane was back to the world of the living.

The medics gathered themselves and quickly slid in beside her. They placed a mask over her nose and mouth, giving her much needed oxygen. Her eyes were tightly pinched shut, and her hands were feeling around, surveying everything that was happening.

I knelt beside Hannah Jane and took her cold hand in mine. I offered her a genuine smile. "Welcome back. We missed you," I said.

"We need to get her to the hospital, sir," one of the medics told me. They gently lifted her onto the stretcher.

Hannah Jane squeezed my hand the best she could. She mumbled something, but I couldn't tell what it was. She pulled down the oxygen mask so she could be heard.

I understood her this time. I heard her clearly, and it made me smile.

I helped her put the oxygen mask back on. I nodded to the medics, and they wheeled Hannah Jane away to the waiting ambulance. They were gone after a moment, taking Hannah Jane to the hospital to make her well again. She's such a strong-willed young woman. I know in my heart that she's going to be just fine.

The graveyard crowd consisted of firefighters, police, news crews, and even bystanders who always seemed to gather when something interesting was happening. The action was now over, and many of them looked at each other as if quietly asking: *what now?*

What happened next came out of the clear blue. The massive crowd surrounding us began to applaud. It started with only a few spectators and then grew like a wave of excitement at a ball game. There were even stout whistles echoing throughout the cold graveyard.

I slowly turned and watched them. I looked at every face. I don't think I recall ever seeing so many people expressing pure happiness. It was definitely a sight I will never forget.

I turned and saw Harper was smiling wide. He seemed as if the weight of the world was suddenly lifted from his shoulders.

I smiled and applauded along with them. Harper deserves this gratitude. The years of cat and mouse hunting is something these people will never know about, but I knew it all. I appreciated everything that Harper and the men and women just like him do every day. They put their lives and even sanity on the line day after day to keep the rest of us safe and sound.

We walked back to the car. The evening show was over.

Reporters quickly trailed behind us. An exclusive story in the palm of their hand, but they wouldn't get details from either of us. The police stopped the group from even coming close.

"So, what did Hannah Jane whisper to you?" Harper asked.

I smiled again. "She said, 'I dreamed of you. You were calling me and telling me to come back. I left that place because you told me to come back to the people I love.'"

"Huh, weird."

"The weirdest part, I didn't say those words, but I had thought them. I had thought them very hard," I said with a mystified smile.

"Devine intervention, perhaps."

"Perhaps," I agreed. "Maybe someone is trying to make a believer out of me after all."

"It couldn't hurt, Jack. Believing in something is a good thing. It always seems to be there just when you need it most."

"So, where do we go from here?"

"You go home. I'm not sure where I'm going. Maybe I'll get a little break to ponder what exactly I learned from all this. We finally beat Azrael. We finally won the game, and I can't tell you how pleased I am about that. Unfortunately, it won't settle well with Azrael. He's going to want compensation for our success. I think we may have upset him a little."

"We'll just have to wait then and see where his plan takes us next. For now, I'm going to do as you said. I'm heading home for a little while."

"That's a good idea, Jack. Go home and see your family. It's Azrael's turn. Unfortunately, all we can do is sit on our thumbs until he makes his next move."

It was a good idea. I had somewhere important to be tomorrow evening.

I said, "I heard Cinderella would be in Atlanta tomorrow night. More important, there's a silly fat mouse that's the comic relief part of the show that you just have to see. You should come."

Chapter 51

I carried a light heart on the night of Reanne's play. I was possibly in the best mood I've been in for years. Hannah Jane was home safe and sound, and that's a happy ending. Of course, the word *ending* is only a relative term. We still weren't any closer to finding out Azrael's whereabouts and capturing the monster for good. It bothered me that he was still on the loose somewhere along the roads of our fine country. I didn't doubt that his wicked ideas are now in overdrive.

My mind quickly gathered all the thoughts of Azrael and Rita Sowell's disappearance and temporarily locked them away in an impenetrable safe. It was a bulletproof, nuclear warhead resistant, and even deflects coffee stains kind of safe. Nothing is going to spoil my mood tonight.

The Clairmont Elementary School parking lot was packed. Inside the front entryway was an abundant amount of parents and students shuffling around. The parents were immersed in joyful conversations. The children were playing and laughing without a worry in the world. The sight of this brought pleasant electricity to the event. I met up with several parents I had associated with through other school functions. We spent a bit of time conversing about the play and how delightful it was going to be.

Caroline had arrived at the school earlier in the evening to help set up and coordinate the school production. I began searching for her as soon as I entered the small auditorium. I figured she'd be backstage along with several of the teachers seeing to last-minute details.

I went up the stairs to the right of the stage and found Caroline behind the curtain, setting up stage props for the first act. Even though the play is Cinderella, I could tell the production hadn't wholly forsaken the Christmas spirit. Wreaths were hanging across the stage, red and green seemed to be the primary colors of the props, and each child I saw wore a Santa hat or pointed elf ears.

Children were shuffling about in costumes. Some seemed frantic about trying to remember their lines, while others were chasing each other around the set. Just kids being kids, I guess.

"Everything looks fantastic," I said.

I hugged Caroline and buried my face in her curly chestnut hair that smelled so sweet. It felt good to be home.

"Where's Reanne?" I asked.

"She's in her star dressing room preparing for a world event, of course. Wait until you see her. She looks absolutely adorable." She gently took my hands in hers and said, "I knew you'd find Hannah Jane. I didn't doubt it for a second. Reanne and I saw the news yesterday evening before you called home. We saw you at the cemetery, at the end of everything, and we cried together because everything was all right. Reanne was so happy and so proud of you. I was incredibly worried that the case would end in tragedy. It really did turn out to be a special night for everyone."

Before I let myself become too overwhelmed with the moment, I left Caroline to her work. I found a couple of empty folding chairs in the third row. Caroline told me to find prime viewing seats, and she'd join me just before the curtain went up.

When Caroline was finally able to sneak away, she found me among the crowd of eager parents. She sat beside me, took my hand, and gave me a warm smile.

"I can't believe you made it tonight. I'm impressed," Caroline said.

"Of course. I couldn't bear it if I broke another promise. If I did, I would no doubt develop chronic back problems from sleeping on the couch for the rest of my life."

The lights in the auditorium dimmed to a soft glow, and the stage lights went up. Next, the curtain parted, and the stage set revealed. I had to smile. Caroline, the other parents, and the teachers had done such a fantastic job getting the stage props built and setup. It was no doubt going to be a production to remember.

Megan Jefferson played Cinderella, who happened to be a close friend of Reanne's. First, we see Cinderella at the beginning of her struggles. She wore tattered clothing, her hands, face, and hair covered in grime. She was kneeling and scrubbing at the hardwood floors. The lights quickly dimmed to a deep crimson. Darkening music boomed over the speakers as the stepsisters and evil stepmother entered and began to belittle Cinderella to the best of their wicked abilities.

As the production went on, I felt myself becoming more focused on what was happening before me. It was entrancing. Happily ever after, so the saying goes.

I felt Caroline tap my arm. I leaned in close as she whispered, "Reanne will be coming up at any moment."

Cinderella was curled up on the floor and crying. Hope had shattered now that there would be no elegant dress and no Grand Ball. Every hope of something greater now lost.

But when the darkest times come, that's when you can see the tiniest sliver of light breaking through, a rebirth of hope brought on by saints, or in this case, a squadron of mice. As they came to the stage one by one singing a song, I searched for Reanne. I hadn't seen her costume beforehand, but she told me she was Gus, the goofy fat one. There was no mistaking that mouse for any other. After a moment, I realized no other mice appeared from backstage. One was missing. Reanne.

I turned to Caroline, and I could tell by her expression that something was wrong. Reanne had missed her cue.

"What's going on?" I asked with obvious concern.

"I don't know. Reanne should have come out with the others. It's her first scene."

"Maybe she developed a case of stage fright. It happens sometimes," I offered.

"I don't think so. Reanne was all pumped up for this. I don't understand. I'm going to see if she's all right."

Just as Caroline stood and excused herself down the row, something happened that wasn't part of the production. Someone backstage began screaming.

Chapter 52

The play came to an immediate standstill. Parents and teachers sprang from their chairs in surprise. We all looked around for some sort of explanation for the disturbance to the play.

I followed close behind Caroline as she weaved a path through the crowd. We headed up the stairs and passing the children in costumes. I felt a sharp jab of panic hit me as we made our way toward the back of the auditorium. A crowd had gathered, and I could tell by the facial expressions that it wasn't good. Children were huddled together and crying.

"Make some room," I said as I bullied my way through them. I *had* to see what they saw. In the crowd's center was Principal Art Jennings kneeling beside third-grade teacher Frieda Diego, Reanne's teacher. She was lying on her back, clutching a blossom of crimson at her lower abdomen. I didn't know if it had been an accident or if someone had attacked her. She was still alive, and that's all that mattered at this point.

I grabbed the phone from my jacket and handed it to Caroline. "Call for an ambulance."

She put all her emotions aside and did as I asked.

I knelt beside Principal Jennings. "What happened?"

"I'm not sure. Someone attacked Mrs. Diego. I was on the other side of the stage when Ms. Cartwright started screaming."

"Who attacked her? A parent? One of the students? Who?"

"I told you, I don't know! Ms. Cartwright, who did this?"

Jean Cartwright seemed lost in the moment of disbelief. Her eyes were bug-shot as she stared at the pool of gathering blood.

"Ms. Cartwright!" Principal Jennings shouted. "Who did this to her?"

"I don't know. I didn't see anyone!"

I turned my attention to Mrs. Diego. She was still conscious, but her breathing was shallow. Her eyes shifted from one hovering face to another. She was in a state of shock.

"I need you to move your hands away so I can get a better look," I gently said to her.

She slowly pulled her trembling hands away from the wound.

Mrs. Diego was stabbed. It was a narrow slit that made me think that the blade couldn't have been much bigger than a pocketknife. I grabbed one of the cloth covering from a first act stage prop and used it to apply pressure. We needed to slow the bleeding until the paramedics arrived.

"Mrs. Diego, can you hear me okay?" I asked.

She wasn't looking at me, but she nodded.

"Can you tell me who did this to you?"

She shook her head, and then she looked directly at me and started crying. "I'm so sorry, Mr. Calloway. The Lord knows I'm sorry. There wasn't anything I could do. I tried to stop him. I started calling for help, but then he did this to me."

"It's all right. Everything will be all right. It's not your fault." I tried to calm her the best I could.

Mrs. Diego took in a long, hard breath and winced in pain.

I couldn't help thinking about how much I wanted her to live. I've seen enough mangled bodies of innocent victims in the last week to fill one hundred lifetimes.

"No, you don't understand." Mrs. Diego said and grabbed my hand, our grip slick with blood. "I tried to stop him from taking her. I tried to fight him off, but he was too strong." She started to cry harder. "Oh, God. He took your daughter. He took Reanne."

I think I heard Caroline drop the phone. I think I heard the entire crowd take a unified gasp. I felt my heart momentarily stop. I felt euphoric for the briefest of moments as my mind tried to grasp the concept of *He—took— Reanne*. It was then when everything came crashing together as I realized the full extent of what she had said.

The monster was here.

Azrael kidnapped my precious little girl.

Reanne is gone.

Chapter 53

He took Reanne.

It was those words that continued to echo in my mind as I stood. I left Mrs. Diego, Principal Jennings, the teachers, students, and even Caroline all behind. I was racing through the rear door of the auditorium and into the frigid embrace of the winter wind. I scanned the parking lot and the streets that bisected the school property with the surrounding neighborhoods. There were over one hundred cars, vans, and SUVs in the school parking lot. I didn't want to believe that Reanne was already gone, but too much time had passed.

"Jack!" Caroline came running out the back door, calling for me. She was thrusting my cell at me. "You have to take this. I think it's him! You tell that bastard I want my daughter back right now!"

I snatched the phone from her. I heard a deep laughing on the other end.

"She certainly has lost her composure, wouldn't you say, Jack? I suppose right now you're asking yourself, *why didn't I see this coming?* And the answer would be what?"

"Because you're the grandmaster of all things fucked up in the world," I told him as my eyes continued to scan.

"Not exactly what I was looking for, but for the sake of argument, I'll just say that's close enough."

Caroline was intently watching me, following every single word spoken. She tried to grab the phone from me, but I held her back. I needed to hear everything the madman was saying.

"What are you planning to do?"

"Who said anything about plans, Jack? Why wouldn't you believe that something this dramatic was taken on a whim? I hate plans. Did Harper put that idea in your head? You and Harper missed important clues along the way. I would say it's simply astounding that you ignored so many important things during our game of cat and mouse."

As I listened to Azrael, I also listened for sounds beyond him. I couldn't hear an engine humming as it traveled down some mysterious city road. I couldn't hear the sounds of tires on the pavement as they thumped across the creases in the concrete. I couldn't even hear the noise of passing traffic. I couldn't hear anything at all.

Azrael wasn't fleeing the scene of the crime because he wants something more. He wants to taunt me and to see the anguish on my face. He wants me to understand that Reanne is so very close, and there's nothing I can do about it. He's in total control. I felt him watching us right now.

I removed my Glock from my shoulder holster. I slowly walked through the parking lot, turning every which way and watching for any movement. I glanced at each parked car, studying the interior for a figure behind the wheel, hoping for it anyway. I crouched down and peered underneath every vehicle. Where the hell is he?

I was anticipating something terrible was about to happen. I was feeling it vibrating throughout every nerve, making my entire body tremble.

Caroline was half a step behind me, watching and waiting.

"You won't ever know the feelings I have, the hatred, the loneliness, and even the satisfaction I've experienced throughout the ages. A mind such as yours simply couldn't

215

comprehend it. It would drive you into a tangent of self-loathing and madness."

"I don't think you should be the one to tap the conversation of madness right now. As far as I'm concerned, you're a couple of tacos short of a combo platter. It must be from all those years of hating your very existence."

Caroline grabbed my arm with an iron claw. She was warning me not to antagonize the monster.

"I wouldn't say such things if I were you, Jack," came his calm reply.

Suddenly a blinding flash of lights came on at our left, and an engine roared to life. I couldn't see a thing as my eyes wouldn't adjust quickly enough. I held up my Glock but didn't fire.

I heard the squeal of rubber on the asphalt. I shoved Caroline out of the way. She cried out as she hit the parking lot and rolled to safety. I shielded my eyes with my hand and got a better look at what was trying to run me down. It was a late model SUV, large and heavy, built to withstand a hell of an impact. I tried to spin away, but I wasn't quick enough. I was expecting the vehicle to crush me, shattering bones, separating muscles and tissues, and blink away my existence.

At the last second, the SUV swerved left, purposely avoiding a direct blast with me, but the front fender still caught my hip. Excruciating pain coursed along every nerve. I pin-wheeled down the entire side of the vehicle. My cell flew from my grasp, but my Glock stuck fast.

The SUV collided with a maroon minivan. Steel crumpled. The SUV then spun away toward the parking lot exit. I couldn't let him take my daughter away. I couldn't let him steal one of my most precious things.

Even though my hip screamed in throbbing agony, I gained my balance and somehow threw myself forward. I dodged between the rows of parked cars. I was trying to cut off Azrael at the exit. I was going full force, anger overriding pain. I crossed another lane just before reaching the parking lot exit. I was going to beat him there.

The SUV headlights found me waiting for him. I heard the vehicle accelerate as he wanted to slam me into the pavement. A second later, I side-stepped to the right, avoiding another painful collision. He hit the street, and straight ahead was a row of trees. He had to turn left or right. I had my money on the left. Heading left would lead him to bustling streets, and there was more traffic to disappear in and the opportunity to hit highways and interstates.

My snap judgment paid off. The SUV made a drastic left turn that nearly caused it to flip over. As he fought to gain control, I made my move.

I charged at the vehicle. With a desperate leap, I hit the driver's side with a bone-rattling force. My right hand seized the metal roof rack. I held on as my body beat harshly against the side, flapping like a kite in a cruel wind. My dangling feet were able to find the driver's side running board. I positioned myself the best I could as I reached for the door handle and found it locked. I could hear Azrael laughing inside as the psycho was actually having a good time!

I looked in the deeply shadowed cargo area. By the glow of street lamps, I saw Reanne partially buried under a bundle of blankets. She was unconscious, oblivious to the insanity that befell us.

I pressed my face close to the glass and looked at the Angel of Death. He was wearing a black mask that only exposed his lips and eyes. I looked deeply into those pale green eyes. He smiled.

Suddenly the vehicle made a hard swerve left, right, left, and right again. I almost lost my grip. Almost. Azrael crossed lanes, hit the curb, and the vehicle bounced onto the grass. Tree branches slapped relentlessly at the side of my face. I was determined to ride this horrifying roller coaster to Hell and back again as long as Reanne would be safe and sound.

It was then when something happened that I wasn't fully prepared to handle. It was something that I was utterly helpless to control. We were approaching a major intersection, and there were cars everywhere.

Chapter 54

The traffic came like a relentless force. I don't think any of the drivers could comprehend what they were seeing. I heard some of the vehicles slamming on brakes far in advance with anticipation of the horror about to unfold. I couldn't possibly think of a quick escape from this particular picture of damnation.

My eyes widened. My heart pounded. I was sure I was going to die tonight, right here, right now. Inescapable.

Tires were screeching, and horns were frantically blaring. A white Explorer was matching our pace as Azrael entered the intersection at a sideways skid. He was banking hard to the right. The Explorer was trying to pass the maniac. I thought that it might mean certain death for me.

Briefly, as we careened out of control, I glanced at Azrael, his cruel smile glowing in the traffic headlights.

I watched the white Explorer come so very close, my mind calculating every possible scenario in record time. I made my decision. The likeliest chance of survival lay in the hands of I did next.

I took a deep breath and reluctantly let go.

I collided with the hood of the Explorer on my knees, giving me enough control to slow my momentum. The action gave me a better chance of not becoming a giant slab of muck on Fifth Avenue.

My life didn't blink away in a second flat, but I was going to feel pain. I knew it from the moment my knees skidded off the hood. I tucked my arms in and rolled as my body hit the pavement with force hard enough to steal my breath. I wasn't sure, but I thought I felt bones on my entire left side give way under pressure. The back of my head cracked against the street. A storm of yellow and white sparks filled my vision. I heard other vehicles quickly braking, trying to avoid running over the figure rolling in the street that somewhat resembled a man.

When the tumbling finally ceased, I felt nothing except a surreal sensation that this was more like a horrifying dream than a moment of reality. With great relief, I was finally able to catch my breath. I didn't know what parts of my body were broken, fractured, or even punctured, but I managed to roll myself onto my stomach and watched the red SUV tear off down Fifth Avenue. Reanne was leaving me. My eyes focused and flashed a picture-perfect image of the license plate. The plate number was the only way of finding Reanne before it was too late. I repeated this number to the many people hovering over me. I said it again and again. I wanted them to remember. The police or even the FBI needed to know this number. It was perhaps the only way of catching the Angel of Death and finding Reanne alive.

An unsettling blackness pulled at me, and I reluctantly followed.

Chapter 55

I blinked or thought I had blinked. My eyes had opened and closed so quickly it was hard to tell. The only thing I knew for sure, I was still alive. The thunder of pain that coursed throughout my entire body told me so.

I forced my eyes open as much as I could. I was in the emergency room, and people were leaning over me. Through a gap in the surrounding bodies, I saw Caroline, and she was crying. I wanted to reach out to her. I wanted her to know I was still in the game of life.

"Mr. Calloway, can you hear me?" a young man in a white coat asked.

I'm not exactly sure what I said.

"That's good. At least your eardrums aren't broken."

I thought the doctor, or whoever he was, might be making fun of me at my own expense. He shined a small flashlight in my eyes.

I was attempting to say something else when I took a hard slip downhill from consciousness. My mind took a joyride into that damn blackness again.

When I later woke, I was in a private room. I didn't know how long I had been out, but the pain I felt earlier was gone. My nerves were in a calm place, probably induced by drugs. I feared that my head strike against the unforgiving pavement had done enough damage to toss me into a coma.

I shifted my sight and saw Caroline slumped in an uncomfortable-looking chair in the corner. Her coat draped over her like a blanket. Her head was cocked to one side, and she was fast asleep, no doubt knocked out by pure exhaustion.

"Hello, gorgeous," I said in a whisper.

Caroline heard me, and suddenly her eyes popped open. Confused, she looked to the door of the room and then to me. She offered a weary smile as she came over to me. She looked depleted. It was apparent that mental strain has hit her hard.

"Back again? Are you going to stick around for a while?" she asked.

"Huh?"

"It's Wednesday morning. You've been in and out of consciousness for several days. Just when I think you're coming around, you slip away again."

"Wednesday?" I couldn't believe I had been out that long. My mind, even though it felt as if it had been used as a punching bag, was still working. "Reanne? Did they find her?"

"You need to relax, Jack. You've sustained a severe concussion. The doctors wanted me to let them know if you came around again." She reached for the nurse call button, but I gently seized her hand.

"Please tell me. Where's Reanne?"

Caroline slowly shook her head. The mention of our daughter's name brought the tears, and she angrily wiped them away.

"You did the best you could. You nearly died trying to get Reanne back. I got a hold of Harper and told him what happened. I also gave him the license plate number you got off the vehicle and repeated to someone before you blacked out. The vehicle owner reported it stolen earlier that day, but law enforcement hasn't found it yet."

I figured Azrael and Reanne were long gone. I feared what he might have done to her. If Azrael hurt Reanne, there was no corner of the world where he could hide. I'd find him and punish him to the fullest extent a human body could tolerate. He might only be the soul of a fallen angel, but as long as he's trapped in a human body, I could deliver pain like he's never before experienced.

I squeezed Caroline's hand. "I'll get her back. I won't give up as long as I have breath in this body. I love you and Reanne so much. I won't let this family deal with another loss."

I was crying now. Even though I fully believed what I said, I knew all too well what kind of evil my daughter is facing. I've seen the awful and disgraceful things Azrael has done to innocent people. He has no regard for human life. He's the perfect destroyer of humankind.

I kissed Caroline, and, even though it hurt like hell, I wrapped my arms around her.

"But before I get started, I need to know what kind of condition I'm in."

"I'd say you're in as good as shape as you feel."

After I composed myself, I said, "Like shit, I guess."

She pressed the call button. "I'll let the doctor explain most of it. The *Reader's Digest* version is that you have a hell of a lot of bumps and bruises and a bad concussion. You don't have any broken bones at all. Your guardian angel was luckily close by."

"I don't know about a guardian angel, maybe pure dumb luck. If a concussion is the worst of it, I'm just going to rest for a moment and get my mind a little more coherent, get dressed, find Harper, and end this thing for good."

Even though Caroline knew I shouldn't leave the hospital, she also knew I wouldn't let my brain being scrambled a little stop me from getting our daughter back.

"You might like to know that you have a neighbor. They're keeping Mrs. Diego next door. She's doing just fine now. The first day was rocky for her, but she pulled through like a champ. Reanne will be happy that's she's going to be okay."

Reanne will come home again. I would stake my life on it.

Chapter 56

Caroline may not have verbally protested my early dismissal from the hospital, but the doctor sure did. He tried to convince me that my injuries should be taken seriously and bed rest was necessary. I told him that nothing short of an atomic bomb being dropped at my feet would stop my departure. I think he knew about the ordeal with Reanne and that I was going after my daughter at whatever the cost.

Although it was policy to use a wheelchair when being discharged from the hospital, I kept the staff off me long enough to maneuver myself to the entrance. It was difficult to maintain balance as I walked through the hospital front doors. I had to use Caroline as a makeshift crutch, but I left on my own two feet.

"Jack, look," Caroline said.

As we exited the building into the cold daylight, I saw Harper walking up the steps to greet us.

"Man, you look like you ran with the bulls and tripped over your shoelaces," Harper said.

I missed his blunt sarcasm.

"I am the adventurous type. It's nice to see that you finally made time to stop by. You didn't even bring me flowers or chocolates, you selfish bastard," I said.

"I did stop by once. Caroline and I spoke for a long while. I think she's got a thing for me." He offered a quick smile and then to business. "I've brought something much better than flowers or chocolates. While you were spending the last two days lying down on the job, I've been a busy FBI guy. I think I know how to find Reanne."

Even though my head throbbed and my vision seemed as if I were viewing the world through fish bowls, Harper had my attention.

"You found her?" Caroline asked.

"Not exactly, but I think I know how we can trace Azrael's steps. He left a trail in a roundabout way, and we should be able to pick it up. I've already traced it so far, and I was just about to hop the plane to the trail's end when Caroline called me to say that you were awake."

"If you don't mind me holding onto you like a two-year-old with bad balance, I'm ready to go."

"I'll make sure we have a kid's seat on board."

I turned to Caroline. She knew too well the look on my face. I was on my way to save another child—the most important child of all.

"You know what you have to do. I know you'll bring Reanne home safe and sound. I'll be waiting for both of you."

I hugged and kissed Caroline goodbye.

Harper and I slid into the sedan, headed for the airport, and would fly to the gates of Hell again. I'm going to bring my daughter back from Hell. My life for hers, if that's the price to pay.

When we boarded the plane, I quickly took my usual seat. The private jet took to the air, which happened to make my head even loopier.

When we reached a cruising altitude, Harper said, "I'm sorry this came down on you and Caroline. Azrael has never gone this route before. I thought your part in this chase was over when we found Hannah Jane."

"You couldn't have anticipated what he was going to do. It might have been a last-minute plan. Azrael's pissed that Hannah Jane didn't die. So he struck out the only way he knows how. He went after my loved ones."

"Truthfully, I think kidnapping Reanne was part of the plan from the beginning. That's one of the things I've figured out in the last two days."

I stared at Harper. "Why would kidnapping Reanne be part of his plan?"

"I think it's a contingency plan. I've told you before that I've never won the game. I never saved the person Azrael held hostage. He always had everything calculated perfectly with the odds in his favor. I could never beat his clock before. Except this game was different because I was working with you. It's because of your ability to help me quickly decipher many of the clues that allowed us to save Hannah Jane."

"Am I blushing?" I asked.

"I believe Azrael knew this one was going down to the final minute. I think he figured out that we had a strong chance to win. That's why he wasn't there for the finale. Well, not from what we could see anyway."

"So because there was no showdown and he's still living in Hunter Jacobs' body, the game is continuing? Are you saying he plans every game like this? You think he has an alternate ending worked out in the unlikelihood that you do save the girl?" I said.

"That's exactly what I'm saying."

I leaned back in the seat and tried to take in everything. I wondered if it were possible that Azrael had planned to take Reanne on the off chance that Hannah Jane lived. Just when I thought his mental instability level couldn't be more deceitful and complicated, he proved me wrong.

Two things were bothering me, and I dished them out to Harper.

"When he took Reanne at the school, he was wearing a ski mask. Why would he do that if he already knows that we uncovered his identity as Hunter Jacobs? What would there be to conceal from us?"

"That's a good question. I didn't know about the ski mask. It's an interesting question that's hiding an equally interesting answer."

"Could it be that we're wrong about Hunter being Azrael?"

"I couldn't say for sure. The clues we followed led directly to Hunter. From what Virginia told us about his recent death, the strange behavior, and the trip to L.A., I still think we're looking for the right man."

"There's something else. I'm not sure if it's just me, but I seriously feel like the whole thing with the murdered cop was unfinished. What I mean is, Azrael killed Christine Daniels and Father Richard James, who was involved in the murder. We then pieced together the clues that the officer's wife may have been involved as well, and so Azrael kills her next. He rubbed our faces in the fact that he solved an important cold case, but I think he was trying to tell us something more. I understand how the clues led us from one person to another, but we completely jumped the tracks when we went from Nora King to Nolan Windell. We know that Nolan knew Azrael and following those clues led us to Hannah Jane. But as far as we know, Nolan and Rita Sowell had nothing to do with the officer's murder."

"I'm glad your mind went in that direction, Jack. I'm at that same point as well. I need a little help figuring out the rest. Here, I want to show you something," Harper said and opened his laptop.

Chapter 57

"We can only speculate that Azrael is using the body of my old partner, Hunter Jacobs. Hunter's name isn't found on any airline manifest in cities where each murder has taken place, except for L.A. We already knew Hunter was there because Virginia told us. So, I searched all airlines for the same name arriving and departing in our four target areas where Azrael had killed and left clues. In the case of Father James, I searched the airlines in Albuquerque since that's the closest major city to Treagan. I had a hit on one name that traveled to each area in the specified timeframe. Anyway, I believe he's using the name Ian Matthews."

Ian Matthews, I thought. Something clicked and fell into place in my mind, like the lock tumblers of a safe moving in unison, ready for someone to rotate the lever, pull the door open and see what mysteries lay inside.

"Ian Matthews?" I said in a distant whisper. My thoughts were breaking the posted speed limit, cruising down the intellectual superhighway at breakneck speeds.

"Yeah, that's what I said. I don't believe in coincidences, but Officer Andrew King's partner was named Ian Matthews. It just so happens that the night Officer King was murdered, Mr. Matthews had called in sick. I called his precinct while you were in the hospital, and his captain said he's been AWOL for over a week. No one has the foggiest idea where he's gone or if something terrible happened to him. Azrael had to have known that we'd search the airlines and come up with his name. I think it's a clue because I think Ian Matthews might be Azrael's next target. I have no idea where we'll find Officer Matthews, but he's the reason we're going to New York City. We're going to the place where Azrael has been directing us from the beginning. All the signs are pointing to New York."

Clues and ideas were colliding together inside my mind. The name Ian Matthews flashed a bright light in a dark place, a place where exciting things lay hidden. Something dwelled in that darkness that I hadn't thought of before.

"I see the wheels cranking, Jack. What are you thinking?" Harper asked with extreme interest.

"Doesn't it seem a little odd to you that some of Azrael's victims have a name relating to a book in the Bible? At least I'm sure they are books in the Bible. It's been quite some time since I've been to Sunday service. I'll point out one exception, which would be Hunter's mother, Beverly Jacobs. Her name isn't a book in the Bible. Now we have Ian Matthews, the Book of Matthew. I agree with what you said before. I also think this is still the original game we started in Los Angeles. I'd even stake my right hand on it."

A light I hadn't seen before suddenly and dramatically flashed in Harper's eyes. The cobwebs that had been woven and collecting dust over the files in Harper's mind marked as "obvious stuff you should comprehend the first time around" were suddenly blown free of debris.

"Holy shit. You just might be on to something here." Harper moved his hand to his inside coat pocket and removed a Bible with a worn white leather cover. It was apparent that Harper thumbed through it regularly.

"Do you always carry that with you?" I asked.

Harper glanced at me and smiled. "Always. My wife gave this to me just before she left. My wife and daughter never knew about my cases. They never knew I was chasing a fallen angel. I wanted to tell them. I wanted to explain to them how important my work was, but I couldn't. If my superiors found out that I leaked that kind of information, I'd be removed from the case, stripped of my badge, and thrown in prison. My wife most likely wouldn't have believed such a thing. She probably would have thought that my mind had completely gone off the deep end. She would have left me either way. Anyway, my wife gave me this and told me that I needed to keep it close to my heart and keep the faith that everything that's meant to happen eventually does."

"It sounds like solid advice," I said.

Harper flipped to the contents page and said, "Take out a pen and paper and write this down as I read it off. We just might figure out something important. Maybe the direct path to Reanne."

I was all set. "Okay, good to go."

"Victim one, Christine Daniels. Daniel is the 27th book of the Old Testament."

"Got it."

"Victim two, Father Richard James. James is the 20th book of the New Testament."

"Got it."

"Victim three, Nora King. There are two books of Kings, which are 11 and 12 in the Old Testament."

"Got it."

"The next one is speculation at this point, we know Ian Matthews is AWOL, but as far as we can tell, he still might be alive. But in any case, he's part of the clue nonetheless. Victim four, Ian Matthews. Matthew is Book 1 in the New Testament."

I leaned back in the seat and tried to collect everything we had brainstormed so far. I wondered if we're meant to use both numbers from the Book of Kings.

"We have the numbers 27-20-11-12-1 in the order they died with the suspicion that Ian Matthews could be deceased as well."

"What the hell? Is Azrael trying to give us upcoming lottery numbers?" Harper asked.

"The only one I'm confused with is Beverly Jacobs. She was the first victim, and the last one found."

After a moment of thought, Harper said, "I think that in the case of Beverly Jacobs, her death was because Azrael wanted a crafty place to hide Hannah Jane for the finale. The clues told us that he was Hunter, which led us to his mother's house and then to her grave. I also think that's the only part Mrs. Jacobs had in this ordeal. This extension of the game doesn't involve her, only the players of Officer King's murder. Hopefully, in New York, we'll find out where Ian Matthews is, alive or not, and pick up the next clue that hopefully leads to Reanne."

"Maybe these numbers are a strange road map leading us to Ian Matthews. I'm not sure if it's from the concussion I received, but this run of names and numbers is giving me a fierce headache," I said as I closed my eyes and massaged my temples.

"I've got you beat. I've had the same nagging headache for the last four years, and no doctor can prescribe something strong enough to knock it down. I've gotten used to it. It reminds me that my head is still attached."

"We need to figure out the connection of these Bible numbers and what they have to do with New York and where exactly they're pointing us. That is unless I was pulling things out of my ass in desperation. The victim names might be coincidental with the books in the Bible."

"I just told you moments ago, Jack, I don't believe in coincidences."

Chapter 58

My legs were starting to cramp as I sat in the passenger seat. We'd been staking out the area for nearly three hours. I was beginning to think that my theory of following the books of the Bible in the order Azrael had laid it out was nothing but a shitty pipe dream. It completely baffled me that Azrael had been so prepared and created each step so precisely and with shockingly accurate timing.

I stared at my notepad.

27-20-11-12-1

Harper and I had so far been unable to track the current location of Ian Matthews. So we decided that our next step was to figure out the number combination Azrael had cryptically left. After an extensive Internet search during our run across the friendly skies toward New York, Harper and I knew it had to be an address in New York. We decided that 2720 W. 11th Street was the destination to search. We also decided to drop the number twelve because there are two books of Kings, and it seems likely to use the number eleven because there was no such address of 2720 W. 12th Street. As for number one, we hadn't figured that out yet.

The building that bore the address of 2720 W. 11th Street was a music store called *Jammin' Jams* of all things.

On arrival at the address, I immediately began to regret the route my mind had gone. I couldn't possibly understand what a music store had to do with this madness.

"At the end of everything, four victims linked to the murder of a police officer. Those victims also happen to have a last name coinciding with a book in the Bible. How the hell could Azrael have figured all this out and left his clues accordingly?" I asked.

"Simple. Azrael has nothing but time mounted on top of time to come up with this crazy shit to play his games. I have to admit what you thought of, Jack, was brilliant. I don't think my brain would have ever wrapped around the possibility that the Bible somehow came into play. I think I've been chasing my tail the entire time. You're the one who has been picking up all the clues," Harper said and took a pull on his cold coffee.

"I'm not sure if it was brilliant. We're staking out a music store, for crying out loud. Besides, you've done as much as I have, and you know it. We've done well together. The fact remains, if you hadn't gone mad and hammered your way through that cinderblock wall and found Beverly Jacobs buried within, Hannah Jane would have died for sure. We were so close on that one that if we had even spent a few extra minutes at Beverly Jacobs' house looking for some sort of clue, Hannah Jane wouldn't have come back."

"I suppose you're right. We make a pretty awesome team. Of course, I'd like to point out that if you hadn't recognized the tattoo in the security video in Atlantic City that led us to Nolan, Rita Sowell would have died for sure," Harper said.

"Okay, so we're agreed that we were able to save a few lives along the way. Unfortunately, there were others that we simply didn't possess the power to save. Fifteen souls were all taken by the hand of Death. In the end, Nolan wound up taking himself out. Hannah Jane and Rita's lives were spared. Of course, we still don't know what has become of Rita since she went missing. All in all, fifteen people died for the sake of one. It hardly seems fair."

"Not fair at all," Harper agreed.

"I can't cope with the death of another child, Harper. I can't. I won't. I refuse to lose my beautiful child at the hands of an angel gone sour. I would forever turn my back on God if that happened. If my punishment for that were an eternity in Hell, then so be it. I won't place my faith in something that would torment Caroline and myself with the deaths of two daughters. After saving so many children over the years, and Caroline saving lives at the hospital, we certainly wouldn't deserve something of that magnitude."

"I don't blame you for being bitter, Jack. I've questioned my faith more times in the last four years than you can imagine," Harper said.

I ran my hands down my face. I was exhausted. I needed a little time alone to process everything. "Okay, I'm going to stretch my legs. I'm going down to the café and get my espresso injection started. You want anything?" I asked as I slid out of the car.

"Yeah, sing me a few verses of *Jailhouse Rock*, and I want to hear some compassion in it."

Despite everything that has unraveled so far, I had a little humor in me at the moment. I sang several verses and even did an impersonating dance on the sidewalk in front of dozens of onlookers.

"Good God, Elvis is cringing in his grave, I think," Harper said after his laughter subsided.

"So you're telling me that the FBI admits that he *is* dead?" I asked and closed the door before he could respond with another wisecrack or maybe a confirmation that I didn't necessarily want. I like to think that the possibility of running into that old hound dog down the street while I'm getting a refill of coffee should always remain open.

I glanced across the street to the small music store we were intently watching. It seemed so strange that such a carefully organized plan constructed of numbers from Azrael's kills to the names of books in the Bible had brought us to this section of New York. I was sure that there was something here to follow. I had to be right because my daughter's life depends on it.

Chapter 59

There are times when the mind seems to play games. I'm not sure if it's a part of the brain that made us such strange and charismatic children, and we never really shook it off as we approached adulthood. When I awoke in the hospital, it seemed to make a reappearance and concealed obvious things that I wouldn't usually overlook. It was in that small bustling coffee shop in New York where my mind ceased the childlike games and dealt everything to me in a perfect hand. Everything about the case abruptly clicked together.

The event hit me so forcefully that the fresh cup of coffee I was carrying to the door slipped from my grip and splashed across the slush-covered tiles. I offered no look of embarrassment, only appearing like a man coming to grips with the importance of a mission at hand. I left the coffee shop without apology and dashed down the sidewalk like an escaping mental patient.

Harper was watching the music store and all the passing people when I yanked open the passenger door. I saw him reach inside his coat for his gun.

"Easy, cowboy, I'm not going to draw on you," I said as I slid inside.

"Haven't you ever heard of subtlety? I could've filled you full of holes."

"That would be a shame because I think everything just came together like a horrifying head-on collision."

"What the hell does that mean?" Harper asked.

"Well, I was speaking with Elvis in the coffee shop when my brain cells placed all of those silly little clues in some sort of order and clarity. I dropped my fresh brew right on The King's blue suede shoes, excused myself, and came running to you."

"You should do one of those public service announcements for 'This is your brain on drugs.'"

"I'm talking about this whole game Azrael has been playing. Most of it is making perfect sense to me now. It isn't the music store we're supposed to be watching."

"It isn't?"

"Huh-uh. It's what's above the music store that we're supposed to focus on. We know the books of the Bible led us to this address. But we never considered the apartments above the music store. Maybe it's because we're both so damn tired or that the clue was so obviously in our face that we overlooked it. The music store's address is 2720 W. 11th Street, but the upper part of the building has the same address, only with apartment numbers. We couldn't seem to place the number twelve, so we dropped it altogether. We figured only the first Book of Kings should be used. I think twelve is the apartment number we'll find our next clue, or hopefully, Reanne, *if* God is good."

"As I said before, I like the direction your mind goes," Harper said with a degree of admiration.

"It's time to fasten on your thinking cap because I believe I have most of it figured out. I'll still need your expertise to work out some of the wrinkles. Okay, I think it all started with a well-constructed plan brought forth by Nora King. We know that Christine Daniels and Father Richard James, of course, they had different names back then, were primary players in the death of Officer Andrew King. Richard James kills the officer with a rock to the skull, and Christine helps him hide the body. First, we thought the whole thing was a moment of panic at the thought of going to prison for soliciting a prostitute. He freaks out and kills the cop to avoid prison time. Honestly, I'm starting to think that the whole thing was a setup."

"So you're saying that the prostitute and the john planned on getting caught by this particular cop as a way of getting him out on some dark road and purposely killing him?"

"That's what I'm saying. Only I don't think they did it for the sheer hell of it or just for some sort of mad thrill. I think they were paid by Nora King to murder her husband."

"Yeah, we already suspected she had something to do with the murder. But I'm having a hard time believing that Nora King was a part of it. She sent her daughter to a good college, and then donated almost every cent she received from the insurance policy," Harper said.

"Remember, Azrael primarily goes after people who turn away from evil ways and reinvent themselves for the better. I think Nora gave away her possessions and money out of guilt because it speaks guilt to me, anyway. Officer Andrew King had a one million dollar life insurance policy. It was in the report you gave me. I read through the entire file as we flew here to New York. The authorities suspected Nora initially, but she was attending a party and had a concrete alibi to back her up. The investigators turned their attention elsewhere. Just because she didn't physically murder him doesn't mean she wasn't a part of it."

"I think I'm starting to mentally catch-up with you, Jack," Harper said.

"I'd also like to point out the fact that Officer King's partner Ian Matthews was sick the day Officer King was murdered on that dark road. Officer King was alone and vulnerable to this well-conceived plan. The fact that Officer Matthews had the sniffles on that particular night seems too much of a coincidence. I think he was also part of his partner's murder. We have four people connected to this murder, three are suddenly dead, and the fourth has gone missing. It just so happens that our missing guy has the same name that popped up on your airline list."

My head was buzzing from what I had just churned out. The whole thing had been so damn complicated that my mind had to shift into overdrive to process all the information with relative clarity.

Harper took in a deep breath. "Okay, let me see if I can boil this down to the bare bones. Nora King and Ian Matthews come up with a master plan to murder her husband for a one million dollar insurance policy. They hire a prostitute and someone else to help out. Ian Matthews knows the route his partner will patrol that night, and suddenly a plan for murder is in motion. Does that sum it up?"

"I think that's as clean-cut as this mess can get."

"So, all this went down because of money?" Harper asked.

I shrugged. "A hefty check like that can motivate almost anyone into doing something incredibly ignorant. People have killed for much, much less. We know that Officer King was a decorated cop, but we don't know anything about his home life. He could have been an abusive drunk toward his wife or screwing around on the side. Something that simple could have set her off. Who knows, if Ian Matthews was also involved, we could assume that Nora was having an affair with her husband's partner, and together they constructed this insane plan. We can only speculate at this point because almost all of the key players are dead, and I'm sure we won't get any statements from them unless we come up with some serious smelling salts.

The only person who remains is Officer Ian Matthews," I said.

"So now it boils down to the fact that Ian Matthews could be Azrael. We know he's been crisscrossing the country ahead of us. Is that the final clue? Ian Mathews is Azrael, and apartment twelve is his hideout?"

"I honestly don't know for sure. But there's another thing I just thought. We couldn't seem to place the number one in the series of numbers we uncovered. If you take Ian Matthews' initials and the number, you have *IM the 1*. Maybe that's what we're supposed to understand from the numbers. We have an address and proclamation of the real man behind it all." I said, mystified.

Harper closed his eyes. I saw him trying to get a hold of everything mentally.

"Then what about Hunter Jacobs? We were so sure that he was Azrael. Now, I'm not entirely sure what the hell is going on."

"Neither do I. What if Hunter Jacobs was Azrael, but at some point during all this chasing around, he killed Ian Mathews and took over the body? Another point I'd like to make is that you once told me that Azrael always works alone. Except in this game, we know that Nolan was an accomplice. What if there are more players than we know?"

I watched Harper closely. He looked worn down like an old flint that rarely gave any spark. I could see it in his eyes. Harper seemed like a man close to the edge of a mental breakdown. I wanted to help him end this. I needed to find my daughter, and I wanted to help put Azrael down.

Harper said, "The thing about Azrael is that he's highly unpredictable. There's never a constant path he follows and certainly no set of rules. Azrael shakes things up because he can. One thing he hates most is keeping things relatively easy for us to decipher. As far as I know, he's never before brought in civilians to help him. It's all new to me."

"I guess Azrael's true identity is irrelevant at this point. My daughter is the primary goal here, and if we put Azrael down in the process, that's all good, too. Regardless, the body he's occupying won't hold him forever, and he'll eventually be able to start another game. My daughter comes first. Capturing him is a distant second in my book."

"I know, Jack, finding Reanne is my goal, too. We're close. He wants us here in New York. He sent the cryptic message that brought us to this point. But I still don't understand why."

I quickly poked Harper in the ribs and pointed to a figure halfway down the block.

"That's Hunter," Harper said enthusiastically. He suddenly bolted upright with new life.

Hunter Jacobs was young and handsome. He seemed to carry himself different from the way Harper had described him. Hunter appeared hard-nosed and supporting a grudge that couldn't be satisfied. He looked as if the world had sapped all the goodwill within him that once flowed so freely. Hunter was carrying a brown paper bag and walking toward the door to the left of the music store leading up to the apartments.

Harper and I slid from the sedan and stepped onto 11th Street.

Chapter 60

Without a second thought, I stepped into the street, and a taxi nearly plowed me down as it screamed through a red light.

Harper and I were quickly on the move as we weaved a path through the waiting traffic. I ignored the glaring eyes and the blaring horns. The people had no idea what we were up to and probably didn't care.

I lost my balance in the slush and came down on the hood of a Lexus. The driver responded with a fierce burst of the horn and curse words I couldn't completely hear. I gathered myself and was in pursuit again. Harper was a dozen yards ahead of me. I was sure we were going to get our man.

Then the worse thing possible happened. Maybe alarmed by the horns, Hunter Jacobs looked in our direction. He saw us coming and drawing our guns at the same time. He then did something I didn't expect. He smiled at us. It was one of those smiles as if he had expected to find us at this very place and time.

Hunter dropped the brown paper bag he'd been holding, shoved pedestrians out of the way, and ran from us. The chase was on, and we wanted him bad.

I glanced down at the dropped bag as I hustled past. Inside was a ruptured gallon of milk, a box of cereal, and several packs of doughnuts. I wondered if the groceries were for Reanne. I hoped that she was in apartment twelve and eagerly waited for me to come to the rescue. But right now, I couldn't leave my partner's side. I had to help Harper catch the monster.

The crowd of people on the sidewalk parted as they saw us running after Hunter. They saw our drawn guns and wanted no part of the action. I was thankful no one tried to be a hero and attempt to take down Hunter as he passed. I didn't want anyone else hurt. Besides, I wanted to take down this asshole myself.

Hunter took a right at the corner. We were gaining on him, and he knew it. He did the only logical thing he could to get away from us. Hunter lunged up the stairs of an apartment building and disappeared through the front door. We followed him inside. I didn't see him, but I heard the pounding of his footsteps. We ran down a short hallway, turned left down another hallway, and followed the sounds up the flight of stairs.

The building was five stories. The chase through the streets and up the stairs had slightly winded Harper. I had to pass him on the stairs in order not to lose Hunter.

"There's nowhere he can go," I said to Harper as I reached the third-floor landing.

"I think he made this an escape route. He seems to know where the hell he's going," Harper said.

I didn't see how that was possible. Had Hunter prepared for a chase in the streets and buildings of New York? Or was he making up the game as he went along?

"No, I think he's trapped himself. Maybe he's going to take a hostage. Come on!" I yelled back at Harper. I felt my blood surging.

Hunter laughed as he hit the top floor. He overheard what I said, and I wondered what was so funny.

I quickly got my answer. The apartment building was only five floors, but stairs led to the roof access. Blinding sunlight flooded the staircase. I ran up the narrow metal steps and onto the graveled roof.

To my left, Hunter was hauling ass across the rooftop. He picked up momentum as he ran right for the edge of the building. Did this fallen angel believe that he could still fly? In one fast motion, Hunter launched himself from the rooftop to the brick edge three feet up and took flight. He sailed through the air like he did have wings. Hunter just leaped the ten-foot gap from one building to the other. He hit the other side and barrel-rolled across the roof surface. Then he stood, brushed himself off, smiled, and took a bow.

I wanted to shoot him. I wanted to put one right between his arrogant eyes, but I couldn't. I needed this bastard *alive*. So, I did the only thing I could think. I charged forward and followed him.

"Jack, don't!" Harper called out from somewhere behind me.

It was wrong from the second my foot left the edge. I didn't have enough power behind the leap. Even with the adrenaline pumping, I was exhausted from the chase and powering up the flights of stairs. I wasn't going to make it.

I let go of my gun as I hit the opposite building, and my hands seized the brick edge with an iron grip. My body slammed hard enough against the building that momentarily stole my breath and blurred my vision. I forced myself to stay conscious. If I blacked out, I'd fall for sure.

Hunter peered over the edge. He still wore his arrogant, smug smile. What he did next baffled me. Hunter thrust out his hand.

"Better take my hand, Jack. Take it, or you'll die."

My grip was loosening on the brick edging. My feet kicked around, searching for a hold on something. I looked down at the alleyway below. There was no fire escape, no crisscross of wires going from one building to the other. There was nothing to catch my fall. Below me was a littered alleyway and nothing more.

"Go on and take my hand. There's no shame in it. You want to live. You want to see Reanne and Caroline again. I completely understand. Just reach out and take my hand. It looks like the concrete below will be unforgiving if you fall," Hunter said.

"I can take him, Jack! Hold on!" I heard Harper lock back the hammer of his gun.

"No, Harper!" I shouted.

"Shame, shame, Harper. You know better. You haven't figured out things far enough ahead. I promise that you won't find precious little Reanne with me dead. She'll starve to death, and no one will find her body for weeks. Now take my fucking hand, Jack!" he screamed at me.

I didn't have a choice. My fingers were loosening, so I reached up and seized the outstretched hand of an angel.

Hunter's smile broadened. He said, "However, this has been extremely fun for me, but I believe your part in this play has come to an end. Goodbye and Godspeed on your journey, Jack." His hand opened, and I suddenly felt the surreal sense of falling through open space.

I remember screaming somewhere between the fifth and first floor.

Chapter 61

My eyes were spasmodic behind the lids. There was blackness with random star-like flickers of white. There was a voice calling out to me, not the voice of God, but the voice of Harper.

"Jack, Jack, holy shit, can you hear me, Jack?"

I could hear him clearly, but I couldn't answer his question because my voice wasn't there. I felt oddness throughout my body. It wasn't so much a thundering of damaged nerve endings, but rather a harmonic vibration of liveliness that was more a delightful feeling than that of awe-struck shock.

As my eyelids finally opened, small slivers of light stung my eyes. I saw only blurred images. It was like viewing the surface from the bottom of a swimming pool, distorted colors and shapes passing my field of vision. Something hovered over me, tilting to one side and then the other. It moved in close and then pulled away. Other objects were floating in the distance behind the main object. I realized it was a person. More in particular, it was my partner.

There was something in his tone of voice pulling me from the haze. It was a monotone of both disbelief and unquestioned faith. As my eyes flickered from object to object, my sight became clearer. I finally understood where I was and what had happened only minutes before.

I had fallen. More to the point, I had fallen *five* stories to the paved alleyway floor. I wondered what had stopped the death-defying drop. I hadn't seen a dumpster filled with garbage or anything such thing to catch my fall as I gazed madly from above.

The blurriness gave way, and my normal vision returned. Harper and many others were standing over me. Stunned disbelief covered most of the faces I saw. I didn't understand what all the commotion was about.

With a whisper of tenderness, Harper said, "Jack, can you hear me? Can you respond? Do you know where you are?"

"Yeah, on the ground," I said in a raspy voice that burned my throat.

"Okay, more importantly, do you remember what happened? Can you tell me where you're injured?" Harper asked.

I heard sirens approaching from down the street and wondered if it was me they were coming to help.

"I think I fell. I'm not sure if I'm hurt. Everything feels weird, like a strange dream."

I started to sit up. Harper used a hand to try to keep me down, trying to keep me from moving. I lightly brushed his hand away, letting him know that I was perfectly all right. Nothing in my body screamed out in agony as it usually would if I had bones punching their way through the skin.

"Jack, take it easy. An ambulance is here for you."

"I seriously think I'm okay. Just help me up."

Reluctantly, Harper took my hand and pulled me to my feet.

"I'll be goddamned," said a man with a deep and baffled voice. "Motherfucker did a cannonball from way up there. Did you see that?" he asked another.

"Praise Jesus," said the woman beside him and crossed herself.

"I think that sums it up for you, Jack," Harper said.

I looked toward the sky and spotted the place I'd been minutes before. On wobbly legs, I turned around to face the alleyway. I now understood what the commotion was about. Nothing had stopped my fall. Nothing had even slowed the descent. I struck the alleyway ground with such a velocity that the concrete had spider-webbed under pressure. It looked like a small boulder had fallen instead of a vulnerable human body.

People were backing away from me as if I were a host to a plague. They watched with both suspicion and curiosity. I couldn't compute what had happened any more than they could.

"Judging by the fall you took, we should be able to squeegee you into a puddle and put you in soup cans. I don't even believe it myself, and I saw the whole thing. I saw your impact. There isn't even any blood, Jack. You're completely unscathed."

It was all too overwhelming. I buckled to my knees, and in front of a hundred or so witnesses, I threw up whatever contents were in my stomach. I couldn't remember the last time I ate anything, which must have been quite a while ago, because not much came out.

I was alive. I didn't know exactly how, but I was still walking and talking. I wasn't bleeding from anywhere that I could see. I didn't sense any broken bones, and my brain was thankfully still inside my skull. Besides a fierce headache that was rapidly approaching and joined with a full-body ache, I was undamaged.

I was still hunched over and waiting for nausea to pass. I gripped Harper's ankle and squeezed. "Tell me you got him, Harper. Tell me we have Azrael, and we'll go get Reanne the second I can stand up."

"Jack." Harper paused and searched for comforting words. "Even when you fell, I couldn't shoot him. I kept thinking about what he said. What if this wasn't the final step like we thought? What if Reanne isn't in apartment twelve? I thought that I lost you, and the only thing I could think of was not killing Azrael and finding your daughter. It would have been the least I could do for you. But don't worry, we'll get him, and we'll find Reanne."

I was feeling slightly better, and I pulled myself up with Harper's help. My legs were shaky but kept me upright. I walked over to where my Glock had fallen. I picked it up and inspected the damage. I was amazed that the gun was still intact. A nasty dent was on the steel slide and a hell of a lot of scratches across the black finish. I couldn't tell if the inner workings were shattered, making the thing nothing more than an expensive paperweight. I yanked back the slide and released it. The unfired round ejected from the chamber, and another shell rammed home. I couldn't test fire the gun here in the alleyway with so many people around. I just hoped everything was still in good working order. I'd have to rely on the belief that it wouldn't blow up in my face when the time came to use it.

"You should know that I made a call as I ran down the stairs to you. It's a call that initiates an action to section off a ten-block radius from the point of my cell phone. We have a protocol for cases such as this. When you're an FBI agent who primarily chases a killer angel that loves to destroy lives, you get an immediate response when the call goes through. Cool, huh? All available units will block off all streets around us. No one is going in or out without clearance. New York swat teams will gather and prepare for whatever Azrael does next."

"You threw down a net on a major section of New York?" I asked. I thought of the word "net" and how many holes they usually have.

"It's no guarantee. All of the units have a physical description of Hunter and what he's wearing. I hope someone spots him quickly."

Two paramedics with a stretcher in tow finally broke through the thick crowd and entered the alleyway. They stood there looking from me to Harper to the empty narrow alley.

"Where's the body?" asked the younger of the two.

"Turns out it was a crank call," I said and tried to bustle my way through the mob.

I got about fifteen feet in the crowd when I heard the man who had made the cannonball statement. "The body? Do you want to know where the body is? It just strolled that way, dude!"

We approached one of the many cruisers parked around the scene and overheard the CB radio crackle with a voice that didn't conceal his excitement.

"I think I've spotted our guy! I'm sure it's the man we're looking for. He just jumped off a moped and went into the subway station on Houston Street! Copy that?"

Yeah, we copied that.

Harper approached the officer beside the cruiser, flashed his FBI badge, and told him that we'd be commandeering the vehicle for a short joy ride. Harper and I were sliding into the empty cruiser before the officer had a chance to protest.

I had just plummeted five stories and landed uncomfortably on a slab of concrete. I was still alive for a purpose I wasn't completely aware of yet. I've had experiences in my life that have made it rather difficult to believe in a God who oversees everything. Sometimes, like today, things happen that flip my perspective a perfect one hundred and eighty degrees. Something marvelous and unexplainable happened to me only moments ago. I figured I'd just have to run with it and see wherever the craziness might lead me.

Chapter 62

We were rocketing beyond the limits of sanity down West Street, trying to get to the Houston Street subway station and catch up with Hunter before he made another mysterious getaway. I was gripping the seat edges with iron claws. Harper, who seemed to be guided by an intellectual force in the universe, dodged his way through narrow traffic gaps.

Harper kept glancing at me as if I had suddenly transformed into a slimy green alien sitting compliant in the passenger seat of the police cruiser.

"For the love of all good things in the world, would you please keep your eyes on the road?" I finally snapped at him.

He glanced at me again just as we weaved dangerously between a taxi and a light pole. If we happened to catch a patch of ice, the sudden disruption of wheels from the pavement would undoubtedly send us spinning out of control and careening into one of the office buildings.

"Are you sure you're all right, Jack? You don't need to go to the hospital?"

"I was in the hospital earlier today. I've got more important things on my mind right now. Believe it or not, but I feel fine. Watch out!"

The cruiser sideswiped a Honda, and there was a shower of sparks and the groaning twist of metal. The cruiser jumped to the left as Harper overcorrected from the impact. We nearly took out a bike messenger blazing down the sidewalk.

A fury of curses came from those we left behind.

"Sorry about that."

"Don't apologize to me. It's the Honda owner you'll need to send a Christmas card."

"You don't think you're one of those—" Harper cut himself off.

"One of those, what?"

"You know, like one of those X-Men? Maybe you're like one of them. Maybe you're unbreakable."

"First of all, you do realize those are movies and not real life, right? And second of all, fuck you for thinking I'm a mutant."

"Well, I wouldn't use that word. I'll just say that you're something special."

"This isn't a movie, Harper. I assure you that I'm not anything special. I've broken bones before. I've been cut and bled, and it took the average time to heal."

"By all accounts, you've died three times now, and you've come back to the world of the living. In my mind, that makes you indestructible."

"Three? No, only twice."

"Three, Jack. You were dead when I raced back down the building and knelt beside you. For reasons I don't know, I checked your pulse. I knew you had to be dead because no one could have survived that kind of fall. Hell, there was even cracked concrete where you hit. But there wasn't any blood, and none of your limbs looked twisted in an awkward position. I hoped there was a possibility that you had miraculously survived. I even prayed for it."

"I don't understand it any more than you do," I said.

"Perhaps you're meant for something great. Maybe it's something that you can't understand just yet."

I gave in a little. "Maybe. I guess we'll have to wait and see how the rest of my life plays out."

"The subway station is just down the road. We'll be there in a minute," Harper said.

I was impressed at how well Harper knew these streets. Azrael must have brought him to this part of the country before. I was happy to hear that we were almost there. I did something I haven't done since I was a child. I don't think I did it out of sincerity, but maybe it was a subconscious mocking gesture toward Harper's driving. I crossed myself. I didn't even realize I made the action until it was done. I wondered if the motion was my heart trying to wake up my brain, or maybe the other way around.

"I saw that," Harper said as he power braked with both feet and slid the cruiser to a halt in the middle of the street.

Harper sprang from the cruiser, and I followed his lead. Drivers and pedestrians alike were watching us. It was probably the most exciting thing they've seen all day. Several patrolmen disappeared down the stairs of the subway station ahead of us. I wondered how many men were hot on the trail of Death. I had hoped it was a thousand, but more likely, it would only be a dozen.

Harper and I barreled down the gray steps two or three at a time. The sunlight gave out to the dull station lights. I felt like we were following Hunter into the greater depths of Hell. I thought this was likely part of his plan, after all.

What if Reanne isn't in apartment twelve? What if she's down in this awful darkness? Is he leading us to his destructive finale?

Chapter 63

The platform was busy with commuters patiently waiting for the next train. I saw patrolmen walking calmly through the crowd, trying to pick out one particular face. Some people realized that something was up because they kept a watchful eye on the patrolmen and whispered to the person next to them. If they weren't Hunter Jacobs, then they should have no worries.

Harper and I casually made our way to the platform edge. There were no rails to prevent someone from slipping and falling onto the tracks and being gruesomely dismembered by the sudden arrival of the train. Another thing, there were no railings preventing someone from purposely leaping down onto the tracks and disappearing in the blackness of the tunnel. I thought Hunter would have considered this method of escape. It was possibly suicidal or dangerous, at the very least. It sounded like the kind of action our man would take.

Harper must have read my mind or watched the travel of my eyes because he said, "I think we have a super-sized rat scampering down these fair city subway tunnels."

"I think we need to get some extra strength rat poison and chase after it."

I gazed over at the patrolmen mingling in the crowd. It was apparent they hadn't found anything of interest. Azrael wasn't hiding in the group of innocent travelers. He was gone.

Harper and I slid off the platform and onto the tracks. I could barely see a damn thing. The light flowing from the platform reached fifty feet into the tunnel and lost its battle to the overpowering darkness. There were subway lights overhead traveling the tracks' lengths, but they were extremely dim, and it seemed like there were more out than lit. I was practically blind, clueless, and dreading what was coming. It seemed like a bad combination.

I reached out and groped for Harper's coat. "Harper, if we can't see very well, then neither can Hunter. He might be preparing to spring a trap, so be careful."

"If he suddenly jumps out at us, will you throw yourself in front of me, pretty please?"

Harper wasn't letting go of the idea that I'm somehow indestructible.

I quickly came up with a plan. It was a poor plan, but a plan nonetheless. I thought that if Hunter was lingering in the darkness nearby, I might be able to antagonize him enough to flush him out of his position and come at us.

I spoke loud and clear. My voice ran down the length of the tunnel. "You know, Harper and I were just talking about how much you fit in down here with the rest of the mutated rats, giant roaches, and other freaks of nature things dwelling in these sorts of places. Of course, the difference between them and you is that they can't help what they are. You took a universally beautiful thing and pissed it right down the drain. You allowed the so-called Prince of Darkness to control you to do his bidding. If you had just kept your anger against God in check, He wouldn't have banished you from that perfect place, that heavenly place. You're just as sad as Satan himself."

"I recognize the voice, but it can't be who I think it is because his heart should beat no more. Did God catch your fall? Did He save you so that you can find your precious little girl? Don't pretend you know anything about me. Don't even assume you have a sliver of a clue about the kind of things I've been through, Jack."

Azrael's voice in the blackness had startled the hell out of me, and probably Harper, too. Wherever he was, it was too close for comfort.

"Oh, I think I've learned a lot of things since I joined Harper's quest to bring you down. I think I understand now why I'm here and why I've died three times. Each of those deaths was a test. God has tested me, challenged me to see if I'm the one He's looking for."

"The one?" The voice was so close it seemed like a thought in my head.

I was spinning in small circles. I figured Azrael was about to make a move. I feared he'd take us down without either of us getting a shot off.

"Yeah, I believe God sent me here to destroy you," I said confidently. I truly believed the words I had spoken.

I heard a train rumbling in the distance.

"Uh, Jack!" Harper yelled from somewhere to my left.

My foot hooked beneath one of the rails as I tried to work my way to my partner. I went down on jagged rocks that bit into my knees. I quickly got up. Although I couldn't see them clearly, I followed the sounds of Harper and Azrael struggling in the dark.

A gunshot went off with a concussion that temporarily struck me deaf. The muzzle flash may have lasted only a fraction of a second, but it gave me an exact location. I ran forward in the bleakness of the subway tunnel and grabbed Azrael. I felt Harper's grip let go, and I heard him collapse to the ground. I feared the shot had found my partner.

I threw one of the hardest punches of my life. I felt my fist connect brilliantly in Azrael's left eye socket. He staggered back, screamed out in agony, and then charged me.

I delivered two more. The first completely missed as he ducked to the right, but the second punch caught him dead center in the nose. I heard the cartilage crunch and give way under the force. It felt damn good. I heard him stumble backward, but he didn't go down.

The adrenaline surge powering me for the last twenty minutes finally found the bottom. My legs were shaking as I went to Harper.

A train roared into view from the opposite direction we had entered the tunnel. The headlight on the train lit up everything God awful in that tunnel. I got a clear sight of the Angel of Death. His nose was drooling blood down into his mouth, and he appeared as if he could barely hold himself up. He didn't seem so tough after all.

"You've both been played from the beginning of this game. Remember how the game is always changing, Harper? Remember how deceiving we can be? You won't figure it out until it's entirely too late. You've just killed her, Jack. You've killed your little girl."

Before our perplexed eyes, Azrael stepped between the tracks of the oncoming train. He was smiling. It was probably the most insane smile I've ever seen.

"No!" Harper and I simultaneously screamed.

The sound of the train's horn nearly ruptured my eardrums as the conductor saw Death on the tracks in front of him.

Azrael impacted against the train. If it weren't for the harsh squeal of the steel wheels on the tracks, I would have thought that the compacting sound might have matched that of a body falling to the concrete from five stories up.

"Harper, are you all right?" I asked after the train, and whatever remained of Azrael was gone.

"Yeah, just depleted."

"Hopefully, that shot didn't find you."

"No, I fired it. I think it must have been a millimeter from Azrael's head."

Maybe it's from our long struggle with Azrael coming to an end, or because Harper was thrilled with the idea that for once, he wasn't the one who had to finish things with a bullet. In any case, two friends and mad partners began to laugh.

"Azrael has never terminated himself like that, not that I know of anyway. I didn't even think they were allowed to suicide the bodies they occupied. Azrael always made the authorities bring him down," Harper said.

We exited the subway, got in the cruiser, and made our way back to the start point.

"You've said Azrael is always changing the game. You said he's highly unpredictable. I don't think even the Angel of Death can predict everything that will happen and every move we might make," I said.

"Yeah, I know what you're saying, but something doesn't sit right. I knew the game would probably change again, but I never saw the abduction of Reanne coming, and I never saw the possibility of Azrael stepping in front of that train. I'm sorry to say, but I don't think that was the end of the game. He has something else planned, something we're not expecting. He wants to see someone die at the end. Reanne, so far as we know, is still alive. That isn't his idea of a finale."

From what I understood of Azrael and the games he's played for thousands of years, I think Harper has a solid point. I initially hoped that I'd find Reanne alive in apartment twelve and that this madness was over for us. Now, I'm second-guessing *everything*.

"Right now, we need to focus on one problem at a time. Let's go find Reanne, and then we'll take step two," I said.

News vans were coming down the street, heading for the subway entrance. I wondered how the vultures had slipped through the barricades. Maybe they were already in the area, covering another terrible crime only blocks away. Hatred and destruction always seem to be right around every corner these days. The armies of fallen angels are winning the long-running war, and that scares me more than I care to say.

Chapter 64

Harper and I were bounding up the apartment building stairs. Apartment twelve was on the third floor. The hallways littered with garbage, children's bicycles, and even several people slumped against the walls.

The people on the third floor saw us approaching with our guns drawn and didn't seem to register an alarm. They eyed us suspiciously but didn't even shift positions.

"Time to find another place to chill," Harper told them. Figuring that we weren't here to arrest them, they all moved to the stairs and disappeared below. Harper and I were alone again.

I glanced at the door and silently prayed that Reanne was alive inside. My heart has a long jagged tear, and it would only mend with my adorable little girl gathered in my arms.

We had our backs to the wall. I didn't hear any noises coming from the apartment.

Harper reached out and tried the doorknob. The knob rotated smoothly, and with the squeak of the hinges, the door swung open.

The apartment seemed abandoned. There was a dirty brown sofa with holes placed against the far wall of the living room. That was the extent of furniture as far as I could see. In the small kitchen, the refrigerator rattled. The place smelled like a city dump, which it had apparently become. There were pizza boxes and various fast food wrappers scattered everywhere.

Harper and I slowly made our way inside. I kept my attention on the hallway where the bedroom would be and the area behind the kitchen counter that I couldn't quite see. Harper motioned for me to inspect the kitchen while he took whatever lay beyond the hallway.

I came around the end of the kitchen counter. No one was waiting to spring at me. I moved to the pantry closet with my finger tensing on the trigger and slowly pulled the door open. There was nothing but an empty trashcan.

Harper startled me when he called out from the bedroom. "Jack, are we clear?"

"Yeah, clear in here!"

"You better come take a look at this."

I hurried down the hall to the bedroom. Harper had his back to me. To my great relief, the bedroom simply contained a filthy bare mattress. It didn't appear as if anyone was captive here. I began thinking that Reanne was never here in the first place.

There was something else, and it was obvious when we stepped in the room as if the person who wrote it wanted it immediately noticed. There was graffiti written in red spray paint across the wall.

It read: John 8:44

I looked in the bedroom closet and found it empty. The bathroom was empty, too. The apartment was completely vacant. Of course, it had been vacant until two bumbling fools charged in and now stood staring at the wall.

"What does it say?" I asked.

"It says John 8:44."

"Thanks, I wasn't sure," I said sarcastically. "I meant, what do the chapter and verse say?"

Harper slid his hand to his inside left jacket pocket and withdrew his tattered bible.

I took the book from him and flipped through until I found the chapter and verse.

I read it out loud. "John, Chapter 8, Verse 44. *You are of your father, the devil, and you want to do the desires of your father. He was a murderer from the beginning and does not stand in the truth because there is no truth in him. Whenever he speaks a lie, he speaks from his own nature, for he is a liar and the father of lies.*"

"So does that mean that some of this game was a lie? Is that what he's telling us? Was Hunter used as a diversion or a method of misdirection? Is Azrael telling us that he wasn't Hunter Jacobs?"

"It's just another level of deception," Harper said. He took the Bible from me and flipped through the worn pages with watchful eyes as if the answers were written inside.

"One thing stands out to me that happened in the tunnel. Hunter said, *remember how deceiving we can be?*" I said.

"Yeah, I caught that as well."

"He said, *we,* not *I.* We could have been right when we brought up the possibility that Azrael is no longer playing these games alone. You told me that an entire army has fallen to earth. It seems feasible that over the countless years Azrael has been bound to earth, chances are strong that he's come across members of his forsaken army. Don't you think?" I asked.

"I think Hunter was a different fallen angel. I think Azrael is telling us that he isn't working alone in this game. I think Azrael wanted us to kill Hunter and understand that times have changed again. I knew there were others, but their psychotic profile is almost non-existent compared to Azrael's. I knew that something wasn't sitting right with the way Hunter stepped in front of that train. I don't believe Azrael would have done that. He wants to see this thing to the end. If he's now teaming up with some of the others, then our future is more screwed than I thought. With an army like that, they would be unstoppable."

"Yeah. Not a positive outlook for us," I said.

"We followed the clues he carefully laid out. Azrael wanted us to reach this point and for us to realize exactly how clever he is. There has to be a clue here, something to follow to the final step. He wants you to watch Reanne die. He'll then kill you, and after that, he dies by my hand. It would be the end for him, the end of this game, anyway. Right now, Reanne is still alive, and the clue we need to find her is somewhere in this shitty little apartment."

It wasn't a great motivational speech, but it got me going. Harper and I flipped over the mattress and prodded it with our fingers in search of something that didn't belong within. We moved to the living room, pulled the stained cushions from the sofa, and dug our fingers in the creases where the springs were hiding. We gripped the sides of the couch and rolled it forward so that it was now upside down. There was nothing but more discarded fast-food wrappers underneath. I pulled away the sofa lining to reveal the inner structure and nothing more. All the kitchen cabinets were completely bare. Besides stained and cracked ice trays, the refrigerator was empty as well. The groceries Hunter had been bringing here would have been the extent of his food supplies. The apartment was simply a squatting place for Hunter to wait until the Bible clues brought us here.

"There has to be more to this," I said with a severe degree of irritation. I was slowly spinning in place, eyeing everything. I was looking for something else to fit within the puzzle.

I halted as my eyes caught something. Ordinarily, it was a thing I wouldn't have even noticed if I weren't so desperate.

The something I spotted was seemingly unimportant, but my mind wouldn't dismiss it. It was a missing screw.

The small empty hole was on one side of a smoke-stained air vent at the upper part of the wall where the sofa had been.

"Help me flip the couch back over, please."

I climbed up the back of the couch, grabbed the loose side of the vent, and pried it free. When it came to leaving clues, Azrael always did it with a sense of mystique and outright puzzlement. Inside the vent was a framed photograph of Hunter Jacobs and another man I've never seen before. They were both dressed in camouflage. Hunter had his arm curled over the other man's shoulders as if they were lifelong pals. I wondered if Azrael's soul is possessing the unknown man. I handed the photo to Harper.

"Jack, the other man is Ian Matthews. I told you earlier today that while you were unconscious in the hospital, I researched Officer King's murder. I was trying to figure out what Azrael is telling us. There was a photo of Ian Matthews in one of the newspaper clippings I saw. That's why he's gone missing, because sometime recently he died, and Azrael slipped inside. We were right. Ian Matthews. *IM the 1.*"

I stepped beside Harper. We stared at the photo as if the two men inside it would suddenly do a magic trick. I took the photo from Harper. I flipped it over and peeled off the back of the frame. I had hoped that something was secretly awaiting discovery inside, but there wasn't. I threw the frame pieces down and looked at the photo again. There had to be something else to it.

Behind Hunter and Ian was a dense forest of snow-covered pine trees. There was a sliver of a mountain peak in the distance curving over the treetops. At the very edge of the photograph was part of a log house, and dangling from the corner of that house was a colorfully woven dreamcatcher.

Curiously, I asked Harper, "Do you recognize the background? Does it stick out in your mind at all?"

Harper stared intensely at the photo, looking beyond the murderers in the foreground. What was behind them didn't reveal much. However, the old saying about a picture being worth a thousand words rang true to Harper at that very moment.

A look of sudden recognition and astonishment found Harper's face. A smile filled his features. It was only the third time I've seen genuine happiness on his face in the short time I've known him. The other two times were when he had a guitar curled in his hands playing to a barroom full of strangers, and when Hannah Jane began breathing again.

"You know where this is, don't you?" I asked with excitement and revival.

"Jack, I know where he's keeping Reanne. I know exactly where this place is. We can be there by nightfall. Come on!" Harper said and ran out of the apartment.

"Where are we going now?" I asked as I chased after him.

"We're going back to the beginning. The beginning of everything," Harper answered.

Chapter 65

We had crawled in the private jet again and raced to a destination unknown. It was unknown to me anyway. I grimly wondered how many hours I've killed in the last nine days leap-frogging the country. The only thing I knew for sure, the next plane ride I take better be one with Reanne at my side, destined for home sweet home.

The beginning just happened to be a remote area in the Sawtooth Mountains in the heart of Idaho. The mountains were famous for winter powder skiing, summer hiking, climbing, and whitewater rafting down the many scenic rivers.

Just as Harper predicted, our plane touched down on a freshly plowed runway at the base of the mountain range as the last of the sunlight slipped away.

Harper had made arrangements for three Sno-Cat vehicles equipped with front plows to be ready on our arrival. Harper had also arranged for local police and several emergency crews to follow us into the great unknown. It never hurt to have reinforcements ready in case something went terribly wrong. However, the team trailing us were instructed to stay clear of the immediate area where Azrael was suspected to be. They were only authorized to rush in when Harper or I radioed for them.

Harper pointed to the right and said, "I'm pretty sure that's the road that cuts up to the ranger station where Azrael took the picture. That's where they'll be. I'm sure of it."

I didn't see a road, only a partially snow-covered sign. Truthfully, I couldn't see anything across the landscape except a thick white blanket. I kept my faith in Harper's knowledge and willingness to see this horrible game to the end.

Harper cranked the wheel of the Sno-Cat, and we left the empty highway. Our headlights uncovered fresh track marks in the snow leading deep into the mountains. Azrael was here, and hopefully, Reanne as well. They were waiting for us in the darkness.

"As strange as it turns out, we're heading to the exact place where Hunter and I took down Azrael the first time. I can't say for sure why he's leading us to this place again. I'm terrified of what he has planned."

Confidently, I said, "It's a challenge to the highest of levels. For me, Azrael is trying to find out if my wits and strength are strong enough to save another daughter, where I had failed before. For you, maybe he wants to see if you've learned from possible mistakes made the first time around. Maybe there was something you could have done differently. It's his final test to see if both of us are cunning enough to save his innocent victim."

Harper turned his eyes to me, and without hesitation, he said, "We will. You have my word on that. Reanne is going to live."

A treacherous thirty minutes later, the Sno-Cat rolled to a stop. There was an empty all-terrain vehicle parked next to a small ranger station. As I studied the building, I saw the partially snow-covered dreamcatcher we saw in the photo.

Harper pointed to a gap in the trees.

"The Salmon River is right down there. There's a spot along the river where people drop rafts in the water. That's where it ended the very first time. It's where Azrael will be waiting for us," Harper said.

"You do realize that I probably won't make it out of here alive," I nervously told Harper.

"Always keep in mind that we can take him down, and we'll get your daughter back safe. Faith, Jack, just try it on for size. You might find that it fits perfectly."

"He took my daughter. An angel cast down from Heaven has kidnapped my little girl and is threatening her life, Harper. How can I love a God who would allow such heartache? Azrael wants to kill me. The chase is over, and Reanne and I will probably die. He wants to finish it here and now. You're going to be the only one to walk out of these mountains alive," I said.

I felt sick to my stomach. I believed everything I was saying. Reanne, Azrael, and I were going to die tonight. Except Azrael would return as always. Reanne and I wouldn't. It didn't seem fair from any crooked point-of-view.

I thought of Caroline and how much I missed her. I longed to touch her again. I needed to kiss her sweet lips and look deeply into those sparkling green eyes and tell her how much she's always meant to me. I wanted her to understand how her unquestionable love has saved my life more times than I could count.

"I do have faith. It's with my girls—the support, happiness, and unconditional love. That's faith for me because it's always guiding me like an invisible hand."

Harper smiled and said, "It's everything I've been trying to make you realize this entire time. The truth of whether God exists is only answered when our souls depart from this world. You have faith in something, and that's all that matters. I don't want you to worry anymore. You'll get your daughter back. You can then put this

271

whole mess behind you and continue saving those who need it. I envy you, I really do. Your devotion to helping others has gone unmatched by any of those I've met before."

"Thanks, that means a lot," I said.

"That's why I apologize for this in advance."

The action Harper made next caught me off guard more than anything else I've experienced since we met. Harper pulled his gun from its holster and swiftly slammed the metal against my forehead.

For the second time today, I found myself tumbling into cruel darkness.

Chapter 66

Thankfully, the dark and bitter cloud didn't hover very long. The Sno-Cat was still warm from the reminiscences of the heater that ran full blast during our mountain sprint. As my eyes began to focus, I realized that I was alone and slumped against the door. My head throbbed with a steady spike of pain.

It took only a moment to recall what the hell had happened to me. Harper and I were having a civilized conversation, and then metal clanking against my skull, only to leave me unconscious again.

I believe I understood the reasons behind Harper's harsh act. Harper has seen far too many good people destroyed by the hands of Death. I'm one of the few people Harper possessed the power to remove from the equation. Even though we're partners, Harper must have felt reassurance in his abilities to get Reanne back. Maybe he had a strong belief that he could complete the task at hand by himself and spare me a brutal death.

I didn't blame him for this, but I certainly wasn't going to idly sit around as he tried his best to beat Death at his own game. I opened the Sno-Cat door and stumbled out.

I found myself following the freshly pressed footprints. From what I could determine, there were three sets of prints preceding my own. One of the prints were small, the shoe size of an eight-year-old.

I was guided through the woods by the sliver of moonlight breaking through the cloud cover. My feet crunched on the snow, and low hanging branches repeatedly slapped my face as I ran faster. It was incredibly cold, and the light wind only made things worse. I could barely feel my fingers and toes.

I didn't have the details of the final battles Harper and Azrael have played over the years. I was aware that Harper has always shot Azrael to death and ended the chase, but Harper never won the game itself. Every battle ended with the death of a young, innocent girl.

I slid down an embankment, nearly losing my balance. I slowed my pace a little when I heard voices in the dark woods. I began to tread lightly. I didn't want anyone to know I was approaching, but I might have already blown my surprise attack.

One of the voices I heard was Harper. I've never heard the other voice before. It was Ian Matthews, now infested with the soul of a killer angel. I was sure that Ian Matthews had been one of the key players in the death of Officer Andrew King. The truth behind the murder is forever lost. Everyone who knew the facts of the situation is dead. Azrael saw to it. I thought maybe Azrael had taken over the body of Ian Matthews because Ian never repented for the murder of his partner. Christine Daniels, Father Richard James, and even Nora King had later walked away from the suspected murder and turned their lives around for the better. As I said before, we'll never know for sure. We can only speculate. I wouldn't dare take Azrael's word on it because his word is foul, and he is the father of lies.

I came down on my knees in the snow. I shuffled my way to a large pine and used it for cover. I slowly cocked my head to see around the tree and catch a glimpse of what was happening. I couldn't believe what I saw.

Reanne was there, and so was Harper. The madman was there, too. He had a gun pressed to the side of

Reanne's head. I tightly closed my eyes and hoped this was simply a horrifying image my mind had drawn up in expectation of a disastrous situation. But when I opened my eyes again, the view remained the same. My daughter was in the grip of Death.

Azrael and Reanne were halfway across the bridge, standing against the metal railing. Moonlight washed over them, which seemed to throw shadows in every direction.

I shifted forward to the edge of the tree line, trying to get a better view. That was when I did the worst thing possible. My body settled on a fallen branch, and it snapped with an echoing crack in the still woods.

Azrael, Harper, and even Reanne turned and looked in my direction.

With my cover blown, I stood from my position with my Glock out.

"Jack, no!" Harper yelled.

Azrael then did the unthinkable by creating a finish to this game that Harper and I couldn't have anticipated. He calmly shifted the gun from Reanne's temple, pointed it at Harper, and fired two quick shots.

Reanne screamed.

Harper had no time to react, no time to even get a shot off. The only thing he could do was catch two slugs directly in the chest. He staggered against the bridge railing and gripped the frozen handrail to keep himself upright. Harper drew in a labored breath, and when he exhaled, he did it with such violence that the snow-covered bridge spotted with crimson.

I knew Harper hadn't been wearing a vest. He gave up that measure of self-protection years ago. Even from this distance, I saw a blossom of red. Maybe he finally wanted things to end between Azrael and himself, dissolving an unfit relationship. Azrael wouldn't let Harper quit the chase, so maybe this was the only way that Harper thought he could free himself. He was letting Death finally take him after all.

Harper's legs were wobbly, and with carefully placed steps, he staggered along the edge of the bridge. His knees gave out, and he collapsed in the snow on the opposite side of the bridge.

I ran down the embankment. I think I was screaming. I wanted to squeeze off several shots and slay the monster. Unlike Harper, Azrael has protection. He was using my little girl as a shield.

I was pointing the gun at his head. I felt the need to fire and take a chance. Otherwise, Reanne and I were both going to die out here. If I fired now, there was a sliver of hope that we could both walk away from this ordeal. For reasons unknown, I couldn't take that chance, no matter how much my mind told me to.

I heard the rumble of the Salmon River below grow louder as I carefully approached the bridge. I couldn't chance a slip in the snow and lose my fix on the only shot I had. I stopped twenty feet from Azrael and my terrified daughter.

"I think I'm going to miss that old fool," Azrael told us.

Chapter 67

"Despite what you might believe, this was always meant to be the ending to the game," Azrael said as he pressed the gun to Reanne's temple again.

"So, how do you want this to play out?" I asked.

"I think you know how this will conclude, Jack. The one thing I can say for certain is that you will live. You're the one I've chosen. I was sure that your intelligence was extremely high, and we both know that your determination is right up there as well. I honestly didn't think I'd be as impressed with you as I am right this second. I spent many months researching individuals I wanted to challenge. You were the one who stood out above all others. You could say that I became a mentor to Nolan Windell for the single purpose of having him convince the senator that you were the best choice to bring into the case and save Hannah Jane. Much to my surprise, you did just that. You're far wiser than I anticipated. It's the reason the clues led you here. This place is where Harper and I first met and have played so many wonderful games since. Only now, Harper's a tired old man, and he simply doesn't have the enthusiasm that used to push him in the chase. You're going to walk out of this place, Jack, because you're the one I've selected to take Harper's place."

My mind kept shifting focus from Reanne standing in the middle of winter's vicious bite with little clothing and then to Harper, who had fallen at the opposite side of the bridge. I then looked at the maniac in front of me, who began it all. I was sure that I had heard Azrael say he has chosen me to replace Harper, but I couldn't completely understand it.

There's no possible way to picture living my life as Harper has lived his in the last four years. I didn't have the kind of mental strength to push me through one bloody crime scene after another as the hands of time ticked along, and all the important people in my life faded away. I also thought of the events that transpired earlier in the day. Had Azrael known that Hunter had allowed me to fall from five stories up? I was sure that the action of my third death hadn't been part of Azrael's plan. I briefly wondered what his reaction might have been if I hadn't shifted from Death's front door again and back to the mysterious ways of the world.

"I won't replace Harper because I'm going to stop you here and now."

"I can't be stopped, Jack. You know that. Not you, not Harper, and not the thousands of others throughout history could manage it. Not even the right hand of God can stop my destruction. God made his grave mistake by placing the others and myself in these flawed, helpless human forms for all eternity. God cannot undo what He's done without serious consequences."

"I'm cold, daddy," Reanne said. She was hugging her-self, shivering in the freshly fallen snow. She was only wearing a long-sleeved yellow shirt, gray sweat pants, and tennis shoes. It was the clothes she'd been wearing be-neath the school costume.

"I know, baby. It'll all be over in just a moment. Daddy loves you, sweetheart," I said.

I was trying to conceal the trembling in my voice. I didn't want Reanne to know that I was scared shitless of what might happen. I could lose one of the people I love most in the world. I could also lose a new friend and partner. I even thought that I might never see Caroline again. Her sweet smile. Her soft, loving eyes. Her gentle and kind touch.

"How sentimental. I think I have goosebumps all over. I can try to shed a tear in this heartfelt moment," Azrael mocked.

"You wouldn't understand the human concept of love. You don't know anything about it. You only care about destruction. Do you even remember what it was like to feel God's love?"

"Of course I do. I also remember feeling God's hate, anger, and wrath. These are far more effective and potent feelings than His love. He took away that love from me and gave it to you. You have no idea what that can be like, Jack."

I saw movement in the distance. I was trying to keep my eyes from looking in that direction. I didn't want Azrael to know what I knew. My peripheral vision saw a head bobbing up from the drift of snow at the end of the bridge. Harper was there, alive, and I thought he was going to make a move.

"Do you believe that killing thousands of people will place you back in God's good graces?" I was trying to keep Azrael's attention fixed on me.

Azrael gave a deep-throated, maniacal laugh. "You've got it wrong again, Jack. Millions, I've destroyed millions of lives throughout history. I've taken them one at a time, and I've slaughtered entire armies. Mankind always has and always will be easily corruptible. So that you understand, it isn't good graces I'm seeking. It's revenge. I'll continue killing. As long as God punishes me, I'll punish you. This world will never be rid of me."

Harper was standing, staggering in place to keep himself upright. I didn't know how he was holding himself up. Maybe it was sheer willpower to see this thing through to the end. Harper was desperately trying to open a doorway out of this hellish situation for Reanne and myself. Whatever was driving him, it was working. With wobbly legs and the muscles of his entire arm badly shaking, Harper raised his gun.

I kept my eyes focused on Azrael. I was preparing myself for the best and the worst of things to come. I could fire a succession of trained shots in a second flat.

I looked at Reanne, and her terrified face stared back at me. I didn't want to lose her, not for anything in the world. I couldn't bear to lose another child, not like this, not again.

"There's just one thing you forgot to calculate into your equation. There's one tiny fact you've overlooked. A simple misstep you made that changed the way *this* game will end," I said. My blood was thundering, pounding from the balls of my feet to the hollows of my ears.

"Why don't you enlighten me, Jack? Let's compare your forty-two years of life experience with my millennia of expertise."

"It's simple, you see. Something you couldn't possibly understand. It's called human determination."

Just then, Harper fired three shots in the air. It was a perfect diversion.

Azrael loosened his grip on Reanne as he spun around in surprise. His gun raised and searching for whatever the cause to the interruption of his perfect grand finale. His aim found Harper, who had already collapsed to his knees in a complete state of exhaustion.

I saw Azrael's finger tense on the trigger. Reanne managed to slip from his grasp and hit the snow-covered bridge, her hands wrapping around her head. *That's my girl.*

It entered his mind seconds too late. Azrael turned back to me, but my aim was already set. I hammered two well-placed rounds into what had once been a man named Ian Matthews, only now the soul of Azrael, the Angel of Death, occupied.

Azrael rocked back from the hits, and then he let out a series of raging grunts. He released his gun, tottered forward and back again. He stumbled against the bridge handrail, suddenly pitching backward and vanishing over the rail and down into the swelling blackness of the river below.

Chapter 68

I don't think I have ever run faster in my life than I did at that moment. I came down hard on my knees in front of Reanne. I leaned in close and took hold of her. She was shivering badly, and tears were streaming down her rosy cheeks.

"Sweetie, can you hear me?" I asked in a trembling voice.

She looked up at me. She was unable to speak between the sobs but managed a nod.

I unzipped my coat, pulled her in close to me, and wrapped her up. She was shaking so much that I could barely hold onto her.

I managed to retrieve my phone from my coat pocket. Our back-up team was not far out of view. They were instructed to remain out of sight until we called in. I was glad they stayed clear even when the shooting started, but I needed them now.

"This is Jack Calloway. I need the team to move in right away. I need paramedics and a Life-flight helicopter here ASAP. Agent Caster is down with multiple gunshot wounds. Move, move, move," I said and then hung up.

I looked down at Reanne. "Sweetie, I love you so very much. Everything is okay now."

Her grip tightened on me. "I love you, daddy. I knew you'd come for me."

"I'll always come for you, no matter what. I'm not going to put you down, but there's something I have to do, and you're going to have to come with me." I was already walking toward where Harper had fallen.

"Are we going to make sure your friend is all right?"

"Yes, sweetie, we need to check on my friend. He saved our lives. We need to see if we can help him."

"I'd like that very much, daddy. I want to thank him."

"You're my brave little girl with a heart of gold." I hugged her tighter.

The event had drained everything I had left. The cold had stolen some of that energy, too. But I needed to get to Harper. I hadn't seen or heard from him after he fired random shots in the air to distract Azrael. It was his final act allowing us to finish the game.

I heard vehicles approaching, followed by footfalls in the snow coming up behind me. The cavalry is here.

I was down on my knees again in the snow. I saw two holes punched through Harper's coat. Two chest shots. I didn't see wisps of white exiting his mouth. I didn't see his chest rising and falling. His eyes were closed, and he was unresponsive to my calls.

Two paramedics with a gurney quickly came up behind me. The ambulance back-up beacon sounded as it rolled onto the bridge to get as close as possible. One of the paramedics was saying something to me. I didn't hear what he said. I was in a state of shock.

A paramedic began pulling us off to the side. "Sir, I'm sorry, but I need you to move aside so we can work on him."

They lowered the gurney, lifted Harper onto the pad, and then moved him into the ambulance. I thought they would take him to the clearing where we had parked the Sno-Cat, load him into an arriving helicopter, and quickly make way to the nearest hospital.

Before the doors slammed shut, I saw one of the paramedics beginning CPR as the other prepared the defibrillator to jolt some life back into my partner.

I know a little something about death, about dying. I hoped it was going to be quite some time before it came around to find me again.

I also hoped it would let go of its grip on Harper. He didn't deserve this kind of finish after all these years of cat and mouse games. He deserved to live a long life.

"Let him live, please," I whispered.

I don't know for sure to whom I was speaking. God? Maybe. It was worth a shot. Perhaps Harper has started to make a believer out of me after all.

"Oh, daddy, no," Reanne said as she turned her sight from the ambulance. She pressed her tear-streamed face into the crook of my neck.

It was no surprise, but I cried, too.

Chapter 69

I wanted nothing more than to sleep for the next twelve hours. Fifteen hours sounded even better. My body ached, and my mind fizzled out like an old fuse, but I had somewhere important to go today.

I let my thoughts wander a little as I drove down the streets of Boise. Truthfully, it was quite a fantastic city. Wherever your trails ran, beauty always lay before you. I hadn't intentionally come here to take in the scenic beauty. I came to this area for the single purpose of pulling my daughter back from the brink of death. I'm pleased to say I had accomplished that feat. Now that my mission was successful, I found myself absorbing my surroundings and breathing deeply like a man with few worries in the world.

I always believed that someone should learn something with every major life experience. It's especially true when dealt with something as dramatic as I had experienced. I was trying to figure out precisely what that was.

After the extensive tests the doctors had scheduled at the hospital, they determined that the worst of what Reanne brought down from the Sawtooth Mountains was a mild case of frostbite on all her fingers and her ears. Physically, Reanne was going to be just fine. Her greatest challenge would be mentally pushing through these recent moments. With Caroline and me helping along the way, I knew she'd eventually break through that obstacle as well. She's the strongest willed little girl I've ever known.

I called Caroline when Reanne was admitted to Mount Haven Memorial Hospital. I explained nearly everything I could. The only thing I left out was that we'd been chasing Death himself.

On the phone, Caroline spent five minutes crying tears of joy and telling us how much she loves us. I explained to Caroline that I needed to stay in Boise for a few days. Caroline claimed that she wouldn't wait for our return. She immediately booked a plane the following morning and reunited with our family.

Hannah Jane was safe and sound. Reanne and I were safe and sound. It's something I enjoy often saying because I think those simple words speak volumes.

Safe and sound.

The madness has come to its end. Roll the credits and then draw the curtain closed. This story is over. We could all move on with our lives now. We would take in this experience for what it's worth and get back into the swing of normal life, or as normal as we could make it. Love, live free, and then love some more. The most important thing of all was to enjoy what we have while we have it. We never know when something so personal to us might be taken away in the very next moment. I think part of me sometimes took that for granted, even after the events that took away my first daughter, Regina. I wasn't going to let that happen anymore. I know what I have, and I'll enjoy every waking second I have with those I love most—my sweet girls.

I had left Caroline and Reanne to explore Boise and the many pleasantries it held. They needed a little time to take their minds off the terrifying events that had unfolded and journey the winter landscape of this delightful city.

I reached the guest parking level at Mount Haven Memorial Hospital. My heart quickened a little as I walked to the elevators. For reasons unknown, I was feeling slightly nervous.

What was I going to say as I looked into his face? What possible rational line of thinking would enter my mind as I walked into the hospital room, gazed into those eyes, and said the things I was thinking? Of course, it has to be done. It's a necessary action to speak from the heart.

I walked down the busy hallway of the ICU. I briefly consulted with the head nurse, and she allowed me to proceed to one of the private rooms. As I entered room 214, I smiled when I caught sight of Harper sleeping peacefully. The heart monitor beeped with a steady rhythm. He was alive, of course. He was a tougher-than-steel son-of-a-bitch if there ever was one. When you boiled everything down, Harper hadn't surrendered to the clutches of Death because there was just too much beauty left in the world to explore.

Harper *had* died on the battlefields of the Sawtooth Mountains. His heart ceased motion saving Reanne and myself. However, if I'm now going on my fourth chance at life, then Harper deserved at least one more chance. It was precisely what he received. Mysteriously, Harper's still heart began to beat again. The baffled paramedics sustained his condition until he was airlifted and delivered to the skilled and caring hands of those at Mount Haven Memorial.

On Harper's third day in the ICU, the doctor wouldn't allow any visitors yet. He said the following day I could stay for a short while if Harper were awake. I gave the doctor a sealed envelope and asked if he would place it at Harper's bedside.

The note explained the events that happened after Harper's collapse. I saw the letter on the bedside table had been opened. Now Harper has all the facts. I wondered what his thoughts were when he learned of what became of Azrael.

I pulled a chair close to his bed and watched him for a few quiet moments. He could finally rest easy. The nightmare case has found its end. It was this thought that allowed my tired mind to drift off as I watched Harper. Sometime later, I woke from him gently shaking my arm. I sat up and smiled.

"Welcome back," I said as I rubbed the sleep from my eyes.

"I didn't realize I went anywhere," Harper said in a dry, hoarse voice.

"You were close, too close for comfort. You almost went away for good. You spent some time on the other side. Someone must have decided that you have a little more living to do."

"Maybe. Or maybe I'm just a lucky SOB."

"Maybe a little of both. In any case, I'm glad you're sticking around."

This case brought us close together. I wanted to know so much more about Harper. I didn't doubt that we'd be friends to the end of days.

I smiled and lightly fingered the fresh bruise and shallow gouge on my forehead.

Harper said, "Yeah, sorry about that. It was honestly a last-minute thought. I couldn't bear the idea of Azrael killing you. I wasn't positive that we'd get Reanne back alive. I just kept thinking that Caroline needed someone to come home to her."

I said, "It's all right. I understand why you did it. Maybe if I had been in your place and went through all the horrible things you have, I might have taken the same steps. We still would have been able to work better as a team. Together we might have spared you a hole in your chest."

"I was curious about the afterlife anyhow. I got tired of you having all the bragging rights."

Harper took in a long slow breath and winced as he did. He was still in pain but mending quickly.

I turned my sight to the nightstand and the white leather-bound Bible resting there. The cover had a jagged hole completely wiping out the letters IB. I gently placed my finger on the surface and slowly circled the hole. It was the BIBLE that Harper kept religiously in his coat pocket and close to his heart. The words of God had stopped the bullet that would have obliterated his heart. There wouldn't have been any coming back from that. However, the second shot punctured his right lung and collapsed it. That shot had briefly taken him from this world.

"The nurse told me earlier that my wife called yester-day. She's bringing our daughter up for a visit. It should be interesting, I think. Who knows, maybe now that we finished this whole mess, I can get back to a little thing called life. I can get a fresh start with the FBI. No more killer angels or anything like that, just ordinary bad guys," Harper said.

"Sounds like you might just have it all worked out."

With the mention of Harper's wife and daughter, I thought of my own family eagerly waiting for me to rejoin them and then make our journey back home. The emotion was overwhelming, and it hit me like a full-blown tidal wave. I put my hand on Harper's arm and gently squeezed.

"I owe you everything. I can't tell you how grateful I am that you helped me get Reanne back. I don't think I could have done it on my own. You put your life on the line for a little girl you didn't even know." The tears were slipping faster now. "If ever you need something, great or small, just ask, and I'll be there for you."

Tears were beginning to well in Harper's eyes. He gave me a warming smile. "I was just doing my duty, Jack Everlasting."

"Above and beyond the call of duty. I mean it. Anything at all."

"There's one thing you can do. How about getting the hell out of here and getting back to the girls you love."

"That, Special Agent Caster, I can definitely do."

A short while later, I quietly closed the door behind me and left Harper to rest. I walked down the hospital hallway at a hurried pace. Some visitors and nurses glanced at me as if I were an escaping patient, running for freedom.

I wanted to grab my girls and catch a plane home. It's where the heart is, they say.

As the elevator doors opened, a huddle of people unloaded. Two people stood out to me. I didn't know them, but I was sure I knew of them. Clara and Kaylee Caster. The mother had her arm wrapped around her daughter. They were crying softly, a cry somewhere between relief and sadness.

I held myself back and let the elevator doors close. I quietly watched them hold each other and make their way down the corridor. They paused at the nurses' station and then made their way to room 214. They opened the door and vanished inside.

I smiled. Another family reunited. Once torn apart and later unintentionally mended by the hands of a fallen angel. Life seems to go in circles sometimes.

I hit the elevator call button. I thought of something Harper had said, *Maybe now that we finished this whole mess, I can get back to a little thing called life.*

It sounds like a good plan to me.

Chapter 70

Home sweet home. It's my favorite place in the entire known universe and beyond those borders, if there is such a place. Not only am I home again, but the most wonderful part of the year has come. It's Christmas morning.

The previous Christmas seasons were always joyful, of course, but this year seems blessed with more excitement and a greater sense of love. Our family is together, and not even a battalion of fallen angels can break that bond. Love *is* the most powerful kind of glue.

I had awoken around six in the morning. A wicked kind of dream had shaken me from my peaceful sleep. Damn those dreams. I carefully slipped from the bed, not wanting to wake Caroline, and headed down to the kitchen.

I brewed myself a pot of coffee. I busied myself by planning a delightful Christmas morning breakfast for the family. Making breakfast was the least I could do for my girls because I broke a promise weeks before. I was still sore about going back on my promise to take time off. However, I didn't regret it. Harper and I saved Hannah Jane and brought her home safely. I briefly lost Reanne to the grip of Death, but she, too, had come home unharmed.

I prepared scrambled eggs as a skillet of potato hash browned, slices of bread toasting, and sausage links sizzled in another skillet. Pancakes and fresh-baked muffins were already sitting on the table. It was a buffet fit for a queen, a princess, and the court jester.

Through the excessive noise I was making, I heard footsteps coming down the stairs.

Caroline and Reanne stepped into the kitchen with eyes of wondrous delight at all that awaited them. No doubt, the glorious aroma had snuck its way upstairs and stirred them from sleep.

"Good grief, did you happen to invite the entire city over for breakfast?" Caroline asked with a crooked smile.

"No, but I could make a call."

"Daddy, you cooked?" Reanne said loud enough that the neighbors had probably heard.

"What? Can't the most wonderful dad in the world make breakfast?"

I picked up Reanne and bear-hugged her tightly. She snuggled back.

"Mommy, group hug!" Reanne said and giggled sweetly.

Caroline joined in. I was so happy at this moment in time.

After a minute, I broke up the small group because the toast was burning, damn toast.

"If I'm not mistaken, I think today is a special kind of day, isn't it?" Caroline asked.

"Christmas! Christmas! Christmas!" Reanne chanted while hopping in place.

"Then I guess you better get some breakfast down lightning fast so you can tear into those humongous presents I saw under the tree," I said.

After we had stuffed ourselves, we headed into the living room. During my time off work, Caroline and I had done a lot of Christmas shopping. We bought an excessive amount of white and multi-colored lights, a plush snowman, Santa, and reindeer stuffed animals placed around the house. We had bought so much extra stuff that our tree was no longer visible beneath the explosion of twinkling lights, tinsel, and music and motion ornaments. It was indeed a winter wonderland.

Caroline and I settled on the couch. I wrapped my arm around her and held her close. We watched Reanne read each present's tag and then dig into the ones with her name on them.

My eyes traveled around, exploring everything this perfect little house has to offer on Christmas morning. I studied the long row of Christmas cards on the mantel. We had received well over a hundred. The cards were from family, friends, and those I've saved over the years. It's always wonderful to receive such thanks years after I've done something good and brought loved ones together again.

One card stood out above all the rest. The photo was of Senator John Hillcrest, his wife, and their son and daughter. Hannah Jane had several cuts and fading purple bruises marking her face, but those genuine smiles were priceless to me.

Senator Hillcrest included a check inside the card. The amount, well, let's just say that the amount made my heart flutter and caused Caroline to find the nearest chair because her knees had gone weak.

Even though it was the happiest time of the year, an evil little thought had slipped into my mind at that moment, and I silently cursed it. I didn't want my mood to be spoiled, not here and now, but there's something I have to do soon. I don't understand the reason behind it, but something pushed me, and I have to see it through. I'll eventually answer that nagging mental call. But I figured that little mystery could wait a while. I gave that dirty, rotten thought a minute of my time, only a minute, and then I shoved it into the deep cobwebbed area at the back of my mind.

"No way!" Reanne screeched.

She frantically tore away the wrapping of her biggest present. I had called in a favor to a close friend to build an incredible dollhouse. He went above and beyond in replicating the gift after our own loving home. In my opinion, it certainly put one of those plastic dollhouses to shame.

Reanne slowly ran her fingers across the yellow lap siding as her eyes took in everything the playhouse had to offer.

"I love it! It's the best present I could ever get!" She ran over to us, leaped onto our laps, and continued the group hug that was earlier interrupted. With the love we have for each other, there's no obstacle we can't overcome.

John Lennon had once sung, *All You Need Is Love*.

I believe that man was on to something good.

Chapter 71

The cold rain started as I slipped from the rental car. It was early springtime in Baltimore, a time for rejoicing, rebirth, and all things beginning with a new sense of purpose. Yet, I felt no pleasure for this time of renewal and no sense of wonder or excitement. What I felt instead was a lingering dread deep in the core of my being. I hated what I was doing today. The fact is, I gave in to something I swore to myself that I wouldn't. I had let that little demon of impatience and overwhelming curiosity get the better of me and whisper those crude and commanding words in my ear.

I stood in front of the big, brightly lit building. In the blackened night, it called like a menacing entity beckoning me to come inside and play. Rain pelted my clothes and streamed down my face as I looked up at those bright yellow windows. I hoped some satisfying answer would peek out. I could then turn around, go home, and blink the memory away like a horrific bad dream. The answer wasn't looking out at me. It was hiding inside and always waiting because, for some of us, time stands still.

I calmly made my way to the entrance of the Wilmester Institute for the Criminally Insane. The facility is one of the keepers of the great and many things wrong with the world.

Wilmester is the largest facility in the U.S., housing nearly three hundred of the country's most dangerously mentally disturbed. Now it housed the leader of them all.

Azrael, the angel of death, is now a permanent resident.

A guard handed me a towel to help blot away some of the dampness when I entered the front security station. I passed through several more security stations, showing my identification and waiting to verify my clearance. Guards thoroughly searched me at two other checkpoints before I reached the outside room where Azrael was temporarily staying. I didn't make a fuss or a single complaint about being held up. In fact, it made me feel greatly relieved. I suspected that it couldn't be easy for a killer angel to escape this place.

I hope.

Two armed guards stood outside the room, and two more were inside. I'm told this would be a luxury for the institute's newest member. This containment method was only brief. The great minds of the FBI had another idea for the man called Death. Until the next stage of Azrael's stay went into effect, the FBI wasn't taking a chance at this deceptive bastard finding his way out of confinement or out of the body.

A crackling voice came over the guard's radio. I had been cleared and was able to proceed to a sublevel of Hell. The guard turned, punched in a code on the electronic keypad, inserted a key in the deadbolt, and unlocked the thick metal gray door.

My heart was racing a little. Do I need to go through with this? Do I need to inject myself with any more of this demon's evil? I think I have to this one final time.

Without a single creak, the door swung open. What I saw inside sent a river of chills racing up my spine.

Azrael had no doubt been waiting for me. When the door fully opened, he was standing in the center of his cell, offering that awful sadistic smile that only he could manage. Somehow he was expecting me. Does he already have an inside source at the institution?

"Ah, Jack," he exclaimed. "I've been awaiting your arrival for quite some time. It pleases me to see that you finally gave in to your curiosity."

The room wasn't large, only about twenty feet by twenty feet. A cage that could be found nowhere else in the facility was housing the fallen angel. A simple, sturdy cot with a pillow, a blanket, a composting toilet, and the uniform on his back were all the possessions Azrael had in the entire world. He wasn't allowed music, newspapers, supplies for drawing and painting, or even literature. His only order from the FBI and the administrator of the facility was to sit and rot.

I stepped closer to the bars.

"Keep your distance, sir," one of the guards warned.

"Yes, yes," Azrael confirmed. "Don't let yourself be coaxed too close to my dirty little clutches. The man has spoken, and you'd be wise to obey."

Maybe out of defiance against Azrael and not the guards, I stepped forward. I wasn't afraid of him, not anymore. He could no longer do any harm.

He smiled at my disobedience. "Tisk, tisk, Jack, you don't want to invoke danger, do you?"

"Don't get me wrong, but I'm certain that I'm quite safe from you."

"You wouldn't want to come too close. Not close enough for me to reach out and seize your pathetic little neck and squeeze. Perhaps the guards would have to follow orders and shoot me dead on the spot. Wouldn't that be a tragedy?"

"You don't have to worry. These guards won't kill you, seeing that's what you want. But they will inflict a great deal of pain. I know you can feel pain. Their orders are to keep you alive at all costs. Isn't that right, gentlemen?"

"Shoot? Naw, but they gave us these nifty Tazer guns. I've heard that five-hundred thousand volts going through the body hurt like a bastard. It makes you fall to the ground spasming like a tortured bug. It leaves your body aching for days after. I'd love to try it out sometime soon," one of the guards said.

I said, "Sounds pleasant. You see, Azrael, even you're safe and sound. At the end of all things, I saved you as well."

It only took a split-second for his exterior to fracture. He ran forward and rammed hard against the steel bars. It's been over three months since I put a slug in each shoulder. Wounds from hollow-point rounds punching through muscle and splintering bones always take a long time to heal. I knew it had to hurt like hell. However, he showed no signs of pain, only a rage I will never understand.

"You didn't play the game correctly, Jack," he hissed through clenched teeth. "I was supposed to die on that bridge, and your daughter was supposed to die, too. Whether it's two weeks or two years from now, you're going to be Harper's replacement. I speak the inevitable truth, and you know it."

He watched me with cursing, penetrating gray eyes.

"I played fair. I followed the rules and clues. I'm just smarter than you. As it turned out in the end, everyone lived, even our good friend Harper. Your Father saved his life with words of faith that Harper kept close to his heart. I guess it was all my fault that I ruined everything for you," I said and felt a smile creep out of me.

Azrael quickly collected himself. He had actually seemed a little embarrassed that he had lost his composure.

He was now self-assured again, with a bit of cockiness thrown in.

"How's the family, Jack? Has Reanne started therapy sessions yet?"

Chapter 72

He was trying to get under my skin, trying to bring my emotions to the next level just as I had done to him. He was pathetic.

I slowly paced around his cage, inspecting it for any type of flaw. Thankfully, I saw none.

His suspicious eyes never left me.

"Oh, you have no idea how strong-willed my girl is. She's already over what happened. To her, you're nothing but a distant memory. The FBI made sure the public didn't learn your entire story. The only thing the public knows was that you were just another raving lunatic out for attention and that we put you down like a lame horse. The people have grown bored with the stories of how you failed to kill Hannah Jane and how the FBI outsmarted you. The newspapers and newscasts don't even mention you anymore. You're like, well, you're a has-been. Your fifteen minutes of fame is over, and no one cares anymore. It's all in the past, and that's where it will stay."

Azrael began a laugh that gave me goosebumps.

"That's where you're wrong, Jack. The quest will continue. It's simply a minor setback. Give me a little time, and yes, there's always time I have to give, and then things will resume as they always have. It's a never-ending cycle. Just like the sun rising and falling with each passing day. I *will* kill again."

He was right. I had known it from the moment the authorities found his battered and nearly frozen body alive.

The river ran his unconscious body a hundred yards downstream. Maybe by the will of God, he had hung up on a tangle of fallen branches at the shoreline. If it hadn't been for his clothes getting snagged, he would have never been found and would have died. His soul would have been free again.

What he said was stuck in my mind. He *was* going to kill again. Nothing but the hand of God could stop it. This type of prison was only a temporary solution to our dilemma.

Azrael stepped to the steel bars and curled his long fingers around them. He said, "I was in Europe when the Nazi hatred demolished millions of lives. I was part of it all. I assisted in the destruction of those hopeless beings. I was dancing with pride at all the chaos I had created. I'm a god among you. Hitler and the hundreds before him were simply puppets to which I alone controlled the strings."

"As far as I'm concerned, you won't be pulling any strings for at least, let's see, the next fifty years or more. Actually, I wanted to let you know that this prison is only temporary. You'll be moved next week from this room to a more pleasant one. They're going to give you a shot, and you won't ever wake up again."

"Enlighten me, Jack," Azrael said with extreme curiosity. His eyes were dancing.

"They're going to place you in a drug-induced coma. Basically, you're going to fall asleep and stay that way until your heart gives out decades from now. However, you don't need to worry because you'll be fed sufficient nutrients intravenously, everything your body needs to reach extreme old age. They don't want to waste time or resources on you anymore. I suspect you'll have plenty of demented dreams to keep your mind occupied for the next fifty years." I smiled plainly at him and gave him a wink.

I wasn't sure if it was a mistake at this point, but with Azrael in a coma, I did agree that a chance of a prison escape was unlikely. We were also taking away the possibility of Azrael killing someone within the prison, someone who got careless and stepped too close to his cage. More importantly, we couldn't take the chance that Azrael would figure out a way to kill himself or get someone to do it for him, which would make all our efforts pointless. We had to play the odds, and I was beginning to think it was probably the smartest choice of all.

He gave a smile that was more to himself than to me. "It sounds pleasant, falling asleep, and only awaking when my soul moves into the next body. Yes, this body will eventually give out, but the soul will live on."

Damn, why did I really come here? Was it to be bombarded by this cocky, arrogant asshole who could one-up me after any clever remark I had? What was I hoping to find here?

The answer was, of course, right in front of me. All along, I wanted to know for sure that it was over. I wanted to know that the Angel of Death was trapped inside this human and only escaping in death. That seemed kind of ironic just then, Death escaping in death. God has a wicked sense of humor, I think.

I turned my back on Azrael. I couldn't bring myself to look at him anymore. Because looking at him was like staring into the face of our annihilation.

"Jack," Azrael called after me.

The guard punched in the code, and my hand was on the door lever. Against my better judgment, I gave in and turned around.

I watched him contemptuously.

"There's one thing you're forgetting. I realize that you only spent a little over a week playing my exciting little game, but with all the experience Harper has, I'm sure one evil thought entered his mind. You once thought that Nolan Windell was your man, and then you were positive that Hunter Jacobs was your man, only to realize that you'd been misguided twice. Now, you've incarcerated me, still positive that you have the right man. My point is, who said I was Azrael?"

It's the reason I came to the institute. A level of uncertainty was in my mind at the very end of everything.

I didn't react to his statement. In fact, I gave him a look of boredom. "I guess then if you're not Azrael, and simply one of his drones, or one of the other members of the fallen army, then I suppose we'll catch him the same way we got you."

The fact is, I was ninety-nine percent sure we had the right angel. I didn't trust any words that came from him because he's the father of lies. He had told us so. Of course, there was always that tiny percentage that picked away at my mind enough to drive me mad.

"I'll be seeing you real soon, Jack," he said.

"Unless you're a reincarnated Houdini, I don't believe we'll ever meet again." I turned around and walked from the room without another word.

I was wrong. I could tell from the flicker in Azrael's eyes. The facts always tell the story—Death eventually comes for us all.

But not right now. Hopefully, not for a long time. Someday when I'm an old man, having only a couple of marbles rolling around upstairs, and after giving my love to a handful of grandchildren and watching them grow, then I'll be ready.

For now, I have too much to live for and so much love to give to the world.

I'm going to take another week or two off work. I'll then return to one of the things I'm best at doing.

This moment is where the story ends for me. I'm going home to my girls. I'm going to get on with a little thing called life. I'm heading home safe and sound. That might possibly be the greatest saying in the free world.

Epilogue

It couldn't last forever, not really. Nothing ever does. This place, this land of exile, is simply a stitch in time that eventually ushers one toward another level of existence.

It was such a shame that Harper and Jack had failed to realize this. Honestly, there were quite a few things they had overlooked. There had been one thing, in particular, the biggest clue of all.

Winter had come and gone like the quick flick of a switch. Early April came around to something spectacular and brought out the liveliness in those it embraced.

Sitting on the park bench this fine spring day was a person no one here ever laid eyes on before. Of course, she altered her appearance for the sake of mystery because she's methodical and has been so for thousands of years.

The woman's eyes traveled to the mammoth of metal that constructed a jungle gym with slides, monkey bars, and swings. The thing twisted from the ground like partially buried dinosaur bones of a species so monstrous and mysterious that the only ones to discover it were those who played among the wondrous remains and believed. Children were running about, screaming in delight. Parents sat on benches and chatted with one another as they casually watched the kids raise all hell.

"Higher, Daddy, higher!"

Rita Sowell shifted her sight to the middle-aged man and the girl he enthusiastically pushed on the swing. The girl wanted to rocket into the sky and maybe find that far off place with angels of unquestionable kindness and just maybe a god who gave a damn.

Good luck on that one, kid, Azrael thought.

However, she wasn't just any ordinary kid. Her name was Reanne Calloway. Azrael had been more than eager to bring her to the place she now so desperately desired. Of course, that entire plan had come apart at the seams, at the very climax of the event that he worked so feverously to prepare.

It doesn't matter because what's done is done. It's strange to think in such a way, but Azrael was astounded and inspired at the last game's outcome. So many lived when so many should have died. It certainly was something that intrigued him, and he could even accept the conclusion for now, just for now.

The events were an inspiration that began the wheels of deceit turning again. Azrael would need to come up with something more maniacal the next time around. When the next time came for Harper and Jack, Azrael couldn't say for sure, but it would come someday.

Reanne leaped mid-swing onto the sand and began running around with a group of children. Jack, obviously winded, found a seat next to Caroline on the park bench. They were a lovely couple, and combined with such a beautiful child, made a picture-perfect family.

Azrael wanted to kill them and extinguish the happiness within. For the time being, they would continue to breathe.

Perhaps the feeling of being watched, or even picking up the vibrations of hate seething through Azrael's skin, made Jack turn his sight from Caroline and to the altered appearance of Rita Sowell.

Azrael offered him a half nod and a sly smile.

Something about the eye contact apparently troubled Jack. After a moment of studying the older woman, he excused himself from Caroline's company. Azrael watched as Jack passed between the empty swings. As he crossed the sand, two children collided with him, sending one of the small boys to the ground. Jack helped him to his feet, smiled, and said something that made the child laugh.

Azrael pushed himself from the park bench. Using a cane for visual purposes only, he began to make his way to the parking area.

"Excuse me, ma'am?" Jack called from behind.

What was it, Jack? What tiny thing about the old woman on the park bench drew your attention so much that you felt the need to pursue? That's what makes you such a worthy contender. Your instincts are so unbelievably strong. You and Harper are practically indestructible as a team, but apart, you're as frail as any other human.

For a time, you thought I was alone in this game, didn't you? Did it surprise you when Hunter died in that subway tunnel, and you later realized that he might have been one of the elite soldiers who had also fallen? Did you also have a hunch that the angel now residing in Wilmester Institution, wasn't me? We're uniting, Jack. I'm finding them one by one, and someday soon, there will be an epic battle.

I want to tell you a secret, Jack. I want to inform you what you really don't understand. All of us, the entire army, we're all Death, every last one of us. We've brought the hatred and invoked the fear within each of you. We're all the bringers of death.

I want to turn, Jack. I desperately want to look into those caring eyes of yours and confirm what you already suspect. I know you went to the institution and spoke with my comrade, but did you know who he really is? I strongly feel the need to tell you that you have the wrong man, or rather, the wrong angel. I want to tell you the truth.

I was a face you never knew, not until now. I saw your advancements and struggles at each stage of the game. I was a face in every crowd, and you never realized it. I even watched from the dark woods as everything found its end in those lonely mountains.

Without the reporter, Rita Sowell, I wouldn't have uncovered the truth about the murdered police officer, and the game wouldn't have been played.

I had honestly planned on Nolan killing the reporter, but you were clever and spared her sad little life. I hadn't planned on taking and later becoming her.

There was a fork in the road, Jack. You chose the path laid out by Nolan's death that led you to Hannah Jane.

Bravo, bravo.

However, there was another path, the one less traveled. If you had realized the significance of Rita Sowell, her path would have eventually led you directly to me.

In any case, your efforts were all for nothing. Kidnapping and later killing the little bitch of a reporter was so easy. Slipping my soul into her wasn't a trick, but real magic.

Azrael could hear Jack's footsteps falter as he gave up his pursuit of the old woman. Jack had let his curiosity slide away.

Smart move, Jack. You'll live longer. Take your wife and daughter home. Laugh, play and enjoy life, because someday soon we'll meet again, and then I'm going to show you real magic, and real magic has a wicked, wicked heart.